Zoe

Honey Rovit

authorHOUSE®

AuthorHouse™
1663 Liberty Drive
Bloomington, IN 47403
www.authorhouse.com
Phone: 1 (800) 839-8640

Published by AuthorHouse   03/08/2016

ISBN: 978-1-5049-8424-9 (sc)
ISBN: 978-1-5049-8423-2 (e)

What use such gifted music from the
lyre, dear friends ?

See how my flesh is wrinkled now,
my lustrous hair turned white.

These legs which were a fawn's legs
once, can scarcely hold me up.

But what is that to me ?
It cannot be undone, —

no more than can coruscal Dawn
not end in somber night,

or cling to her immortal lover
who crawls against the earth.

Yet, I adore the exquisite, —
and, for me, beauty and light

are as one, — are the same as
my wanting the sun.

                              Sappho/ Lardas

Anais Nin
P. O. Box 26598
Los Angeles, Cal. 90026   To WHOM IT MAY CONCERN: I INTEND TO WRITE A

PREFACE TO HONEY ROVIT, 'S BOOK BUT NOT HAVING THE MANUSCRIPT AT

THE MOMENT I CAN ONLY COMMENT ON THE IMPRESSION IT MADE ON ME

AT FIRST READING. I FIND THE NOVEL WRITTEN WITH GREAT FEELING

AND STYLE. IT SHOULD HAVE A GREAT APPEAL FOR WOMEN. I

WAS TOUCHED AND MOVED BY IT, BY CONTENTS AS WELL AS THE BEAUTY

OF THE WRITING.

Anais Nin

ZOE

Around me it's not April but pain in my intestines, heaviness in my legs, burning in my eyes and head — a tactile season which is beyond my talents for suffering. And all about me is not Paris, but rather a disagreeable landscape where two old armchairs, an unused drawing table, dressoir and bed have taken root. On this bed where I sit, I also lie, my nose towards roses which are always in fanatic bloom. Oh! I want to spend my last days in hotel rooms, waking up completely lost!

And you really intend to leave here in your condition?
I've made up my mind to it.

My heart — always ready to explode — does not explode, so with his professional disdain for anatomy he evokes my liver, my stomach… all my failing organs But I refuse to die here in my room. I don't want to die at all. Anywhere. But to whom can I say this? Not to my old daughter who is crumbling like the rest of the debris that surrounds me, or to my agent who'll make a few sous by selling it. Certainly not to this doctor whose concern masks his boredom as well as fleas disguise a dog. To no one. Lacking a husband, lover, friend or God, I talk to myself. And my words follow my words the way, when I was still a woman and deserted by love, my tears followed my tears without sound, without witnesses, without litany or lymph.

I can't of course — forbid you, but since you're so
determined to voyage, I would strongly recommend
a serious cure at Vichy.

Vichy. Vichy. I have to be amazed if I'm to stay alive. I need something to fetch me out of my present existence and lead me upwards, onwards. Perhaps what I see and what I remember will pull together like two horses in a double harness and carry me out of the waste of life. I'll travel through the warm weather and unearth my dead spring times. He doesn't have to remind me how many there are. Nearly four months since I was accosted by my seventy-ninth year and it arrived like a huckster with a choice of goods: an ugly reminder that time exists apart from my wishes; a number which could be applied to many things but adhered to nothing; and a warning whistle for imminent departures. But there is such a fantastic accumulation of details and if my neck aches on my wadded pillow every morning, it's only because I've been bending over them to find expressions, confusions of sentences — who said that?" ..."Wait! I last wore that lavender in the summer of...." And, finally, the gaunt housekeeper of light sweeps them away.

I begin each sleepless night with banal thoughts, somewhat like a performer who displays simple skills before proceeding to more difficult and thrilling ones. The sleeping house in which I'm now denied a thimbleful of wine moves far off; it's an alien present land, like America — settled by savages. A passing automobile enrages me. The sound of street voices tears me from a long procession of vanished people. In a flowered dress, my mother still searches for her little girl. My grandmother, having reached the age of manhood, puts on her dark blue soldier's hat to hide her eyebrows and her hair. A door closing in the flat distracts me from the single face of a man, a longing for the memory of any man I loved, because any man I loved was the *promised* land which led me out of my darkness. And in darkness I find myself again. I thread my fingers through unwound hair, darkened again by the night. The trees outside my window are skeletons of trees, but there were other trees that lined the Boulevard Raspail, and the Russian woman, like an escapee from Carco, is wearing a grey fur hat, some assorted undramatic clothing of which I notice only a silver broach at her thin neck. She receives me like an honored guest, opening the door, seating me. We eat a bouillon with egg yolk swimming in it. "To grow old, to grow old," she says and I flee to a young man with a ravaged beard — a false theatrical beard… he's sleeping, but he's dead, and a younger man with blue eyes turns suddenly to look into mine. I voyage past them, past dream-riven rocks on the ocean, past a pond with one swan on the water, past the incredible bulk of Mont St. Michel stranded in the low tide, feudal towers grown into the moss and the wool of sheep caught on a fence at Avranches. Bruno! I keep moving past. Mose, eternally in love and whoring after fame, says, "What is man? ….. A piece of meat." And Jules, for all his philandering and his painting which covered *"Je m'en fou"* like the pastel scrim on his canvases, is not surprised to see his death so sombre and defined. "I don't understand," Pierre says, "Less do I understand myself." In none of these do I touch goal. But Valery appears…. his hair neatly segmented, his moustaches precise, his heart of cold caffeine, his brain in fugue. "Give yourself wholly to your finest memory," he says." To your best moment." And in an immense salon in Venice, a man in a flowing tie and turned down cellar holds out his arms. Two people climb a stairway slowly, leaning together as though one or both are ill. Candlelight moves towards my room in Basle. At an *auberge* in *St. Moritz* there is a voluptuous dinner of *Meursault* and fish at which I am either too early or too late, it seems at once so continuous and brief, and someone calling "Angela! Angela!" Like a clasp on a large carry-all, there is a locked room with a brown washstand under a gas jet sprouting from a flowered wall….

Such things arrive each night like exiles who speak a language only I can understand, and I take each one because I find that scenes and faces shaded by the grave make better keepsakes than a letter or dried flowers. They occupy me more. But then — my quotidian disaster — I must get up. My bed which had been the quoin of mysteries and sweetness returns me to the room where I'm dishonored by my doctor's visit.

Yes yes I'm listening. You said no alcohol
We pretend that he cares.
The pains in your legs are not worse?

No no, I feel nothing.
But even so, do you think this voyage is reasonable?
Perhaps you are right.

Better to dissemble, to confess they're right. They make me feel my condition more as embarrassment than illness. Soon the whimperings of my daughter will distract me from everything but the ugliness of a house I've come to detest and all at once my memory is like something of the middle ages which has left the gates of its city and is being devoured by wolves. I get up devoted not to taking my medicine, arranging my papers, or even bickering. This is a disguise. I pass my days continuing the long work of my nights, but wide-awake in this hostile atmosphere, it's so much harder. I, who have no more projects — they think - must recover things which come out of my past as I come out of it. I was an artist. One doesn't lose that. I feel the same hypnotic trust in internal design that I used to feel in the midst of a drawing I hadn't quite finished. Certainly there's the same integrity, or necessity, which forces me to change my happy recollections by the shape of events that surround them... then what am I left with? Would I be better working rugs like my poor grandmother whose miserable handicraft had none of Penelope's hope behind it and whose only suitors were the years? Yet so often mother said, "Mutti, you've missed some stitches there... you see?" Was she led away somewhere, like me? Her face startled, had she uncovered some joyous image only to see it rot like an open fruit exposed to the air? Oh late, and seeming so alone, sitting at her prayers, a braid became loose from the coronet and tapped the window glass. And so alone. *Pauvre cherie, ma pauvre cherie,* I failed you at the end. Oh God my God I failed my grandmother. I failed my father, failed my mother, failed my husband and child. I failed. Oh God! God, are you there? So white today, are you sad or spotless?

Down below from Lauren's studio which often disturbs me there comes a music inexpressibly sweet. Let me climb back upon it. Whatever in my eyes began cascading cerulean blue pulls back. Becomes Pavane.

"Give yourself to your best moment!" Valery said. But even of those moments, those "holidays" as I call them which the rest of my life celebrates — those times when like some crazed ten-winged gull in a storm, I broke the circle of continuity and loved a man... the holy times — what's left? Only pictures: he engaged like a workman doing a difficult task which required all his energy; I, lying afterwards in his arms, chaste and sparkling like a small open countryside. That's all. What a pity they aren't made of moss-flowered stone and last nine hundred years like William's tower above Falaise. Even on the day I saw it, Ritter's arm around my shoulders was as provisional as the complex designs on a butterfly which has one day to fulfill its life. I remember that against the view of that tower... or standing before San Marco, or looking up at Byron's empty windows, I felt the same surprised pain of loving something as impermanent as flesh.

Flesh! It's no longer there the mystery lies. It's nothing but menace to me now.

But once I was nude. Once I wanted to take Ritter's bones apart, join them together myself, and crouch down — calm at last — inside them, feeling his blood move around me.

"You're a monster!" my husband said.

Yes, I'm monstrous. Especially on these mornings aged by rain I feel a sorority with tombs. Yet I'm alive. I sometimes think the young are those who die. My child on the day I left. In the garden below with yellow leaves around her tiny, gray face. The little girl who talked all night with my mother in the darkness of the house at Utrecht is a dead girl, but I have a transparent knowledge of her and I must guard it. I'm now these young perhaps. Ritter, fair-skinned and expectant, whose bare shoulders gave me a kind of vertigo as though they were a destination towards which I continually set out and never reached. Janka as she lay looking into my face like a bride reflected in a mirror. Pierre, beautiful and deadly under rain at the pitch of winter. In dreams like unclosed wounds my father looks at me with anxiety, dislike, the sadness of his own unfulfillment.... I'm all there is — like those people of Goya in their endless empty space, so robbed of natural landscape that they become, themselves, the undergrowth and sky and sea.

This carbuncle doesn't please me. Well, what more can I say? Il faut tenir....

Hah! he hopes I will not. And Trudi and Hans. I *am* monstrous. No other thing in nature loses genre as I have. I was so beautiful.... How courteously my face gave way to these hanging cheeks.

How beautiful you are, Ritter said.

How beautiful I was.

I will die without you, I told him.

And I did.

"Il faut tenir!" Why, it was in 1915 I was sentenced, but I've lived on, borrowing myself for all the smaller scenes that came forward, and each time I thought of my lover and his treason my hair got paler; now it's white. Long white useless soft, it's something left feminine to do. My hair was never green when I was twenty, but, rather black in his fingers because... to be a woman was to be in darkness. Never understanding how the milk came into my breasts. Not being able to see the need inside me for a man. An unlit house behind the moon, I felt children growing, and long before my body was punctured by love, before it was torn by birth, it had begun silently to confuse, oppose me.... Now am I supposed to develop an indifference to it? Madonna, Magdelan, cerebrale, bacchante... shall I let these all die? My body is my memory.

...since you seem insensible to good advice!

He shuts his bag of tools as though with that snap! he might close me. "That's all!" the snap says. No more the bitterness, discouragement, pain; no more the risk and the sweetness of living. But his blue coat flapping towards the door I confound with the wonder of natural things — sea-waves, birds-wings, whatever ceaselessly floats, flies, puts itself beyond the day and allies with the solitary traveler I'll be. Let me move straightaway with a motion like that: mount on it through the pageant of myself until the clarity of my "holidays" is blurred — until I can no longer see dark eyes or wide lips or arms held out to me… but only a vague shape to which I shout, "I'm going to die without you!"

They're whispering. I can hear Trudi — that aging disappointment of my belly which is now mammoth with itself. She would prefer that I expire quietly in my room and she sees me dragging off my spite in a second-class carriage heading for a provincial death. They whisper and connive, but they're indifferent and I'm not. Yet… I feel very little compassion for this old woman I've become. If pity's more constricted, it's that. When I see this skin hanging from my arms as though it plans to leave them in the hour, I feel some of the sad protection of a mother for a crippled child. That's all. And surprise. That it seemed to happen in a shorter space of time than the sleepless night I've just passed through. I set out, as it were, on flower-hung horses and I dragged back in the snow, dying piecemeal as age fell over everything, silvering my daughter's hair with ice, staining my furniture, cracking the corners of my best drawings… endless… endless…. As I look into the street I could expect that young woman (hurrying home from a lover? leaving for work?) to change into a hag— her walk slowing, her back bending, naturally, between steps, as though the whole world were sliding with me into decay.

I mourn, yet even as I mourn, I hear a voice slip into my words and I wonder "who is that?" as though something listening is preserved untouched. That's the whole point: there *is* something which is unchanged and only its edges come in contact with my age. Inside my disappointment is the small equipage of hopes that became imprisoned there, and within the desolate disgust for my body, the belief that grew up in its beauty still sings on like a bird which has only the same four-note song.

Moments I'm caught unawares. I look at my etching of Claudel… or did, because now it's gone and for a few months in third-.rate hotels— and I think "Why? I'm very good! One doesn't lose that." And rumbling past my curved white bones, like an ancient lift with gridded doors, excitement reaches my lassitude. "I'll draw today," I say. But what comes of it? It takes me too long to dress, to wash myself, comb my hair, to pull each hour from a swamp of bitterness. I go mad thinking of the drunken concierge who remains lucid enough to leave only *my* stairway unswept. Everyone takes advantage of my weakened state. The butcher thinks I won't complain of the red glue he sent me yesterday in place of meat. Oh, with an energy I don't possess in legs, my heart flew to his counter and I shamed him before all the street. So few things go right. There's my breakfast... but too soon, and like nothing else in my day, it's over. Everything here works against me. When it rains, like today, the steady sound and dimness prolong the sameness of morning and I feel singled out by its malice. I know my daughter thinks me a vicious old woman but how can she understand? "Find something to do," she whines. "Read a book, can't you? Invite people."

People? What can I tell them? There's too much to explain. I used to have the wish to be wheeled down the boulevards holding in front of me my photo which they call "The Modern Giuccioli" enlarged to such a size that it might cover me completely. In those days I still wanted to explain myself, but now I'm finished with the ghouls. They come here to see "the last living mistress of Allevia Ritter" and they find only fragments of a witness too close to a splendid catastrophe. A serious threat to legend on swollen feet pushed into house slippers! A hand as yellow as an old pronouncement! Even the famous ring rolls on my finger like a hoop on a stick quivering with the last vibrations. Look at me! Persephone dressed my hair through the night and left me to arrange these withered creeping shreds. My mirror is cold. Two wrinkled faces scowl their image in my spectacles. They are *real* candidates for paradise. The saints who burned up quickly in an ecstacy of God suffered less than I who have been conscious through the slaughter of my life.... Why am I always so surprised? My beauty like water running downwards, can never return.

Well, and here she is! Jumping about on those wooden clogs that sound like pistol shots.

Need help to dress, mother? Another bad night?

No. Go away.

Yes, I've had a bad night. I went to the four corners of the world and found no angles anywhere. That hoarder, Time, has carried to his overstocked warehouse everything of mine that was beautiful and young: even you, my child. Within the hour a bell will ring and Hans will crook his elbow over the account books. The dining room will be thick with his cologne as he looks dreamily at his birdlike scrolls, as he whirls around my possessions in his pastel suit like a lost cloud. I'll say: "Will you have a drink first?" And he'll answer: "Yes. I believe I will. To the great poet...and our collaboration...." And he'll crook his elbow again, the scavenger. He'll stare at the deviation from my photograph and see yellow teeth which smile into his disgust. He hasn't the stomach for excavation.

Are you sure you're alright, Maman?

Am *I?* She looks so worn, her features as pale as though drawn in soap on a mirror. One eye looks at me and the other is always fixed on that eternal shadow near my ear. Her father should have seen to that when she was younger. Why is she so concerned today? What did he tell her? Or is she guilty for ruining yesterday? The great publisher came with his hat like an elegy between his hands. Even Hans was frozen with respect, looking pained over a nosegay which might just have been plucked from his chest. But she had reproached me for too much powder, for my decolletage, screaming. *"A ton age! A ton age!"* Just as the bell rang. I knew they must have heard. I knew it would end badly. I felt ill to begin.

Malinard pretended he had heard nothing, bending over the sacred relics, brushing my fingers with his mouth. "It must be painful for you to part with these letters," he said. And I agreed: "Mountains and grief change but little." Why did I say that? I felt that something memorable was expected of me. And Trudi dipped the flowers into water and cut the string, ungirding them, so then I saw, wedged between the muguet like some lone apoplectic faces, a few violets and I told him that they were the first flowers Ritter ever gave me. "Fifty-four years ago, Monsieur! It all comes back." Calm and courteous and firm, Malinard talked, but I felt a sharp hail-like shot. It was cold and pierced me to the vitals. My nose was dripping. A hurricane with ledges, the room whirled around me. Trudi's eye was stitched to mine and what a tumult, what a smell! Someone in the building was frying pork at nine? I took a capsule to keep my brain from jiggling. I bent my head to meet the currents which assailed me, but they beat me back. My heart didn't fail me and I only wished that I had wings and could ascend over my faintness, but while wishing this I felt weaker than before. I tried to reach what seemed like the tunnel of a railroad track, but the mass turned black and they helped me up. Trudi reproved me for the single spoon of sugar I had stolen for my coffee. I heard my throat say, "Forgive a poor sick woman, gentlemen," and straight.-away the louts agreed. I had to leave them to urinate, holding to the hammered boards beside the toilet and I felt they'd laugh behind my back. "My dear," Hans said with his spectral smile, "You are in no condition to voyage." But my will my will, like an angel bound shuddering and unwilling to this poor frame, cold and wasted, of whose companionship it has grown so weary, travels with me in a baffled trance. I'll go, but oh, mother, winter's breathing in my shambles. How can I endure it?

And my doctor says I should be thankful that I'm still alive! What what? She'll make my lunch... how solicitous she is today. She wants me to appreciate "all she does." But she doesn't understand that food refuses to continue the lie of her arrangement on a platter; that unlike the artistry it has in charcuterie windows, it reveals its true nature as garbage in my veins.

No no there's nothing left for me here. Time rolls on and what does it bring? To live for oneself alone, to communicate my reflections to none and to be cheered by none, not even to weep, to do nothing, nothing. Draw? Why? I've done it. Stacks of them, folios of etchings, aquarelles, paintings blinded against the wall. Look at the things from my windows? I can still see the Seine. Far away.... Montmartre... hardly distinct. The newly rubbed-to-ochre towers of Notre Dame; they make me cry. I stood up there with Roland on the day before he left and I remember we tried to pick out his old windows on the Quai St. Michel. High, high, dizzyingly over the city.

> *Donne moi quelque chose, je t'en prie. To carry with*
> *me... an amulet....*
> *Tiens, je te le donne.*

I kissed him on the nose, and then I kissed his mouth which was open and my lips touched his teeth. But as a parting gesture, he pulled a blue thread from my shawl....

Je peux? Je vais le garder pour toujours.

Toujours? For him *toujours* was only a few days more. And there we are part of *Notre Dame pour toujours.* I'm not a tourist! History left spaces for my small additions I was included in the vue of Balzac petrified above Vavin, the heroine at Bateau Lavoir, they toasted me at Bouscaret's. Oh, there are a thousand things I no longer want to look at, so grieved am I to see their images propped up like death masks of sleeping poets.

And what came of it all? My mother used to prepare each day with such exigent care— her chignon dressed and tapped with tortoise pins. Men loved me, all my friends had plans... then, they began disappearing one by one like lights around midnight and I had to leave tomorrow like a house that was too large for me all alone. The dead don't know me, the living can't hear me. People have stopped using my name. There's no one left alive who remembers what I was like and for those mean few who see me I have all the essence of a bottle of scent bought at a weekend fair and left unstoppered on a table.... Lilos told me...

> *All dressed! You are quite better then, Madame?*
> *Stronger, eh? It's the plans. The trip. Ca va changer*
> *les idées.*

She's going to make six turns around my bedchamber, at least six, scuffing about with her pail and brushes. Weather report *(toujours pas de soleil*) watchful spy of my melancholy, self-appointed confessor. Still, she's a distraction and I don't mind her patronage. The doer for the served, the superiority of religious old virgins over women who have chosen life and failed. But today I don't feel like talking. It's the depressing weather. I'd like to hang a sign on myself: *Closed During Rain.* She is singing a hymn of praise to her old land of the Savoie…. It will do me much more good than the Midi. Un-nerving surety like an incense she carries in her. We are so at odds —she who has solved all questions while I am still asking them…. A slight inclination of her head towards the door: she has ironed and packet my clothes.

> *The medicine he ordered won't be ready till tomorrow.*
> *I'll put it on top. But, Madame, the best medicine….*

I have much to do today. I'll pick over what's left of my treasures and play Eden. But wasn't it? I hate to sell Kisling's sketch of me— my eyes closed and my right hand like a flower between my breasts. I shouldn't have been anything but enchanted with life when I looked like that but there seems always to have been an internal world boned with anguish. There it is in my portrait of Ritter; but it was mine. There was only distance in his eyes at that time… but who knows that? I painted him too late. There was something disorderly in those eyes when he looked at me. Across the table at the Kuhnle, on a calm winter day, the lights were high in flickering topaz globes and the future closed like stone: "We'll never separate now," he said. "It depends neither on you, nor me. It's eternal."

> *On le detache?*

Hah, I am aware of the contradiction between her disdain for earthly possessions and her peasant disapproval as I sell mine off. I tell her. "We'll see. Not now. For ten thousand I'd let them have even this portrait. If my strength holds out I can go as far as Spain. But stay, there on my wall today, one last time. *Bouge pas,* my darlings I have a surprise for you. Where are you now? Ah, 'vilain'! I have the few images left of you. Here they'll see only your head, your small hands, your torso beneath undefining cloth. He was supple, Madame Morand, without being soft. A very agreeable height, unmeasurable by anything in my painting. Square shoulders, fine ankles and his back... from the bed I saw it in the mirror of the armoire. It was white. I saw it white and unusually long, but he must have changed….. Everything changes.

What shall we do with my shawl, the box of photos, my oval mirror— old mirror of my defeat? Hans will see to everything. I don't have to look at Ritter's photos. I looked at him so long, my eyes open right down to my heart; I will always remember him. I told him that to my death he would be in my eyes, intelligible only to me like the tracings under the stone at Locmariaquer left from some departed religion.

> *Vous ne vous en souciez pas, Madame Morand.*
> *Monsieur Hans will see to everything.*

He deserved condign punishment for his treatment of me and I would have gloried in bringing home to him a grief like mine, would have exalted to burst in on his vision, confront and astonish him, afterwards— one blaze of accomplishments, one cold cruel overwhelming triumph which would have crushed him with regret. When I prayed to God for a personal vengeance, I always felt that the Devil would slip out of Him by a side glass door, stand there— much more accessible— and listen: "Let Ritter fail. Fall from a stairway, pierce his hand with a foul object, and remain unloved for the rest of his days." But my lips flowered on his forehead, and my warm tongue wept with hunger in his hair when we parted. He touched me with his hand and then called out: "I will miss you, Zoe!" It happened fifty years ago and I doubt that I made much use of it. A good nature might have become a saint or a real artist; a hard spirit— like Mimi, whom he left as well— became a lovely demon. I have been a bitter woman. They call me selfish, avaricious... why?

I may pretend that I don't like to peddle my souvenirs, but the fact is I want to sell them all now. Yet *not* for the money. Their very solidity weights them in place with the lost. Yesterday, the trunk open... and my clothes... each dress, shirtwaist... they seemed so treasonable for being the same. I tried to call up other lives we had, but there was no bathing sun of Venice or the milky light of Normandie— only a cruel electric glare falling on some dead cloth. Who'll buy my dead violets? Into what archive will this go. the photograph of me with Rodin? Rose took it. The small dining-room at Meudon. Threadbare, peasant-like, adorned only with the paintings by Russell, what an odd choice. It was over, then, my love-affair, but how pretty I still look. Rodin called me "Esmeralda."

"Some day your line will be more exciting than Ingres," he said looking at my drawings. Here are the three letters from Rolland— especially the one where he writes "...your general loveliness." The card from Valery praising the portrait. My initialed copy of the *Zauberbuch.* Photographs of Ritter and me together— all separating that me and this one who sits alone with such a friendless thumping of the heart. Rolland, Rodin, Valery, Careo, Pascin, Jammes— wasn't there a time when I knew everyone? People like that donkey Hans watched me go by!

I say frankly, I relish the idea of my jade ring lying in a collector's box, or better still, on an unsuspecting finger. I have it when it was given to me. I folded the paper up carefully while Ritter watched, and I told him: "I'll be buried in it." How close death seemed at that time. Imminent, passionate, with no foreign seal of decay. It whirled in the cycle of love and had nothing in it of onset. I would have died for him. Crossing the Marktplatz diagonally, to the Poste when it came to me— with elation!— that if he had to die, I'd go with him. And how powerless my mother would have been to save me, or my husband to forbid me... but there's no one to care now that my life is in port.

Your arm? My canes? No, Madame Morand, I'll wait in here. I have much to do today— and I win from her stone eyeballs a beam almost approving. I'll sit and look at the phantoms of furniture, the wraith of looking-glass, my coffee pot and bowl. The clock just struck some hour and I'll look out my window....

So much activity below. Ah yes.......it's Friday again. Every week the same day suddenly reappears as arbitrary as a playing card that falls out of a deck. Well, down there people are hurrying off to live and I'm dressed and ready for the upright hours like a figurehead above their Friday. What do they think when they look at me? I used to see many old women with geraniums in an open window: opaque spectacles, the small reminder of some lips---something born withered no doubt.. Now I know that each one had a *petite histoire* that she could see as clearly as cathedrals through a stereoscope. And I'm like them. But shall I sit here as though I *am* like them until at twilight only emptiness has filled the space of a day; until my familiar window is a frame around nothing? Should I have death come to me here like any other visitor who ulcerates the silence without changing the arrangement of my room, without doing anything out of the ordinary? Let it chase me on a train like some neophyte adventurer! Whirling somewhere, falling somewhere, let me imagine the last breath on my face a young gallant who fanned me after dancing!

Tomorrow tomorrow....... But what an entourage to see me off! My daughter in her mantelet of complaints and Hans decked in his homosexuality like tapisserie d'Auxerre. Ha! He'll soon be here, his hands trembling with his good fortune. "The photos...?" he'll whisper, "and the ring?" Why not? Why should I keep even the pearls? My principal ornament now is living. Let him rip out the doorknobs, cart away the toilet seat Ritter may have used (he *was* like ordinary mortals, but who'd believe me?). I have all I need. I remember Yasha covering his pallid face with paint-stained hands, saying, "The real memories cannot break to pieces." So, the question "Will I really voyage so far, all alone?" I answer: "No." Ritter said
     "Nothing is ever lost," Zoe,"
     and I was loved once! It can't have left the world. It's there behind a hackney cab with tall wood wheels which stands before our door

near *Martinskirche* as in some photo marked, for others, "Anonyme." It waits for me as it once did at the Basle station when, afraid Ritter wouldn't be there, knowing he would be there, I saw his face... beyond the head of an old woman who pushed her way in front of me. I had to stand there, looking at his smile. feeling not an intensity of something I already knew, but the sudden possession of a new sense— like those suprahuman ones which adapt animals to their medium. And that was less than forty-eight hours after I'd met him. Not two full days from the tuning up, dissonant and fragmentary, in the crowded Rotonde when Pascin said: "Ritter is here," and I put out my hand.

What was it all? Just a re-run of Murger with entrails and I as the role love had decided to play? My dress was blue. Jet earrings hung on silver chains to my shoulders under dark, dark hair.

"You are the most beautiful woman I've ever seen," he said.

I believed him. I can still see myself, through his emotion, as surprise. Like a star pulled through the sky, I was the light unconsciously shed on everyone who saw me until I became the discovery of a poet. "Her to whom I'll give her name." Men had looked deeply into me as though I were standing nude and waiting at the back of my eyes, but I wanted to be embraced Vetue or just with looks and plans. His glance was different. It passed over my hair, rounded the curve of my cheek, and stopped at the parting of my lips as though the lines of the universe converged there. Before him, I'd always had the same image of myself, always facing forward, always the same— like a fashion photo in different clothes through the years, and suddenly his look dissolved it as the huge bouquet dissolved into flowerlets ant fell around me.

"I give you a violet for everyone who loves you," he said, and they rained past my arms, onto the table, over the white cloth, dropping into the darkness and I said, "I can't take them all, I can't," and Colin whispered! "Take them, take them... he's a good fellow and he likes flowers." His whisper drops into eternity like a trinket fallen out of its setting. "Take them… take them…. What difference that it didn't happen last night? My memory it as fresh as a green landscape and these words race through it like black horses. "Take them... take them... take them...." And the flowers fall apart over my arms, scentless, with threadlike stems.

I took them... looking at them... and Ritter was sitting beside me, speaking in his soft, deep adventurer's voice, of love. The low ceiling, the chess ivories, the dark paintings above the banquettes... like fragments of a picture puzzle: my long-ago friends become a smile, a hand sketching, a voice singing Béranger... *"Mon bras si dodu...."* All then, already, so far away from the big house in Lubeck. Hadn't it been enough— my sharing the lavender-blue city with Réjane, cold-faced Claudel, Derain who they say mixed his paint with brains? Would my father have recognised me shivering in Kisling's studio over the café, or sketching beside Yasha at the *Médrano,* walking through the ruined gardens of *Montmartre,* or drinking wine at *Clairon des Chasseurs?*

"Where do you come from?" Ritter asked. "No. Don't tell me. You're like me. You come from nowhere."

I come from nowhere.

He gave me the liberty I wanted from my past. He pulled us up together into isolation and there was no safe way down for me. He pulled me up into love which began in that cafe and ended in a convulsion of unlisted feelings.

Love. What was love? How did it feel? I loved him, I loved him, I remember, but what did it mean?

He *spoke* of love. As everything: the water in the wave, the sound in a voice, the heat in the fire.... There was a slow pacing in his words and between them I could hear the murmur of other voices and the clatter of glasses as though the ordinary were gently sequestering the miraculous.

He told me that life, like the world, was a circle on which man had yet to walk upright and straight ahead, feeding as he went along, like a holy animal, on love.

Love? I didn't know what it meant. It might have been the wine Colin spilled into my cup, or the reflection. of stained glass coming through the lights. I was looking at Ritter's face, at his wide lips and dark hair and eyes, and I lost the hours. Someone said. "Closing time...." and we were all standing up around a white grave that had begun to renew itself in violet. Colin asked Ritter when he was leaving Paris and he answered. "I'm not leaving without her."

We were all there. Pascin's face was a gloomy color he avoided in his painting and he said angrily, "She has a name!"

We were all there. So young. I was so important to them. What a sad miracle that such a lovely scene takes place in an old body so useless for the most commonplace of things. No. Perhaps it must. It's less distracted in the silence left by my vacating senses.

Did Pascin love me then? Did Colin? Kisling? Can't I work more miracles and begin again with each one now I know there are so many paths in youth? How fixed life is! A giant cupboard with everything labeled by a lightning hand. There was my image on the wall of the Rotonde, as ecstatic as Marguerite in the flash of the mirror. Fixed, yet gone in a moment.

Telegrams refold into windowed envelopes. Letters pile in my hotel room. Pleas to be kind, to forget my madness, to return to them— my mother, father, husband, child, my life it was. They're vanished. They vanished as I heard Ritter's saying in the voice of a man who had by desire, fascination, pride, made up his mind. "I'm not leaving without her to whom I'll *give* her name." Colin who had urged me to take the flowers held my arm. No, Jules held me back. I was the trophy. If I'd been made of silver, I would still be there; but I was only lovely to look at. No one could see my veins or the fissures in my mind into which I fell as into dreams belonging to someone else.

"...feed, like a holy animal, on love.

Love? It begins somewhere as a breath before life which one day flies out of the heart and into the features of some one never seen before. The air is thick with miracles. We learn to separate them from the atmosphere when we're old. I looked at a man and in his eyes I saw the bright excitement of the hunter and on his lips I saw a strange half smile that drew me like an animal to a moving shadow. And because I was drawn without understanding it was too much— like holding something too hot or too cold, or running faster than my pulse. That was how it felt. And what did it mean? Jules said. "You will destroy her." That's what it meant.

His phrase cast a solemnity around us and gave a shape to my thousand hands of fear. It took away all the banal steps on which I might have rested until my own life appeared to me again as it had been. And kept my child. And never caused so much hatred. And I went. I went without anything more to follow than my hand closed in the palm of a man I didn't know. A great poet, it was said, but who? Who was he before and afterwards? I followed my hand into the street, and looking up at the Balzac who heaved above us like assent, I felt the glorious suspended like a delicate bridge over the terrible. Because I *was* afraid, and when he put his arm around my waist for the first time, I knew I was entering an order where there was neither God nor other postulants.

Even the warmth on that spring night had vacated for my future misery. March. Still cool enough for Ritter to disappear and re-emerge from the doorway on *Rue Vavin*, of a patroness unknown to me, wearing a long overcoat that gave him the air of an invalid. An invalid with demon strength behind his eyes.

March. Not spring enough to open the top of the fiacre in which we drove along with the sound of excited talk— I chirping like a bird who flies so quickly and so high that the world below seems not to change its place. Did I think to find myself back again at the *Rotonde,* my face radiant with telling, then, returning to my narrow room on *Rue Cassette* where dreams spread over me like awnings over sleep?

We drove on and I never asked to where. When he told the *cocher* to stop by the edge of a wood, I never asked why. It simply never occurred to me to ask. We walked down a path and into his vision because as we moved, he spoke of strange happenings in destiny— such as a man always dreaming of the same particular house and seeing it years later, for the first time, as the villa where his mistress had been born. I remember that I tried to think: What does this mean for *me?* but I was distracted by the sound of his beautiful voice and I heard it without a message just as I might have heard a call—repeated.

We walked on and we sat down when a *banquette* appeared beside us. I had no idea of the time. I had no recollection of how long we had been there when above us, from a hill, an organ began to play and a choir gradually entered the music. Almost as though it had been prearranged, Ritter chanted the words: *"Wachet auf... ruft unz.. die stimne....."*

I believed it to be a *totenmesse* and was taken with dreadful fear. Some pebbles that had clung to the hem of my skirt dropped onto my ankle causing me a strange anguish. Still chanting— almost singing the melody in his remarkable voice— he moved his hand up to my breast. Suddenly in terrifying darkness there was a first kiss, violent and untender as though I had been blinded and pushed into a crowd.

"He means to kill me!" I thought. I wanted to cry out! Yes, I remember that— when gently, gently it seemed he arranged the ribbons of my jumper. Then he helped me to stand. We walked slowly, unspeaking, back to the *fiacre* parked like a decision beside the wood.

Jolting through the streets I heart his disconnected voyages to Warsaw and to Prague, the talk of a war. I was startled by the dim facade of my hotel on *Rue Cassette* and as he helped me down. I stepped onto a sidewalk so incandescent with beginning dawn, I thought my foot would pierce it through. His face had an incredible gentleness which moved me almost to tears.

"You're not too cold?" he asked, and although I was trembling, I said, "No." In the silence that followed nothing passed by to disturb the immobility of the street. Then, without a touch, without a promise or assurances, he said "Will you come and live with me in Basle?" and although I was trembling, I said "Yes."

"If you knew..." he said, "of how I've searched.... of how I've dreamed.... A bird freed from the dark blue of the night gave a sharp cry and I had the feeling he'd waked it.

He gave me details, I believe, of where and how to come— all of which I stored away as I did the clothes I took, knowing when the time came I would need them. And I must have turned. I must have walked the stairway so as not to wake the others with the lift, and it wasn't until I found myself alone in the little room that the rose fell from my bodice. A perfect rose, bruised only where it had touched my skin. He must have carried it in a pocket of the greatcoat, but I never mentioned it to him and I never saw it again. Somehow it disappeared in my haste to pack ant leave my city for his. I can only see myself holding it, putting it down carefully on the pocked wood of the *dressoir*— wondering did he pull it from a vase and was it with or without the consent of someone else. And two nights later he replaced it with three whose branching wires I have to this day.

I could take out those wires folded into transparent paper and look at them now. But what would they bring me? Only the incredible idea that they and I have passed through time like the light from stars that have ceased to shine.

Maman.....maman....are you asleep, are you all right?"

What?...Eh?....No, no... resting.... What is it?"

How alarmed she looked. Did she think I was dead?

"Maman—please think about it. We could go together, rent a caravan, do as we used to do. It's not too late... You mustn't go off alone.. Remember....in 1940... they let us leave the camp... how we voyaged south? How many drawings you did then."

"Stop crying. You unnerve me. Now let me rest. Tomorrow is a big day."

How grey her hair is now. And thin. I've lost everything, Even my child. Yes I remember 1940… He was long dead by then. We had known another war. I spent the happiest years of my life with him in that war.... Did he love me when I went to him? He was a lover of love, of its magic essence, its ability to lift us out of the ordinary— its danger! which he likened to the near experience of death. But the beginning was so innocent… the cab in which he came for me to the station was filled with flowers, and the little rooms to which he took me had been transformed into gardens.

At the joint, at the center of life, love happened and stopped. and its action has forever since governed my responses….After Ritter, small events came in succession and none of them occurred at the axis of my self. Oh I have dreams of petit point stockings, an eternal Liberty hat, a dress of dotted Swiss that shows the top of my breasts, and in white shoes I wait for him again—like the enfant sauvage of Rousseau who goes on setting a place at the table for the man who died. Basle Basle. Motor cars, carriages on the narrow streets. Tram cars brightly-colored as toys, warning bells that make the horses rear up. We were in a cab with the flaps let down, flowers all around me. I saw the *cocher's* head, his haircut which made him seem demented—too closely-cut on the sides such as an institution might require. I could hardly speak and then I saw nothing as Ritter's face bowed towards me. Seeing melted into his arms around me, his hands in mine and I felt as though I was in the branches of a tree and held on fast so as not to fall.

The heavy *porte a deux vantaux* opened wide to admit us into a fragrant courtyard and before it closed I heard some passing hoof beats which for a moment I took to be my heart. At the doorway which I have, again, never seen, he put his mouth over mine and a despair came to me under his lips: my life inside, deep down, unfindable, had shifted out of joint like a vertebra. I had no more plans. Only a stairway stretching up like longing. Endlessly endlessly like sleepwalkers we climbed the dark steps, stopping only to find the kiss from which we were being torn. So many doors left behind us and I never thought of coming town again. There *was* no safe way down for me.

Allevia! I would have died for you that night! When you held my head against your chest. When you kissed my toes. I held your jacket in my hands and looked at all the buttons and the threads as though I had to begin with the tiniest details to know everything. You made me "Angela." Why did you assassinate me then? You said of God, "Be not my Judge, but Muse" and he rewarded you with poetry, while I was left only a name wearing out with the years. Weren't there enough women in hell? You passed through me so quickly on your way to immortality like someone who dines carelessly on the most sumptuous meal to give him strength for his voyage. What was it all — that room darkened by the buildings on the court? I never loved a room so much.

He drew green curtains together over the two long windows. So many intricate things to undo in the ritual of finding each other— his collar coming apart in my fingers, rose ribbons in his hand, as though we were exchanging ourselves, and all the other casings gone, we were left still separate in the flesh which clothed our bones. The hollow O of my mouth echoed his and we found our breaths alike— transparent counterparts which lost their origins as we faded away through them. Two empty round spaces which could accomplish nothing and so we fell into the physical and we were entwined, lost forgotten together, falling into a dark dream with no event but the drumming of the sea in which I drowned.

Why did I live again? How is it I'm left alone with the fingertips he kissed? What was it all? An act so urgent that it had a life of its own with us following or being within it and finding our bodies afterwards— vehicles for the death from which we woke. Finding each other again in a kiss, as though we had been together in a battle, and come through^ had won somehow.

"You don't regret coming here, Zoe?

"Non non."

"You have the face of an angel. I'll call you Angela."

Where do you come from?

Non. Where I come from no longer exists.

"I have a surprise for you!"

He held my head against his chest bared in the opening of his robe and I said, "I will die without you."

"I have a surprise for you!"

It wasn't only three roses growing out of an old peddler's hand. Was it his bed? His row of books, his clothes in the armoire, my name? Was it what it was? Didn't he give him to us, We, *Unz,* with two voices?

Je t'aime.
Moi aussi, je t'aime.
Ah?
Oui. Je t'aime.

Where do you come from?
I come from us.

"I have a surprise for you!"

We drove in a motor cab, he sat across from me on the *strapontin* holding my leg between his ankles, gazing at me, his face radiant with love, affection. pleasure. We had come back from death. We remembered the combination of light-hearted happiness and the dark liquid of non-health; the heartless ruin of tissue and nerve; the sad joy of being forgotten by the world. We celebrated and drank wine and under the beamed ceiling in an unsacrosanct marriage without witnesses, an old *voleur* held over us three roses bound with a silver *riband.* "I'm very happy, he said to me. Didn't he take me for life? Back in that room, in those floating climbing moments at the black heart of the night, wasn't I woven forever into his arms?

I see him holding my child, her head against him, his face unsmiling under his caracul hat, looking as though he would faint. Near Ca' Reggonico, towards the docks where I could smell the burnt straw of the shipyards, there was a glowing candlelit church called San Nicole dei Mendicoli, with a solemn Madonna in a red velvet dress.

"I have a surprise for you!"

"Angela! Angela! Come quickly — I have a surprise for you!"

A ring. A necklace of pearls, the church at Caen with a *couronne* of moonlight. Dinard, Dol, La Points du Crouin, Carnac, Fougères, Geneve, St. Moritz, Florence, Rimini, Venice, Cancale, the cold was new. I became aware of sleep like wizards who discover coals in smoke each time I woke up in his arms. "Look here!" A huge iron gate in Venice with a thick-lipped Moor as a doorknob. Love, which backed my life like a repetitious gloriously carved spine.

"Go back!" my mother said.

"How?"

I remember as he sat nearby and wrote, I washed his shirt under the icy tap and held it in my hands so long they turned numb as the years before. My hair had never been so thick. Was it only a beginning? Everything began: before that time it had only re-occurred. There was the beginning of Bretagne and the ocean. Of the soft Normandie weather that veiled the earth in ground mist. Our cottage lay by several broken farms.

Small. By the sea. The winds up and up to it. Near Cancale, near the headlands ablow with sea pinks, I pick a large flower and scramble down the rock path to his astonished face.

What is he doing there, so far away, on that day? All the world's blue was in that day which he abandoned and which — from the distance, springing— now struck against my breast like an animal that loved me.

It comes to me late, but it comes: there are scrub flowers and *petoncles,* the dank smell of the low tide — so sweet. My dreams are tight with winding. Horizons tipping the white tide towards me, I lay down again by his side where for generations there has not been another summer of 1913. When the sun was so magnificent against an evening sky that fell on the black beach. That summer summer summer covered all over with a tall wild grass.

I laughed as I ran through the long grass which stained the hem of my blue dress forever, back to where he sat. His face was suddenly serious, almost very sad. "You are beautiful like that," he said. "When you run, you look as though you're flying." Our house, low-set, of stone under its wig of thatch: flowery, bosky. Mornings, so early there was no barque on the water, no fisherman in rosepink trousers and round linen jacket walking on the beach; only us and the sea——-- the waves onleaping in an angry gallop, retreating with a slide, leaving behind an-inert crab, a fish partly lost.

"Lie down on your back and look around us," he said, and he put his arm over me. His touch, so manifest of desire resting, held me in place. I saw the sweeping arms of the cone-topped windmills, the black and white magpies which flashed across the sky in pairs, and a rabbit who appeared suddenly like a bewildered tourist. It lifted its eyes and, panting, looked at us as though we were the world in front of its flight.

"Pauvre lapin," I whispered. To be only one.

Oh, time has pulled my memory to pieces, or is it my memories that macerate time? This insane pursuit of my young-selves... seductive, friendly to one another.... They all speak of me, oblivious to my presence as though I and not they had died first. They might be beautiful images hanging in a museum locked up for the night. Or a harem with all the entrances sealed while the master journeys on a mission that has no end.

I understand now how Hans looks at me— at my few jewels he covets, thinking "Such old ears to detain those lovely earrings." Reading over Ritter's letters, imagining with pale excitement and disgust all we did together. Then he looks at me: an old woman hardly able to walk, halting the flow of her direction with a cane plunged into the ground as though to slow her pace towards the grave.

How to keep dignity in the midst of poultices applied and injections given. To leave nature with some grace. I cannot seem to do it. I can't give up the gone like my mother saying, "Poor Mutti. God rest her soul," or my father from whom the years fell like exhausted leaves and people disappeared, thereafter nameless, as under a rigid political system. I have to lift each stone and talk to my loves, have to keep my happiest times. Must still remember what it was like. That joy— which for want of a better word I call love— coming through a sudden opening in the world. Turning weekdays into life. When I die, what will be left of it? Nothing. It's unmarked on any map. What did I accomplish that first summer? Nothing. *Visites de demeures anciennes,* a room with white marquisette curtains, dark wood commodes, a table laid in the center of the floor ant how it was that just to sit and eat with someone should become altered one millionth of a degree to verge on what is most beautiful in living. Towns of straight noses and crooked streets, fortress ruins, an ocean the color of pernod, courts overgrown with grass and forgotten; and at the sight of a beloved face, the feeling of senselessness disappears:. an order is established like Spring which, while one has been away, has sung and blossomed. It's a prolonged present which is too full, and being in love, making love is not enough, but I didn't think to build a monument or paint a picture. I wanted to buy a gift or have a child, I think. I must get it all…. must get it all right.…

Concarneau, the boats, Quimper and its twin cathedral towers, Brest. Lorient, Caen…. Where was it that we had the foaming cups of cider on a platform… I've forgotten, I can't remember, but it was at Plougastel we bought strawberries and ate them, paganly, under the Calvaire. Scenes of travel mingle but each one has a cutting-edge that separates it from another: at Auray we stood on a hillside above the creased river and watched a procession of black-skirted women, their starched Breton coifs like startled gulls; in bright sun-light on the banks of the Ante, he shielded my eyes so that I saw the tower of Falaise through the luminous bars of his fingers.

Under the hood of a carriage, hands clasped together, lighthearted, without a fixed itinerary, we set out to run about the countryside, to sketch, to gather flowers and images, and when we visited chateaux or cathedrals, I looked wonderingly at everything through a mist of love. At Josselin I drew the two castles— one severely upright, its blue-hatted turrets cutting into the sky, the other hinged to it by a band of grass, tremulously merged with the green water. He picked me some yellow gorse on the promontory of Quiberon, and one twilight, among the strange menhirs at Carnac, I walked beside him under his cape.

How many small churches, dolmens, ruins, did I gaze at with enthusiasm "because he loved them and because his words brought out their poetry? To how many terrifying church steeples and old ramparts did I climb because he was walking up in front of me? Were all the towns more than markers of where I was with him? What would Caen ever have been for me if we did not come upon it after midnight, and I did not wake from sleep on his shoulder to see the church white with moonlight? The jolting stop of the carriage, his word, "Regarde!" the mourning cry, flap, and light click on the pavement, and like the piece of stone knocked down by a pigeon, all that was too vague and undiscoverable under the name, Caen, fell down at my feet like something final.

Black clouds piled up on the horizon, shreds of fog around us, lightning and thunder alternating rapidly, and St. Malo suddenly turned into rain are some of my most previous memories.

He bought me an impermeable at a stall in the town and we climbed on the ramparts so that I could remember all my life how everything lost identity, shape and color under the torrent, how the world seemed translated into a foreign phrase without remembering its old meanings: greyer and greyer, grey seen against grey and through grey; even the sea moved wildly— wrinkling up in peaks and sinking down again as though trying to feel itself.

I was speechless, shivering with cold as he tried to warm me, covered me, held the coat together, his lips against my cheek, on my lips, on my head, rain dripping from his hair onto my neck as he murmured tender words of solicitude. Numb and trembling we ran through the cascading water to find a room nearby with intricately parqueted floors crumbling, stones underneath. There was a feather bed, an oil lamp, my drenched chemise clinging to my skin. I saw us in the mirror— neat, beautiful, connected in a fantastic private way made public— eroticism woven into love like a golden warp.... Them I saw his face so close to mine it was like an obstacle and I forgot to stay on my side of him. In no other leap would I have been so courageous, or— for a time— so safe: compared to a man, the streaming day outside, the ocean, were lesser forces that could not divide into two arms.

Was I wrong? Year after year I noticed white hairs appearing alongside my black ones, veins bulging through my skin, and I had the idea that age had got into me by error and was trying to find its way out again. It's because I've never changed and, even now, I can still climb under the shelter of that time and feel hidden from the despair that often comes for me. Even now, knowing what came of losing myself, I'd lose myself again. I was no home-filled woman; I had to follow currents further and further until cast forth in a place where my origin was incidental, and once I was there, it was a laborious happiness in which I carefully reduced my life, the way Cezanne painted with only the most essential strokes— giving my love as solid a form as an apple. It reached up to the spiritual and closed down again in the terrestrial like a circle from which there was neither exit nor entry. There was no room for my child.

I remember that on the day I had promised to be back with her, I was standing in the cloisters of the *Merveille* at *Mont St. Michel*, not knowing whether my joy was on the top and my desperation on the bottom, or the other way. Over the impressive distance of sand, everything was silent, but there was a cold bell in my heart. It's not too late, I was thinking. He loves me and I love him: it's accomplished. I can go home now and take up my life as it was. Loose myself from this tender, frightening, engrossing, interminable mass of feeling which I seem to stand with only my feet visible on the stone. But I followed him down the perpendicular stairway back to our room where a wonderful page of paper with a poem was folded on my pillow and I delayed… was forgetful of the small face at her window far away.

The Island slept, but although very tired, I could not. I kept myself awake— too enchanted by his lying next to me my head on his shoulder, his feet holding mine between them— to replace it all with other dreams. I listened to the sound of *sabots* in the corridor as he tightened his arms around me. His hands grew more passionate as I waited, his kiss was more clinging. Alone, in the quiet centuries-old room, with the sea beyond, a red velvet couch beside the glowing cheminee, he held me by the waist until the sensual satisfaction— an adjunct— was the only place to go; as though entering an incredibly ornate door, one found oneself in a narrow corridor which, yet, offered a moment of repose.

Was it that night in a remaining glow of the dying fire that I watched him stretched out so deeply asleep that he didn't feel me leaning over him and I was free to look in wonder at his beloved face and body? At his broad shoulders and chest in which life took so much space? His wide lips, curved forehead, and his hands which seemed so worthy to hold something as delicate as a magic wand— the whole of him there before me breathing quietly as a child? I watched him while people waited, promises were broken, letters were not written. And seeing the terrible privacy of his sleep, I felt that sense of futility which is like a nodule inside soft hope. I kissed his knuckles and he opened his eyes, smiled— and all my fears flew like wild geese into the sun.

It must have been every night. In every room there was the same glow, the same fear, the same dark ecstasy, the death and return to life. At every breakfast in different cafes the same laughter merged into a single event of joy ant the small changing details were only handles by which I held my happiness. A green two-wheeled market cart on the bridge, orange flowers that seemed too bright to contain themselves and their scent mingling with the smell of cheese. Feeling fresh vegetables in my hand while the sun hit a white wall, a window was flung open, and women picked up green shrubs dropping earth in the market of Auray. The beauty of that and every town with the faces of its people as they went their ways in the place where they belong— just a simple sign of "Oeufs" on a grey shop front— all of it might have been *papier maché* scenery without him. In the spare minutes when we were separated, the picture of the world had no foreground. I was completely animated by his presence like a ghost car run on a nearby motor. It was he who made everything fit, count, take part and sound into a unity where nothing was superfluous.

Again and again we set out, my head on his shoulder, seeing small churches, black-caped women gathering seaweed on the wind-swept furze, girls with velvet ribbons flying and coiffs bobbing, and we return, by short stops, to our cottage, to our home in Basle, to the end. All the scenes are in my mind but it's their loss that makes them flower as though regret were steady rain— giving life, washing it away.

The rain pitted the roof of the taxi. Hans reeked of *L'Heure Bleue*. Trudi was still sniveling. The little extra from Malinard for the letters awarded me a first class compartment at least until Castelnaudary. The most exhausting would be the first part — to Limoges.

"Here's your ticket *maman*. Don't lose it. Phone me tomorrow from the *auberge*. If anything....you know... I'll come."

"Yes yes. I'm not a child."

They stood planted there waiting for the train to start. Trudi, very pale, kept craning her thin neck towards the window, holding up her eyeglasses, tears still shinning in her eyes. She thinks she might never see me again. Maybe not. How many times had I left her? It was chronic. Like a bad habit. All her pleas.... "*Maman*.... Let's go together... rent a caravan...." I'd been afraid of a last minute match of words, buried grievances, and something got between me and an affectionate gesture. Even as she leaned over in the compartment to kiss me, I was mute. For the umpteenth time I left my maternal heart in shreds all over the floor of a train. Hans put my two old valises up on the rack, I said, *"Ne t'inquiete pas,* I'll send a *bleu* from *Limoges,"* and they went out. They waved. *"Auvoir! Auvoir! ... bon voyage Zazu!"* Hans yelled.

With a trembling hand I note: "On the 16 of April of this present year of 1963 at 10h 11, the train has pulled out of the *Gare Paris-Austerlitz* on the way to my journey south to *Perpignan.*

For months it had been spinning in my mind: Get away. Get away. Get away. Getting away had occupied me as if it could lead to... what? Rebirth ? Redemption? But how overcome inertia. The slough of repetitive daily routine. I am sure the decision came with the visit of beautiful young Klaus, my "admirer" from *Frieburg* im *Breisgau.*

"Genädige frau Balard...." His lovely blond curls bent over my hand, *"Mes hommages..."* in his guttural French— the last word turned into "mush". How many years ago was it...when I was invited to the university to lecture on Ritter and read his poems... and the *Ordinarius,* Heyer, assigned Klaus, his best student, to escort me. There was a reception.... Women bowed to me.

"Remember me? I'm visiting friends in Paris," Klaus said when he rang up, and would I agree to a short visit and could he bring the young wife...a painter, and a great fan of Ritter's poetry. So he came, dragging the girl with him... "the wife of my best friend."

Oh really?

With her big, big eyes, so attentive. Young, energetic...in her 20's She asks in English, when she comes out of the toilet, "Did Ritter live here?"

"No. We met many years ago. We lived in Switzerland." Had she been thinking that the great poet put his sacred behind on the same seat where she's put hers? She watched me move, with my canes, across the room.

"I know almost all of his poetry," says the girl with her longing for the romantic. "He understood women very well, didn't he?"

I say, "Sometimes." Which has a bitter taste.

She was looking at his portrait which still hung then on the wall. Then she looked at me. In her eyes I read: "You are old. You haven't long to live. Tell me everything...."

The creature had brought a portfolio of her pen-and-ink drawings. Klaus had told her I was a painter... not just an old mistress.... Looking them over, Hans was impressed.

"Hast du diese hübsche Zeichnungen gesehen, Zazu?" he said to me in his sugary voice. She was pretty. I was irritated. It was sudden. The eruption.

"Yes, yes, I saw!.... She relies on line like a baby!" I spat out, as though her overflow of energy galvanized, injected me.

There was silence. Then the girl said, "It's true. I know. Alexeieff told me the same thing. Someday I hope to be a great artist...like you."

"Stupide stupide stupide," I said to myself. Then to her: "forgive me, what I said is probably rude and incoherent. I am tired. Forgive me." Pushing my chair on wheels, I went to the bookcase and took a copy of my book, *Une Image de Ritter,* and inscribed it to her, with my *"sympathie"*. She thanked me profusely with her big brown eyes in mine. I had let her hold a piece of the myth, let her have a share of her great poet. They left, but her words, "a great artist like you,"

seeing my book again, and Klaus bending over my hand as though it didn't look like a bundle of twigs... made me feel my life needn't be over. I, too, had longings. Yes... she saw me as an old woman who had seen her best days and whose thoughts were with the past and not the present. But the present kept pawing at me like a neglected dog. All right! Down! I'll see to you. And there began my plan. To go away..... I began preparing as though I were crazed. A mad creature, off to some seaside. An open balcony... remote. Where I might make some peace between my past and the dog.

The train picked up speed. "I'll miss you Zoe!" he had said, and he got smaller and smaller.... the still youngish poet with a fair moustache and thin hair, as I opened the window and shouted, "I can get out!"

I was feeling lost in the expanse of open country as we left the outskirts of Paris.. I glanced at *Le Monde*, put aside my thermos, dozed... and suddenly heard music floating in through the window and voices. The train was stopping. In the crowd on the platform, an accordionist was playing. I put on my spectacles: the sign read *Vierzon*.

As the train started up again, I saw a double image: a woman on the *quais,* waving farewell and a sudden me — shockingly reflected on the glass. I'd long ago eschewed mirrors which had once been friends. Ritter loved them. Loved the miracle of repetition in immaterial space. He had a whole vision of another world beyond ours, a world of the dream, of ghosts, perhaps of the dead, and argued that the reason mirrors were covered after someone died was to prevent their coming back. For me, mirrors were constant re-assurances. Ritter spoke of my "mirror-haunted soul—the opposite of Narcissus — that I had constantly to re-affirm myself in the eyes of others. Even, I think, in my own, for at that time I was not myopic enough, and too often in the midst of a happy time, I was standing off to watch myself totally occupied by love. I saw us do nothing but kiss over a table, stroke each other's hair or hand, look at the other's face one moment in a trance of disbelief, the next collapsing in laughter at saying the same thing at the same time. In love, we made love... a miraculous magical life. I saw me parting from him to post a letter, his kissing me again and again before I walked off talking to myself as though I were drunk, saying over and over all the way down the road: "This is happening to me, this is happening to me, this is happening to me."

I see us following the sun or arriving in the middle of a season, because without a village clock to sift the time, particle by particle, the months often surprised us en route as though we were *jongleurs*. January singing adagio at St. Moritz on a morning as high as Chartres, September, delicate, bewildered as a bird that's lost the breeze, appeared in Italy and followed us home to Basle, and with our frequent traveling we confounded, outstripped them. I twisted flowers in my hair and with his arm around me I wandered with my prince of Trouveres — touching new ground every day. In a poem, he wrote to me, "... through our hearts which we have opened / A God passes with wings at His feet." We sometimes lost the world around us and would stop in the middle of a street to look at each other in wonder... forgetting to walk on — as though under an enchantment.

The train just passed *Chateauroux* without stopping. I should have taken a local. We once stopped there in a small Inn where they lent me wooden *sabots,* where, over dinner he said to me, "The patron is curious about us. I am well-dressed and you are beautiful."

"Am I beautiful?" I pleaded.

"Yes, you are." We drove, in a cab, from castle to castle, where near *Azay le Rideau* he fell asleep on the banks of the river, where, looking up at *Chambord* he chose a room for me to paint in and I picked a tower window which would be his study, where...where....

"Where are we going?" I asked on a train."

To drives in the country, to look at beautiful villages, lie in the sun, eat peaches and drink red country wine out of thick glasses. From station to hotel, hotel to station, often exhausted in a new room at night. "Sleep, Zoë, Dors, Zoë." My eyes open as I yearned to follow him even into his restlessness, I waited for those words to which I had become addicted as though to wine or ether or morphine. Words that made up a riddle that enthralled me: *Je t'aime.*

"Angela! I have a surprise for you!" There were acrobats, *gitanes,* a monkey in an egg-colored vest, and we watched them in the little square of *Ischia Ponte*. Hand in hand, he in his cape and straw hat, I with the last spotted flowers in my hair, when there appeared beside us a man with old-fashioned side whiskers who asked me in English. "May I ask where you people come from?" and thought us rude or insane when, taken with mad laughter, we couldn't answer him.

Where had I come from? I had an image in the mirror, a name, my clothes were a certain size, yet I felt myself to be only small things— saliva? sweat. a passage from him to me. When he stood before me in his handsome white body, I was sudden love.

To whom did my family write then? My Paris vacation was long over and I was in Switzerland. I worried people who loved me. My mother no longer believed that I was in Basle to cure ill health. To my husband who wrote that my child missed me, I sent telegrams full of lies and contradictions.

The long down stairway sobbing under my running feet, the small square door that opened with a twist and pull of the spring bolt, the sun in the courtyard over the stone drinking-trough— trembling in the water, varnishing the leaves of the lime tree. Too far away to hear my family now, my feet outracing the order of their days, as I rushed out and found the surprised morning with dew still in its hair... the horses in a trance... the same beggar woman carefully- hatted, leaning on a crutch, her shoes fastened with string, one hand held out? "My beauty^ you are lucky. You have youth," she'd say before I reached into my sac. Always at the same turning, by the steps to the bridge, like my past, I paid her with whatever coin I had and went my way. She bought my guilt. She was repulsive. My heart beat wildly on the days when she wasn't there. And rushing back, the warm breads in my basket, the joy that I had found my way through the wide dismayed world to that door! I had— ah— I had his face looking out at me over the boxes of flowers attached to the sills— the peals of geranium like red bells on the stillness of early morning. It was our own home. I set down my basket on the tiled floor. I untied my hat and called to him. Isn't my voice still buried somewhere in those walls?

I had youth, I had luck. And our own home, so well-lit and the handsome Great Salon! Ritter's desk against the window and all the rooms strung out from his to mine— the smell of ink and turpentine mingling, the scent of coffee, sounds and smells of work and happiness.

The old man had been a painter and left me an easel as indifferent to the change of hands as an oak to birds. We were impressed with his black formality. We told him we would cherish all his treasures and we tried to be subdued, but the day we followed him up was a fragile autumn one, and in that exceptional season of fading, we were too boisterous and brown, too ready to burst into song. The old stairway reproached us with creaking.. He handed us the key, bowed, left, and Ritter filled a mallard vase with mums, their ruddy faces and torn ears giving our first bouquet the air of peasants squeezed into a Sunday suit.

It was our own home— our little charade of husband and wife— daring ambition! A wild joy and guilty fear mixed in the days which crackled with threatening and beseeching letters: threads of my life were still attached to my child and parents, but it was too late to go back, and if my life was divided, I was whole— for what can bind the selves like the mouth and arms of someone you love? Sleeping beside him to wake with a kiss on my hand or shoulder, the happiness of two people who begin laughing and can't stop, and lurking under it the terrible and sweet tenuousness, the feeling of borrowing one's life for a short time which seems very long, on the small high point of love, dizzied.

Friends came to sit under the rosy lamplight within our closed curtains. We sat hours around the table; I told stories, made them all laugh, Ritter sitting beside me, but I didn't have to look at him. I had the sense of our being placed like two annexes of a building in the middle of a city where everything flies. Once Rolland gave a reading while the candles gutted over the remains of a splendid meal. I stood, half-hidden by the door of the foyer, as Ritter showed him out. I saw the old man embrace him, heard him say, *"Felicitations, mon ami; elle est très, très belle."*

These people were as cherished— as landscape— as my furniture and rooms. And when they had left, I felt none of the melancholy that comes at the ends of visits, at the ends of days. I gathered up details of Ritter; the profile which made his wide lips thin into an almost canine smile, his pleasure passing like a shadow behind his face, his arms, his shoes carefully put on and laced— quite as though I were gathering flower after flower, one after another as I happened upon them. But all their miracle vanished if I tried to arrange them into an understanding of my love for them.

Ritter told me that when he had a feeling settled in his mind, he left it, and went around to the side he hadn't yet looked at. But he had the genius for such liberty. Always I had struggled with my random wants for a beautiful tall magic, and when I couldn't reach it, broke off pieces and crammed them, like large hands into small gloves, down in my needs. Now I had it all— the magic— would like to have painted it, put down one of his whispers in two strokes of my brush. But I could only render flesh, place an earring to pull a head forward, round a torso out of flat space, as though by defining the visible. I could calm my astonishment at what I could not understand.

As I copied out his poems, arranged them in folios and listened when he read them to our friends, I knew that what I failed to do in painting, he did with words. Each morning after breakfasting, he went into his study, to the immaculate desk near the bright window, laid out a sheet of the whitest paper, took up his ebony pen and sat several minutes, very formally, as though waiting for a distinguished visitor.

How many times I heard and felt those words: "I have a surprise for you!" A poem. A plan. St. Moritz looking like the windows of a toy shop as we drove from the station in a sledge drawn by two horses wearing bells. "I'd like to take your birthday to a place it's never seen." He lit the fire, we drank a bottle of *Vosne-Romanée,* but I was intoxicated with the pleasure which belongs to people when they rush into the first days of spring. Ritter spread the map out across the table, one full glass untouched to pledge my surprise. The weather had blown leaves around our doorway; they turned ochre and hugged their crisp edges, announcing the frost while I sat in love as though it were a green dome.

It *was* what it was. Gone, gone the past, the old woman, the easel perhaps from my dear room where so often he came up behind me, stretched out his long third finger stained with ink, and we compared the prodigality of the marks our work had left on us. Gone, my parents, but with all its beauty still bearing is that narrow Eden of years in which I lived with Ritter. Old woman waiting at the bridge, old past waiting in the past, I gave them what I could. Go back? To a life in which the unfulfilled stood weeping all around me?

"You are no longer my daughter if you do this," my mother wrote. The world guide of rules and behavior like a closed car on a beautiful road. I had to turn away.

Reason should have told me that he would leave me. Remember his delight with the Japanese artists who changed their names several times in a lifetime to safeguard their liberty? Remember when he suddenly went on a trip? It seemed so natural at the time and yet there was a terrible vacancy as though it were a rehearsal without actors for a real parting. I went to sleep with his coat against my face as though I were a deserted dog.

Reason told me. Reason told me, but my heart was like one of those ignorant *Infantas* whose limited education had taught it only to reign and issue commands, and I obeyed it during these years with him— clockless years that strayed through new-made seasonal summers floored with sand, their highest point a campanile; autumn intoned like a russet sacrament over the high-town; winter cameled by the Alps and all the color of its sky bartered for a silver sun.

"Take us the same way as yesterday!" he shouted to the driver, and we smothered our laughter because we couldn't remember where we'd been; every field had the same white placidity which we demented with our sleigh.

We ruin St. Moritz, leading black footprints, breaking glasslike carpets with our boots, laughing like vandals we escape to our room where the steaming cups of lavender chocolate warm us. He leans his smiling lovely face and head against mine. I loved his smile. If I could hare worn it like the ring he gave me! He took it from the armoire, handing it to me shyly, and as I folded the paper up carefully, I told him, "I'll be buried in it."

> *I have a surprise for you.*
> *I'll be buried in it.*
> *Je t'aime.*
> *Moi aussi, je t'aime.*

We, segmented by two voices, like an angel by the leadings on a church-window. Time has passed, but that day is suddenly here without coming from the outside.

> *Where does it come from?*
> *It came from me.*
> *Like history, my issue are my old events.*

Green summers golden in the dying day, faces wrinkled by birth and smoothed by death play games with living eyes unless we fix the time. I'm suddenly enriched or newly poor as that afternoon appears again with shoulders epaulleted in snow. Its hand raised in a mixed gesture of hello and goodbye, it stays, reluctant as a child, to leave before the end of things.

How fantastic, the survival of all I had and its annihilation from the universe! Or is there some planet archive where everything is stored in transparent boxes... 1913... 1914... 1915... here it is...as the silvery dust— like rubbings from an old Christmas— powders my fingers.... We were gay and hysterical, beautiful, young and hopeful as Europe before the agony of Verdun, the graves by the Somme.

Before glazed hats gave way to helmets and my world splintered like Rheims.

There was no escape. No escape in Venice or in Basle. There was no safe way down for me. And that parting— so much worse for being quiet. Picking up his hat as though he were just going next door. "I'll miss you, Zoë," and walked out, leaving my life ajar.

He made a home, without me, in Neuchatel, remote from battles, writing poems, the suffering of others— of me— was like the oxygen that fed his flame. Sacred monster! He pushed me into ways which brought uncleanness to my mind. I had a vision of detaching my head with its blue eyes and black hair which he had loved; I saw me bringing it to a laundry, sayings lots of water and javel and a little starch— and then I picked it up, wrapped carefully in paper tied with blue cellophane, and found it white white, not new, but comforting, unstained.

"You are still young and beautiful and talented," Janka said. "And you're a fool." She told me that in a time of world destruction, my school girl suffering was disgusting. I thought up ways to change her angry expressions: at Bellevue I held a dying boy against my breasts which he decorated with small rosettes of blood; I mourned Appolino bedded down, alone, in riddled ground at Flandres; I told me: "Zoë, your small defeat is vaulted by the great defeat of war. Be more!"

And every night I went to sleep alone, attached only to my dreams of Ritter as to a short cord which kept me prisoner but nourished. I didn't wake up simultaneously with anyone again. We, Unz, was gone, and like women after childbirth, I closed up again, and became only me, again. I had to go back. "Go back!" To where? It wasn't even where I'd left it. The songs had stopped at *Lapin Agile*, horses tethered to the chestnut trees, Gothas droning over head, Big Bertha waking us each day at five, cavalry bivouacked on the boulevards, Americans, mansions changed to hospitals, and I wandered through the blacked-out streets with Janka. I wore the blue dress bought at Quimper three years before, or my lavender blouse and serge skirt of two years before as we carried thermoses of hot coffee and tea to the wounded soldiers in the street, and I softened Janka's expression.

She often held my hand as we walked, but she didn't know that all the while over me was the numinous hand of a man, above me was a man in a cape kneeling on an embankment... above me, under an umbrella, on a brown slope with yellow gorse, on unfolded handkerchiefs, a young woman in blue and a young woman, in lavender sat amidst smiles and caresses....

Mose caught up with us one day, and under the disapproving eyes of Janka, said, "Let me take you to Grasse, Zoë. The change will do you good." She answered him for me. I listened to them while women in long white nurses aprons —women with patriotically bobbed hair— walked up the stairs to Bellevue. I listened as I looked over what I could keep and what I wanted to throw away. I wanted the tenderness he had showed me when I leaned against him in front of Byron's house. It was sunny. We didn't speak. My cheeks were burned from the heat and his were unshaven. He was a bit distraught and moved, slightly stunned. Later he fell asleep in my arms on the bank of a river— his eyes half-open like a cat's, as though he had to be on guard against what he told me he had never felt before. I couldn't keep the memory of my humiliation at Neuchatel... as though I were sorting stockings with domestic care. "...like using a finely-tuned instrument to chop wood!" Mose said to Janka, but I didn't go to Grasse. I mounted the steps to that disgusting charnel house which used to be a dancing school. Like me, I thought.

Mose took me, instead, to the Chatelet to see" Parade" and I was utterly fascinated by the sense of mission they all had. The gaiety, the gaiety is what perplexed me. The end of the world's innocence, the end of mine, had coincided. And Yanka and I continued to travel miles each day in Paris. "Let me carry that," she said, no matter what small object I held. Her narrow skirt constricting her dancer legs was worn and bulging at the knees; her boots were shining with the cooking-oil she used on them. I counted the brass hooks as we stood in front of the shop window where she wanted to buy me something. "It would suit you...that camisole," she said just above her breath as she often sang over it.

The chambermaid looked after me, filled my lamp without being told. My small room was well-kept, silent, the shatters closed while I dreamed— did I dream it all?— of how I had fled *la Bresse*, the Boer, and myself. How I drove into Paris on a troop filled train. The faded cab at the station smelling of leather, the *cocher's* black hat reminding me... as he lashed the bony horse, the curtains flapping. In the evening Roland gently guided my elbow like the tiller of a little boat towards the lanterns in the *Marais* where the old women gave us a shovel-full of *petit gris*, reminding me.... And a man walked by on *sabots*, reminding....

Would everything remind me?

Yasha and I were to meet in front of the *Rotonde*. I came down the *Boulevard Montparnasse* with my veil blowing behind me, brushing the wet pavement with my dress, weeping. *Rotonde. Rotonde.* I could not get the name out of my mind. Why here? And before me stood my old comrade with his hair neatly combed, his paint-cracked hands held out, saying –

"Eh ben!. T'es beaucoup changée, toi! T'as une toute petite tête, tu sais... t'as été ben malade, la bàs en Suisse, eh?" He had brought me crayons, took me to the *Médrano* where I suffered the spectacle he made, spreading out his tools, moving his palette over the heads of the audience, groaning aloud... all to pack everything: up again and sit with me at *Place Pigalle,* stir his *pernod* with a stick, wipe the stick on his sleeve, tap it against his forehead, his eyes closed, open his eyes, look at the tip of the stick, tell me how badly his new love goes. He had been waiting to tell me all this. In those days he still knew morning disappointments and evening hopes and I was still to wonder "What shall I do with myself?" as I looked at his long cheeks, as I watched his handsome eyes, as he explained to me, as his soiled fingers banged the glass. As he said, "She's no different than the others."

"Dare it!" Kisling said. "Such quaint morality is a museum piece today!" The small unstoppered bottle of ether was passed around, went by my hands— frozen in a small group on my knees— to where the handsome Italian painter lay, half-reclining, with a girl on either side of him. "Did it ever exist?" he asked dreamily, "Even in quaint ladies?" But Roland said to let me be. Wasn't it a quaint morality that he was fighting for. "Like the Catholics," Modi said. "Who go on believing even though the Pope defecates just like us." And I was sorting again, peaches this time, some of which had been ruined by proximity to the rotten. Downstairs, in the *Rotonde,* my violets fester as the voice of the Duchess says, "Come now, little painter, your experience makes it...."

No! I put aside Lilos and all his brothers. I *am* innocent! I think of Roland flying off to die, to see chimeras more terrible than the beasts on *Notre Dame.* I follow Dégas in his battered green hat and shiny coat on the *Boulevard Clichy.* Deaf and nearly blind, he moves gropingly, his face seeming to rage, "Where's the light, the light?" I hear Janka, already ill at that time, singing above the air-raid whistles in her beautiful torn out voice and I listen with the others, sitting out the nights of war. *"Que faro sen-za Eury-di-ce?"* she sings. She liked the baroque ordering of sorrow found in Gluck and in Purcell; anguish peering through melodic bars across its cage. "What will I do without Eurydice?" *Que faro* without this or that, without her or him, and one always finds something, but it's never as good. *"Eurydice..."* she pleaded. *"Eurydice... respondi...... rispondi......"* All the rest of life is excelsior with love packed in the center like a fragile outrage. Over and over, *"Que faro senza Eurydice?"* the repetition eases the pain and delays complete loss.

Ghosts ghosts ghosts ghosts. Echoing footsteps on the cobbled court, Janka walking beside me to the gate. The sky was dropping snow which circled and fell, unattended, around our heads.

"I suppose I'm too brusque with you," she said.

"Non non."

"Oh I am, I know."

After dinner as she made coffee in the narrow kitchen, I had my back against the wall. I said. "But I'd never been happy before." She slid the grounds into a folded paper and answered, "Very well, you've been happy. Now you can begin to live."

Live? How? For so long happiness had equaled living. I woke to the sound of cannon, panicked without my happiness, suddenly remembering it like a coat I'd left somewhere by error. When had I last seen it? Did I still have it when I carried the wine to Lilos? I remember it clearly at... Oh, something as large as that... someone would find it. Wasn't my name written inside?

She walked me out, leaving the others inside. I said, "I'd never been in love before," and she said coldly, "You're lucky. Some people never even have that." But I dreaded the holiday season again without him; the coming of January with the one festival I'd loved as a child— my birthday all covered with snow. I remembered the haystack and the field and the murdered tree at Neuchatel, the cold in my breast and my silk shoes torn by the stiff grass as I walked with him on the day of our parting. I wondered how long it would take for his face to fade; for me to replace his presence in myself with other images, to detach him from the memory of all I had ever read and would feel when someone mentioned "love" and if, without him, my body would ever again reveal itself to me as wonder. Too long: a lifetime, perhaps. cleaned out like a house the moving-van just left.

"Can't people be happy and live, too?" I asked her.

"They don't seem to go together."

In the small electric bulb, a filigree grasshopper of light showed us the paving stones, a branch stripped down for winter like an arm for death; it showed me, for an incandescent moment, Janka's face, a triangle of amber cheek, the beautiful nostril, an emerald eye— her eyes that often looked at me with love — her eyes the color of the sea lightened by afternoon, bountiful but impatient with reflections of the dying day. She presided over my suffering like a lamp which hung in the corner of a very dark room.

I walked beside her in an extra shawl of hers. The long neck with its proud head bent towards the uneven stones... "You won't do anything foolish, will you?" in her deep voice. "You must believe in the mystery of tomorrow." I couldn't speak, although I longed to tell her that I would... or I would try. To make her think me brave, like her. The accompaniment of her steps to mine, her shawl which might enclose me in her strength.

On the street side, we paused a moment in the blacked-out city. She was wearing only a thin cloak thrown on hurriedly when she had left her guests. She hesitated, had a baffled, almost angry look. "All these men," she said, waving her large hand as though they were as numerous as the snowflakes. "They're waiting like buzzards over your weakness. You are too vulnerable. You are too sad."

"J'ai bien le droit."

"Merde!" she said. exasperated. "Your love affair… is that the summit, the end of life— your love? Can't you live without a man?"

"I can't help it if they come to see me," I said.

"Don't you encourage them?"

"A little……."

"Send them packing!" she said.

I heard Bruno say "I love you," and Mose took me for walks. Each night I went back to my narrow bed in ever-widening nights and stored these men away like bottles of preserves in a famine. Roland handing me down the staircase of *Notre Dame* as though I were a porcelain figurine, Jules buying me a *cornet* of *croustillants* and pretending we were children at a fair. I did not want to think too much of them, or too often. I wanted to be content with calm, occasional touches — not too engrossing; not enough to quench my thirst or increase it: calm. Quite calm, and this was the word, the last word I plunged into my pillow every night.

"Come live with me," she said. "I'll take care of you…."

I stammered that I'd see. "Go back now," I said. "You'll take cold."

She pushed a corner of her chopped hair behind an ear and said. "Don't worry about *me*. I'm alright. I've tried. I can't stop you if you want to be an empty boat again and smash yourself against some different rocks."

She kissed me quickly and walked off. I looked back, saw her shove the gate open, and go running into the court.

Death gives her resonance now. At that time she was an ordinary woman who woke up each day.

Her influence acted on my life, and illness, for a certain space, was held at bay. But I hadn't heeded her advice. I went to *Normandie* with Bruno. I gave myself like a gift I'd asked someone else to choose, and so I stood off as he admired it, not able to share in his pleasure. We came down the stairs, in darkness, from his room to mine, and I removed my shoes so as not to wake his grandmother, I shall always remember his taking them from me, tenderly, carrying them on his hands like small black crowns. But it was too soon. I could do nothing with that gesture; there was a wall between acknowledgment and the tenderness of others. So Mose went empty-handed. We dined together one night in February on *Boul' Mich.* The winter atmosphere affected me with a deadly paralysis. "We must only be friends. Do you agree?" I said, and he said, "No." He left me at the mouth of the Metro and I returned to my room, its ceiling as crushing as a slab of tomb.

Slowly. Slowly I unbuttoned my boots and undressed. Roland was dead. All his anecdotes, his charm, for what? Indifference pressed upon me. Fate seemed as blind and bloodless as granite. My spirits were sinking fast. The resolution to finish the painting on my easel fell dead-sick. I paced the floor, wondering "How shall I keep well?" and in the courtyard, for answer, was a barren snow scene, a tree rooted in the center— its arms stretching out to each side like exposed veins on the belly of a grey-white sky. It smote me with revulsion, this stillness; it was death's eye, empty of breath. I sat down on my narrow bed, my head against the wall, a terrible oppression growing in me, my father's ghost rising, saying "You have caused me a lot of trouble, Zöe," my mother's face was turned away, my child taken from me. "You are unstable," my husband whispered in blank space. What was I doing alone in Paris? I was thirty-one years old. How would I get up tomorrow? Where did I. come from? What should I do? I wet my hair, my chemise, my hands with tears, and then I dressed and made my way to Janka's. There were no taxis. The length of the walk filled me with a panic I had never known; inertia seemed to pull me backwards in some dark interval between time as I moved, thinking "How shall I get there?" I waited on the landing for her return, my hands around my knees, when a deep persistent rhythm structured the night, a gong gong gong, trembling but certain, and I closed my eyes thinking, "I'm inside the bells of *Notre Dame*."

She took me, but to speak truth, I compromised matters. I served two masters: I lay in her house, but my heart was elsewhere. She was lovely and I was surrounded by her music. She was not a great artist and her only value to the world, now, is that I loved her. Not enough. She drew me the way convents draw the cast-off mistresses of kings. What fate as glorious could they ever have? Not God, I'm sure it was not God. They crept into the shelter of patience— which is the waiting out of time stripped down of personal surprise. Apart from differently shaped animals, like a herd of calm grey elephants, an ageless dignity could put the world of shame to shame.

But Janka, dear, my stand, my hope, my windscreen against man, it didn't work, my semblable-love. Tomorrow wasn't shaped like me. There was no mystery greater than, my own astonished body of night in arms as pale as every dawn. I was of the prowling kind, and cowardly like most of them; like cats who wander in or out too far and then, afraid, will jump no matter where, trusting to a lightness or instinctive grip to land. So enchanted with my womanhood, I had to see it burned out, reverse, like the drawings from my copper plate when acid touched them.

Ah, if I could have torn myself from men I wouldn't be alone now. What Order would have cast me out at fifty? After Pierre, my face— still a simple Romanesque façade— began to give way under lines like scaffolding in a *chantier* of destruction. And one day I saw that everything had been accomplished; my blue eyes were set in the Gothic complexity of age.

And I'm alone. I'm all I have. I'm buried in it. Devoted to the archaeology of self, no sun-sick German ever found so many fragments of Aphrodisian form.. Shall I renounce, by decency, all my old memories, retire my dead "holidays"......?" No. That supreme chic of knowing how to decline— I lack it, I lack it! I know I'll go to sleep tomorrow in another unfamiliar room, not heavily veiled in unconsciousness, but bared of time... waiting for a scene, a smile... an arm again- mine!- so much rounder than I remembered... before an ascetic morning withers it.

But oh it pains me that in a woolen shroud, jumbled together with images of others, common spleens, erotic conquests, grievances, ambitions— all dissolved and yielding to the flower-roots and the earth, some of the most beautiful things I ever was are lost. And so much of my youth was stored in second-rate memories which have left the world quietly like lamps blown out. Eyes that loved my face have lids of dirt: exiled from the bodies which I often treated with a pilgrim's awe, men wander in my mind.

My heart is full of a vague dread of light— Dégas— of dark mists thinning away into a land where eternal morning is embedded, un-colonized— where everyone lives alone in his stronghold. I'm driven by insatiable longing which stretches up endlessly, endlessly to where I can sit down with my past like two old friends who know all about each other. I must sit down with my selves in that Oriental insistence of seeing one's image in the eyes of others as one drinks, and never alone.

I have watched the years setting out like tumbrels. Now, on a gibbet over the present this old woman of myself hangs apart. Not even God is at home. I must go back, there, where lovers intercede with mortality. I must be distracted by expectations— even those I know— and this will lead me away from catastrophe. I've taken in too much death, and drugged with it, I walk the past to keep myself awake.

"*Wachet Auf,*" Ritter sang, and Janka said that everything could be recovered in music, but Janka dear, there is no mystery greater than your silence. There's no mystery greater than yesterday. Leaving suddenly, the weightless furniture of days overthrown, all the people who loved me in cold vaults now live only for themselves. My mother has forgotten how to braid my hair, and against Ritter's dreadfully bared chest, a passionate decay has replaced my head; eunuched with infinity, he desires nothing more.

But what would they all see if they could look at me now? An old woman with her flesh in tatters like a whore's chemise! I'm almost dead, yet, I can offer sanctuary to some faces which have lost their homes.

1963

5 MAI

The night seemed murmurous and old. Small shiftings, flappings, the constant rustling of whatever could not sleep surrounded me in my own unrest. On long nights youth sleeps on tangled arms. Moist as rain-wet flowers. Only the aged wake before the sky turns pale at roof level. Or sit with a shaded light for company- stiff feet on the boards still cool with night air.

But calling myself still young (it might be the only name he left me) I couldn't share—except in mockery- the emptiness that follows a dream. The dream he had carried away as though it had been a small garden in his life with me still clinging like a leaf to one of many fullblown plants.

Only the most stupid animals seek out for company, those who aren't like them. In this small Inn I had to do with fleas, bugs, unguided bees, roaming cats, the whippet stud that wandered the kitchen garden—backing off on stick-like legs when he saw my own come through the hedge, my hands outstretched with leavings from my meals. I've never been a friend of things that didn't speak; he knew this even when he had forgotten, in his exile like mine, what it was he was born to do.

I stood my last night in the little room, alone; my hands were pressed against the glass door which, while I listened for sounds that didn't change, had gone from cold to the dampness that covers the country dawn in autumn. It was exactly the way I spent my first night there. In the weeks between I had almost loved again.

From the beginning, I had taken to having my evening coffee in a small salon decked-out like a private parlor, but in which there was no evidence of its having been used for living: each chair stood in the same spot each night, and there was not a crumb behind the cushion of someone who had been careless as he pulled his seat nearer the reading lamp or to see a face he cared to see more clearly. The vases stood full of immortelles, dried a week or year or two before; and fresh flowers put out as a convention, in inconvenient places, grew smaller and shriveled without a trace on the waxed tables of any petals that had dropped.

When one can't find a home, one rents something to live in, but what's one to do when looking for a future?

My answer had been to leave mine fixed in Ritter's life almost like the miniature wax of that Bourges banker in the isinglass dome which stood on the sideboard. A gallant page who wavered only under imperfections in his shell, he stood in place each night beside the russet chair I had selected as "my own".

I found a tempting salvation in the garden where I came upon— to the fright of that startled whippet—a wall clotted with chevrefoil and bristles from some English briar roses. This had been allowed to escape from the long dry hand which rented out the rest of the inn. In the parlor, two weeks before this night—my last—I had met another guest who sat in that mock and massive Louis Treize chair from which, I had believed, one could deliver reprisals. He filled it so comfortably that I saw only later that I had been confused by his missing arm in which I reckoned him invalid like myself. Isn't it true that isolation has always made me infirm, and never more than at that time when it was isolation without peace? He was so broad that in my first glance I imagined his arm broken and only held taut within his black cloth coat. It was a full traveling coat, well-brushed, and by its weight, the man seemed destined to remain on his travels into winter. Only minutes later, while he also looked straight at me, I saw that his sleeve was neatly pinned up flat to his shoulder and both sides of his chest were the same depth.

There we sat, and a look from his eyes, dark and heavy as night clouds, passed across the room and struck my face in the shadows. I know I jumped as though my feeling had been something begun while I was still asleep. It was the waking even a small girl knows under a certain glance from a man. But like someone drugged and fitfully dozing off again, I became more aware of him than of myself.

"Good evening, Madame," he said, taking advantage of that peculiar propriety which throws guests of the same establishment into a community as false as their possession of a room which will soon be stripped of their scent. And, in fact, as though he had guessed by some expression of my face what I had felt of this, he went on to add, "It is strange, this---that we take our coffee like friends, one visiting the other, or---"

He broke off, perhaps out of respect for a lady he did not know, and spared me the reference to something more intimate.

"Indeed," I answered him, not looking at his sleeve, but at the fixed smile he had which did seem as useless to him as that sleeve. "Indeed, I find it not strange at all. I have stayed at a hotel before."

It was not his smile which altered, but rather his body which drew back against that massive chair, and I felt that in establishing a proper tone, I had perhaps been too sharp. After all, a lady traveling alone (how grateful I was to him for neglecting that banal opening question: "Does Madame often travel alone?") cannot have the dignity of privacy. It was in that vein of thinking that I almost offered a smile and looking about the room I was impelled to say, following his gaze, "By any means, I should never invite some one to visit me if I had the bad taste to decorate this room, and---" I looked again at him who did seem in fact quite right for the style of his chair, "I wonder that I would visit anyone who lived in such a place."

His head drew back as though he had hit it into something. His smile opened into a laugh so wide that I could see the roof of his mouth illuminated by the hard glare of the naptha lamp. When his head came down he looked at me again. The smile was gone in a moment. In that flicker out, I realized that it was with the slight smile that he disguised his eyes. And to this day, although I saw his face again, I cannot forget how his first look had drawn me up as a flaming sulphur stick held under my closed eyes would have waked me from sound sleep. I retired almost at once to my room.

In the course of other evenings we again had coffee, sometimes alone with one another, or more often with the proprietress who had taken it upon herself to mingle her charges in "play" as though they were children, or she a nurse with patients. Yes, for who but someone afflicted of some hopeless and draining disorder would have chosen this cheerless part of the world as more than a stopping place for the night and at that most despairing part of the year when one season has died giving birth to the other as its character. In the presence of the proprietress, or one of the other guests during those weeks, this man—who turned out to be a Boer and finding I knew a bit of English, would often speak a few words in that language----and I established out of our first meeting the conspiratorial glance of amusement over some new folly on the part of the others in relation to the inn.

One evening, a Saturday, after a large and well-cooked meal, "the station –mistress" –as he had named her in a whisper to which I did not respond—drew up the cover from an old player-piano over which a fringed shawl lay like a deflated sea-monster, its tentacles sadly writhing in the ghostly keys as they began to raise and lower in a Chopin etude. A small round businessman from Orleans who would not stay longer than it took him to go through the specialties of the house, and who always fell into a doze, even at his table, after the meals, suddenly stood up with a vicious expression on his tart-shaped face and ran to the phantom piano shouting: "A little respect. Please! A little respect!" And he threw the shawl like a filthy carcass backwards onto the far end of the table. The rest of the recital found him with a hand, so thick its fingers stood out straight from the palm, clapped over his eyes as he sat in the Louis Treize, his feet—which did not reach the carpet—beating the wood of each chair –leg in tempo with the music. I stifled a laugh and, looking up at my fellow-spy--- for so I had begun to think of him---saw him deadly serious staring right into my mouth. All at once I felt I had no more bones than that chamois which had folded down over the table-edge.

I had tried to prevent myself, in my loneliness and sadness, from any feeling which would have been dishonest at another time. To tell the truth, all the developing society of that parlor had done was to remind me of Ritter again. After banter, a thimbleful of chartreuse, I went to my room on the verge of weeping, for to fill oneself with an emotion can only remind the heart of one it has more deeply felt. The new "friendship" of this armless man rattled in a vaster space left by that beloved who cut down boundaries with a soul that fought always a frenzied battle against his own.

In leaving I had jumped to my feet as though the Boer had physically accosted me. There was no need to interrupt the concert with my parting and I went out of he parlor without a word. In my confusion I turned not quickly enough at the stair and had to go on until I was in the foyer that led to the walk and the carriage-house. What do I remember then? There are steps and turns that escape my memory. I cannot now arrange an order of what passed in the time before he was speaking to me. I am not able to bring back opening words, or whether any were mine. Of that time I can see the unshaven palings of a raw bark fence on which my hand rested, lit up from a lantern in the stables. I cannot humiliate myself by writing again those words he spoke to me, because I knew that beneath the anguish I felt and would feel again for Ritter, those words impregnated and caused to flower in the same moment--- like the mythical plant which grows to maturity at its birth -- a lightless blossom in the dark dungeon earth that I shared with the world of man. This stirring of life---below an anguish as constant and petrified like the sketches of agony Rodin dried in clay---this stirring, like the surprising rustle of a tree nearby on a windless night making one turn in reflex, threw me against him, my arms as though they had blossomed around his neck, my face on that shoulder isolate as I, my lips pressing the cloth of his coat until with his chin he turned up my head and crushed his own lips against them. I felt his long arm curve to my waist, his hand clasped lightly around my side. I thought of nothing.

There are those plants that look tender and yet grow through brick or out of the crevices of stone walls if the smallest space is left, and so what he raised in me that night could smash the barrier to further life that had been built within myself. Some moments, I have reason to know, take longer than a year you chronicle with dates. And lovers plan a whole life with their lips which have no way of reckoning hours. What suns rose and set, more real than those I had not counted in my days that late summer, while we stood melted by the darkness into one curved shadow over life. No. The words that passed between that space for breath between our lips--- words like the same stirring from branch to branch originating at neither—these so engrained in that earth of myself will appear now only after my death as brighter chips of stone in the sand. I did not wonder until later whether my dark and mutilated lover had with a cruder talent caused to flower the small shoot left by a master. No he did not release me. He moved his head back, tightened even more that single hand as though to give it the strength of two, and with a voice deep and hollow said, "Do you mind a man with only one arm?"

His tone trembled at the last, but remained deep—almost majestic. It moved me as an apology from a man can always move, and this was offered not for an inflicted hurt, but as the donor presents a valuable gift just barely scratched by the time which has increased its value. I know I did not answer. It seemed that I had, then. His next embrace had the further genius which can come only after the medium has been formed by the first gropings of invention. But achieving that, he became suddenly restless. He twisted his neck, he pulled me closer, he let his hand fall and lifted it once to my head, pulled out a pin, did not touch the loop of hair that fell, and then without seeming to look where he went, he grasped my hand at the wrist and pulling me after him away from the inn and toward the carriage-house. An electric light was burning; there was no groom to be seen. I walked over some bits of hay which made me turn my foot and stop, but he pulled me past the stalls where a horse stomped and bumped his nose against the slats with a sad and slow persistence.

As though the electric light had awakened in me the presence of invaders, I stopped, suddenly shocked for the first time since I had left that parlor. Was it still standing—that inn? Had summer finally gone? These were the questions which must have come into my mind. The tug made him stop. Then he tightened his hand and pulled me on. Around a corner of the barn the light showed as a dim flare. It was once again dark and I only felt a step with my foot as with that one arm about my waist, he lifted me into an enclosure. I struck a seat on which I I could not really slide and knew it was velour's. A click came over the sound of my own heart. The whole enclosure shook as he came heavily down beside me. I thought to myself, we are in a carriage! It was as though by that I could explain, change, or find my power again to speak or move. What bliss there is after having to arrange one's life and one's dread, to have all option taken away. With that shaven chin by which he must have held so many things, cursing slightly as then, he put my neck and shoulder in what was an embrace, and with his arm h held me on the seat. That hand I had seen slipped into his coat or lifting a glass touched one button of my tailleur, as lightly as a cat who is not sure the object will move away. It was almost a sigh this time with which he drew back and cursed his one arm.

"A woman is not held by arms only," I told him. But my own voice, unused aloud since dinner, could scarcely find breath to finish a whisper. His words I have put aside since that night. If he is still alive---how could he be?---he knows them. He knows them as we remember all things we discover for the first time, and in the way his voice went down, came slowly up, he might have been making the trip himself down a dangerous stairwell, dark, at the bottom of which he too had discovered things hitherto unknown. I had noticed that strange break from his passion which was---like the voice he used in it—slow, steady, the voice of leading. And once a woman gives up her direction, even if that direction is a stoppage, even if it is death, she can only follow. I had begun to do that. Caught at first, not by an order....No. Not by the surety of his voice, but by my first knowledge that he was one of me: a creature wounded.

His restlessness began again and in another tempo he began to plan. "We must leave here," he said. "Tomorrow. At once."

He opened the little japanned door, only to close it again. Then he kissed me quickly, pressing my shoulder with his hand, and he helped me down with that miraculous arm which might have held me above a flood. Perhaps it did that night. Perhaps that is why it was worse afterwards when the memory of it did not save me from being engulfed by a man much less worthy than he. In the foyer the proprietress was garbed in a cotton negligee, her hair under a grey cap. She was carrying a fat tom which I had seen her pick up as we neared the house. Her face wreathed in smiles at the progress her 'charges' were making.

But the consideration I understood him to have did not fail me. He simply said, "Good evening, Madame," allowed that he would have a pipe before retiring, and headed for the salon, his bulk seeming too much this night for his long legs, his head bowing under the low cornice of the parlor way. I only nodded to Madame's notice that the nights seemed cooler already. And as she tossed the cat out into that same night, I was able to look into my friend's eyes which had been waiting for me from the depth of that rented salon----much sadder to me then than before.

Do I only imagine the impulse I had to run to him there? To say, "Don't let us part this might....let us stay together tonight...." How often did I take this up ay the point where my beige boot touched the first stair.....I ran into him...Madame, her arms---free of her animal—hanging stupidly at her sides. Her bare feet, crooked toes, her gaping mouth, her probable expression of- "But I didn't really intend...." She as our setting while I flung myself into his arm, waking that deep step of his, the glorious lips which filled with words I never heard again. And then....braving her look, to which room would we have gone? Mine was too sad. Crowded with tears, full of dreams without sleep. What was his room like? I saw it only when it had become like the rest of the inn....stripped of the idiosyncrasy men drop around them. Is that what his eyes said? The smile had fixed at a lower breadth, but still it did not mislead me. His arm was perfectly straight at his side. It is possible that because I so often took it up at that point on the stairs, that I do not recall what happened in myself that night? I remembered neither asleep nor waking. I do not even know whether I thought of finding his door. The spell of my room was upon me as surely as it had been. My weeping eyes which had fallen shut against the onslaught of tears after I had first unpacked my things, placidly, curious about each drawer, the locks on some---- those eyes had agreed to what the inn was to be for me. I had soon given up on what creatures would be my company. I had found no community even in that impoverished dog. And I knew I had to go too far in time to pass back over Ritter. It would have left me with girls less than half my age. I knew I must seek the starved who had long time since forgotten the pang of hunger. If only I kept on my path.

If it was not during the night, it was in the morning that I knew. When I dressed as informally as on any other day, thinking of my breakfast and a turn about the grounds, I knew. It was not what I saw and heard as I passed the parlor. He was there, his traveling coat brushed free of any dust or hay from the night before. A large black leather case with horizontal straps like those carried by country doctors was set, as though it belonged, on the Louis Treize; and a worn trunk with a name-plate on the top stood on the carpet which I was to walk one more night without him. He held his hat in his hand and put it near the little isinglass dome while he settled his account. I knew before that: I must save. Reasons had no place and I gave none. Too much of myself had I given over in pain. It was a gift that would leave the giver rich unless she were to think it rubbish. Leaving then just a shell which tried to give again….nothing worthy to offer. There stood a man with a destination and mine had been reached.

I walked out into the yard, and while the groom saddled up the horses to the small open caleche, I leaned on the fence, seeing it as clearly as the night before. And not a word have I lost of this meeting. I did not look at him. I did this more for his sake than mine. As soon as I heard his heavy step, I said at once: "I love you and I cannot go with you. It is only while I remain as I am that I can love at all."

Another man might have taken me without my love or consent. I was prepared, but I did not expect this man to do so. Yes, I was prepared to have him turn me, leaving as little choice as I had under that deep step-----to take me loveless without that fund of sadness I had built with the gift of my being. He did not.

"Then," he said in his deep voice, "I would…." He faltered. "You are the kind of woman who needs no arms to hold her."

I felt his lips touch my sleeve and I heard the snap of the whip and the clatter of the gig. There was still dust in the air when I turned to go back to the dining-room.

That night I did not even undress. It truly seemed the last night before winter as I felt the frost on the window.

My despair came back to me like an old friend one had ceased to find peevish. It was before the sky grew pink that I thought about a future away from this place or others like it. In Paris there had been a woman a bit older than myself who never spoke about her life, but who had a lean and spare look which I had found puzzling. Her face had become so sharpened, she might have cut a wedge of cake with it, had she ever felt a taste for things like that.

5 JUIN

I think of Ritter's poem describing winter harvests----the wrenching up of memories muffled and half-effaced by the fall of years--- times---united under the pall of oneself. Memories so fixed. So helpless. Ritter walking toward our house in Basle.

His caracal hat. His coat flung like a cape over his shoulders. His head is down and In the fresh snow he leaves dark prints. Then--- the overhanging balcony hides him and the footprints whiten. I can delay the opening of the door. I can have him begin walking again. He walks toward me exactly as he was and I watch from here, testing with pain the distance between us.

Harvest of age. Images that are unchanged or more beautiful, bringing with them the old commitment even though he has vanished where? Into some place between the changes of the moon where my youth has slid.

But my life, my dear, is not united under the pall of myself. No. Of me there are 20, 30, 40, 50 who disappeared silently, without a name, into the eyes of people on Métros, bathing strips, cafes, who left in the arms of a few young men not even a permanent shape; who died with people. What harvest of age? Leaves blowing over a grave.

Aniko believed that a crack in a mirror led to the land of the dead. Old Agnes was convinced that to see a mirror in the dark brought doom, but for me, in those days, the mirror was a source of nourishment--- feeding my beauty. Now, I sit down behind old eyes from which the future has been peeled away and I see through to his hand on the stair-rail. Autocratic dreamer--- Katherine over my exhausted memories; I rule like virgin queens whose subjects are synonymous with herself.

I call the staircase that seemed to sob under its rug. The foyer, off which there was a small salon and the vase in the shape of a mallard which—after the night I speak of, was never to be there- actually- again. Then the "Great"- as he called it—or large salon which Ritter entered, dropping snow from his boots.

As I embraced him I smelled the wintry air circling his collar like a rival arm. I saw us, as I often did in that room, shadowed together in the glass of the door. I can remember my face of that time: radiant, beautiful, as ephemeral as a woman who might pass me through a train window.

We were happy together, but had begun to lie to save the other pain. He said he wished I'd gone to the concert with him: I said I'd stayed behind to make his tea.

I gave him solitude at the borders, fearing one at the center of his life. His torrents of tenderness were more and more alternating with depressions, sighs, and the increasing desire to be elsewhere.

"The only discord was my spirit" he said. He told me the soprano voice above in the loft, was like a bird that had picked up bits of human sorrow. The uncharacteristic self pity in his talk had increased since our return from Venice and my trip, following. to Lausanne- at my husband's demand. I had been ready to break with Ritter then— yet there had been his letter handed to me before I had unpinned my hat. He asked me to return to him. I carried his letter outside and looked over the embankment at the Protestant roofs – at the un-upholstered spirit which was like Ritter's own. To love him was simple. I must suffer the ugliness of lawyers, the loss of my child, and- I reasoned- my feeling would become greater through sacrifice. I had already become too conscious and, often alone, conclusions became my friends.

It was in a Lausanne café, after the first surge of love and fear that I put my face down on my arms over the dark wood of a table and in the abject position of people sorrowing or drunk, committed my life to him.

I had begun to make the tea and he stood beside me. He was wondering in what season he would die. He continued to talk and I listened. Often – to apply his words to ourselves was like fanning myself in the wind. He hoped it wasn't spring- a crowded season, he said. Then, he told me he had defined his plan to go away for awhile, alone, and I watched, in silence, the white-faced clock, the pile of sliced lemon, the porcelain pot decapitated and spurting steam. It had been an evening like any other. All week he'd been contemplating a short trip, but he had often been away, as I had been. Only that the all the details became memorable as the faces of strangers on the day that ends in an accident. As I continue pouring the tea, I hear Ritter snap shut his cigarette case as though he had never shut it before and as though I was never to hear it again. I see the silver case in his hands, and in the great space around me, I hear it snap. His plans were not precise, he said. He wanted only… "to go through winter as though through an irrelevant act" and arrive at some inward dwelling place.

"Well! Then I'm in time to see you off!" a loud and familiar voice tore into my hearing and I saw Ritter smile, and Lilos, in a fur Jacken, shake his hand.

To me, with broad opera-comique gestures, and unapologetic about his intrusion, Lilos made a bow. Another time he might have amused me. He often did. But more often I had been repelled by something cavernous in his responses. To the building pandemonium in me, to the laggard of chaos waiting inside Ritter's last words, Lilos would add a havoc of himself. I would find no relief, that evening in his absurd fur coat, the skeleton of an umbrella from which he had stripped the fabric and which hung like a sword from his belt.

As he bent over my hand, I was sucked up in that gray breath of the world before rain falls.

"I wish you, Madame Zoe," he said straightening up, "a very good evening" And he gave such a perfect flourish to a non-existent plumed hat that I was taken with a mad laugh which he answered with a shocking white smile. In minutes he was himself again: too dark, too tall, too crushed-looking—as though the pressure of his desires touched mortally on his spirit. He had the head of a young Michelangelo, heron-like legs, and he seemed to exist in that twilight of day when color is disappearing.

Oh, I did not like him—this man who turned "love" into a physical exploit like bicycle-racing and would transform my troubled evening into a carnival.

It seemed never to offend Ritter that Lilos always fell into the room as thought he was hatched above it. He told him, "I am absolutely delighted to see you."

"Ah," said Lilos, "You know there' s no peril like the absolute."

When he told us he had just returned from Paris, I was carried away with sudden questions- of my friends, the Medrano, Gilotte's- but to whatever I asked, he answered, "brave soldiers fall, vomiting, in the streets.." and I turned away from him.

Ettore had said that he'd been different before the death of a young brother he had nursed, but Lilos, himself, said that he was not shocked by the death, but by the pointless growth of so many eyelashes, bones, and tiny nerves. Whatever his history, the dissipated young nobleman was now in my home, removing his jacket as Prometheus might have torn at his chains. He threw it on a footstool and perched on the thin arm of a Bergere opposite Ritter. I see him lean forward to take a few pages which Ritter handed to him--- a poem which I had transcribed that week and which he began to read aloud rather jerkily, ending a line as though there was no other, and giving it a comic effect that made Ritter laugh. Then he put the pages on his knees and began to speak through an onrush of words. A badly rolled cigarette, burning down, the white ash crooked, started me for a moment that I took it to be his finger bent from the heat of his passion. He was complaining of the enmity between Ritter's life and his poems. "I know. I know," Ritter admitted, deploring the uselessness of poetry in such a time of war. But he talked of shoring up ones responses for a better time, of saving the beauty left in the world, and over Lilos' rejections, his intensity expanded. He wanted to rescue the earth from its fading away, and he pitched toward an emotion I had almost ceased to see in him. I was pained to see a stranger bring to Ritter that heightening which, when I loved him less, I once brought.

Lilos, expressing himself crudely, objected to Ritter's phrase of "giving back to God"

"You are too harsh, 'Ritter said. "You could be a happy man if you separated doom from splendor."

"Don't play with me, cher Maitre," Lilos said. "God, since you mention Him, turned the word into flesh they say. You spend yours going backwards."

HE could speak of "going backwards" when he claimed re-incarnation from an obscure Roman. When his only tangible "work" had been the translations of old Roman texts.

"Yet—"I broke in, angrily, as I set the tray between them, "you call him Maitre."

"You always judge me as no more than an overfed dog when it comes to appreciation," he said, looking at me from serious dark-ringed eyes. As it was true, I flushed and began to pour with stiff hands. Amber, steaming, only a thin shell of white correcting it, I handed him his tea.,

They had been arguing over Lilos' mantra that 'violence begets violence'. "Your honesty is irrefutable," Ritter was saying.

Busy with the granulated sugar, the cream…I looked up to see Lilos—with a shock.

His mouth open, the cup swinging rhythmically in his hand, his eyes were fixed on the cross ties over my chest and I dared not move. Without relocating his glance, he put down his cup on the tray, by touch, and launched immediately into an anecdote about meeting N. on his way to us. He talked lightly, his look directed at the beat behind my dress, as though the trivialities of conversation intensified the mystery of our physical selves.

Suddenly he looked away I saw through it all. I saw, again, the inertia tossed like a dead fish by the waves of sensuality in him, and I thrust a fresh cup so precipitately into his hand that it nearly fell to the floor. But he caught and used it so expertly as N. that I laughed before I could catch myself. He took his bottom lip under hard teeth and smiled. Once again, Lilos, gesticulating, altering his voice, hiding his phantasms and debasing his features like a whorish Varieties player, had used every trick to seduce his audience. Honesty! Absolutes. Peril!

"I feel unwelcome tonight..." Lilos said. He looked around the room, settled his glance again on me. "Yes---" He interrupted Ritter's objection.

"Even as I came up your stairs I felt they were rejecting me."

I wanted to say:' Yes. You are intruding!' But he went on. "And you--- he shook a yellow- stained finger at Ritter...were speaking to HER about death. A private tête- a- tête, I thought, but it was too late to turn back."

Liar! I thought.

He grabbed his beard pulling it out like a net to catch his words. "thought shall I hear the poet reveal those mysteries of how love and death meet?"

'Baron, when I reach that point of thrift, in my destiny I might be able to afford your peril."

I bumbled into the silence with talk of Orpheus and Eurydice....

"Perhaps you should write the poetry," Lilos said. "You are always so literary about experience... "however simple her beauty is, "he said to Ritter, "She has very baroque emotions."

"The raven chides blackness," I countered.

"Not at all, "Ritter said, "Lilos has a very simple desperation. Austere. Passionate. Stripped to the bone. Like a deep wound."

Lilos made no response. He screwed up his face and looked at the cup in his hand wondering if his answer was in it.

Apropos of nothing, I thought of Aniko reporting his escapade in the public square, when Ritter began speaking to young Wolfsgerath of what had brought them together: Lilos' studies of the old Roman orgies and rituals. I shuddered. But they were swept off – away from the happenings of the day... Lilos opening life on the side towards death; Ritter standing in the breach with a song of life's beauty.

I left the room to look for food without disturbing Aniko. My sadness diffusing somewhat by the advent of Lilos came back. I connected the "desperate" young man with Ritter's decision to go away and I felt betrayed. I, too, was drawn to the wild wretches that "Neant", just as what bound me to Ritter and me to the same people, books, poetry, vagabondage...everything. But whereas I resisted those people who broke even the furthest barriers of morality—resisted those selves of myself—Ritter was impressed by them. He once told me that he was drawn to the despairing attempts of Lilos, through vice, violations against nature.. to achieve life in the present.

When I came back with the tray, I found they had gone into the small salon where Lilos was curved backwards, like a bow, elbows on the mantle, one cracked boot resting on a cold log. He was muttering…

He grabbed a meatcake which he stuffed into his mouth, his eyes bulging with the waywardness of a space cluttered with tongue and teeth. He wiped the back of his hand over his mouth and leaned forward like an animal about to pounce.

"You want me to say that its' moving?" He twisted his neck around in all directions, as though enemies were closing in.

"You are too moved already, "Ritter said.

"Of course it is. You write wonderfully. Every variety of human suffering…" Then drawing a breath, his face calmed, his lips twitched into sleepy smile. "To write about human suffering? Isn't that an outsiders' hobby?"

"How can.." I began, but Ritter, abruptly and cold: "He is right." And I gasped, "How can you say so?"

"But worse,,," continued Lilos, thrusting his face between Ritter and me, "For everyone of you, and there are not many… there is a maker of artifacts who wants me to share his future over his grave'"

"Or his past," Ritter said, holding up the mallard vase in whose back the grotesque passengers of two marsh willows stood upright. "it may be left to us in a gesture---inconsequential—or in this by an unknown artisan a century ago."

Lilos sneered and tried to knock it aside. But Ritter withdrew it. "Come Baron. Befriend our dead."

"Never."

"Here is his memory"

"Gone is gone."

"The present without a memory is like a candle without a wick." Ritter waved the duck between them..

"You want light. I want to sizzle."

Already finished with the game, Ritter shrugged and was about to replace the vase on the table when Lilos blurted out: "Lust is proof of the impotence of memory," and with the back of his hand he smashed the duck out of Ritter's hand. I screamed as it hit the wall. All the bright colored bits lay on the floor.

When I looked up, Lilos was standing beaming with joy, his head thrown back and his hands clasping and unclasping his upper arms like a happy man freezing to death.

Ritter kicked the pieces into the ash, took my arm and we all walked to the foyer.

"Don't be upset, dear," he said, and fatigue made me lean against him a moment until I saw Lilos watching us with eyes either tearful or glistening.

I realized that Ritter was entrusting him with a few errands, and was incredulous at hearing—almost second-hand- that the departure was set for the next morning, and the place…vaguely Italy. 'This makes it easier for him, ' I thought as I pictured some winter landscape of that summer country. The cold tile floors. The unforgiving marble. It was different when we were together there. Ritter hated plans. He hates scenes. I held in my wretchedness.

Lilos was saying something about going part of the way with him and maybe joining the Germans."

Surprised, I asked, "To fight?"

"No. To die!"

After this tasteless joke the infant terrible opened his mouth so wide I could see his tongue, and laughed loudly. Then he was finally out the door, the bared umbrella slapping against his leg. He was down the stairs which shook under his heavy jump before I realized, that although it was winter, he'd left his jacket.

"He is bizarre," I said angrily. "He is really awful. Childish".

"No, he's perfect of his kind. The true anarchist. His pleasure calls to his despair like a wife at a husband's grave."

"Is that what you call his simplicity?" But Ritter answered me in the second cold voice he's used to me that night. "I never said he had simplicity. His simplicity is just complexity drawn very taut."

I understood only that we were arguing. For the first time since we'd met.

I was lying on the bed, In the aureole of the candle, Ritter's eyes were black. His round face seemed to be borne downwards by his moustaches like the moon by wings.

"Where is your promise?" I asked softly," the we would always live one for the other?"

"Have you understood nothing I've said?" His voice came with a spit like the candle flame and I sat up.

"I understand that I have lost everything," I said. My child. My honor…my reason…." It was cheap. A sordid impasse. I had voiced the rebellion I couldn't utter in simple words to Lilos when he had intruded. The rebellion lost its way and fell on Ritter.

After awhile he said: "I didn't think you would do this."

"Forgive me. You are free to go."

"Were both free," he said in a clotted voice. "We are.. we MUST.. be free."

"I'll never be free again." I didn't cry. Something touched my shoulder and I saw his face reflecting the pain I felt.

"I'll be back soon, dear. You know that." And he blew out the candle.

I remembered his image of 'crossing over love'. In the dark I heard him saying, "I never meant to take your child Zoe." I threw myself against him, begging that drop my words from his mind. I kissed his cheek, touched his hair. From the assemblage of flesh and voice and bone which like a miraculous lodestar had fixed my direction for so long, came the sentence: "You followed me…with your own will."

And the word" follow" dropped into place as the cornerstone of our separation.

"Monsieur est Parti?"

I couldn't answer. Aniko kept sweeping and on the boards she left a yellow straw that separated the time from when Ritter stood on them. I told her how we'd got a fiacre with "torn paper roses dropping from the roof. It pleased Monsieur". But I was thinking that he'd not even noticed the roses. Lilos was pulling the parcels out of my arms. The cocher was ordinary, one of his gloves torn at the thumb as though bitten. I wanted to say foolish things. I love you. I'll pray for you. Don't go, because at right angles to m had been his headless shoulders waiting and he gave me his mouth. It was a light kiss during which one of us trembled. Then, the threadbare carriage was shaking while Lilos walked down the street, waving one arm behind him like a blind man groping for where he has been.

"Pray god Monsieur has good weather or the pass will be closed."

I unpinned my hat and walked into to bedroom to remember. We had spent a happy morning which helped erase the bitterness of the night before. He said how much he cared for me, and would soon return. I felt bereft and beautiful. I spun in the paradox of being resplendently filled with the presence of someone whose absence emptied the world.

I put my face against the towel he'd used that morning and it smelled of sleep and my father. As I hung up his suit jacket, I sniffed it like a dog—distinguishing nothing but a hay-smell of sweat. Impersonal sweat. Everyone's. Then I lay down on the sheets, waiting to imbed myself in his unconscious movements, but Aniko thrust her head around the door, said: "Monsieur Lilos has come back." And withdrew quickly as though she'd seen me compromised.

"Give him his jacken," I called, but she insisted, through the door, that her asked to see me. "Tell him to wait in the salon" as I got up, leaving the sheets with my hand. I remember the light of that day. Even in the passage, and my elation when I thought of Ritter. Of his wide lips—somewhere to come out of as a voice saying my name.

Lilos was waiting. In the shabby comfort of the little salon where he often played cribbage with Ritter and where we had stood the night before. But I realized I was crying and what I could see was blurred.....was one hand red from the cold, clapped on his hip. He was waiting. But for what? I stared at myself in the glass. I looked beautiful and the mirror gave it back instantly. I knew I would do no work that day, but I wanted him to leave. Behind the uneven windows, snow was coming down, white from white as orderly as convent children in slippers. I told Lilos his visit must be short. I had many things to do.

"And how about me?" He stood up. Furious. "I'm not always free! I'm a busy man, my dear. Make a plan with me... I'll go wherever you wish. We'll break the ice and uncover Ritter's swans. We'll ring the bells....... I'd go anywhere with you, Zoe."

The swift passage from violence to something soft in his voice had often troubled me. "Another day, Lilos," I said- thinking I would not see him. Yet- I was not unfond of him. Perhaps it had been his needs over which he stumbled to greet me in that little salon that made me aware of all the foot paths in myself and sped me to people. I was thinking of Ritter, speeding away. I would have asked him if there were times in one's life when standing close to yourself as to a swallow's nest, you can see loves enter like each different bird. Neither surprising nor welcome, just inevitable and free.

All that year since Lausanne, flowers opened in my soul where people had left seeds. Ritter's friends. The women, the men, the old couples, and the young acolytes like Lilos who once brought me a white book as though it had been his single sentiment.

Lilos said, with a smile: "You like me, Zoe, don't you? And...I care for you..deeply."

"There are just times when is simply there for love. Like a ground on which hundreds of acorns fall."

"What? You are beginning to sound like HIM. Where are you?"

"That's nonsense."

"I'm tired, : he said. "I have not slept."

"You are always tired. You never sleep. You are always coming from some cave of ravagement you call pleasure..."

His forehead diminished under his thick hair. His skin was bad.

"Don't be vulgar!" he said loudly. I looked quickly to see if Aniko was nearby.

"Don't judge me…. Don't judge men in that way. You don't know.." Still loudly.

"Lilos.." I hissed. "Be quiet.

He bent his head, affecting to be shamefaced." There is great loveliness in you, Zoe. And vulgarity as well," he said in a soft voice, cajoling me to buy it entire.

"The raven chides blackness, 'I said and flushed- recalling I had spoken the same phrase to him last evening as though it could make a tradition spring up for us, an intimate formula, a code, a combination, Lilos smiled and contemplated me, his fists covering his nose. His black eyes drawing me in like caves.

"While Ritter is away," he said as though in answer, "You and I will see each other."

"I would not be sure of that!"

"It would be stubbornness then that would prevent you…. now you've said it."

"You never speak this way to Ritter. Or..to me when he is with us."

"You know very little of him. You judge only me."

What happened next is confused. I was wondering if I did know little of Ritter. I tried to remember the last sight of his face and the look on it. Worried. A little surprised.. when I sensed Lilos had stood up, came very close. He was talking.

"Go ahead. Judge me. Judge me one hundred and twenty-five times a day if you like. Judge me.."

All the excitement of the night before and now the day…funneled itself into a longing to touch Lilos…. A longing so impersonal and massive that it seemed to originate in some hovering spirit of which I was the medium. I was drawn to the ruin of his youth, to his braggadocio, one evening, that age would have of him only some upright bones sucked dry. I could sense his outlines as he came closer—even that of his square jaw under the wreck of bearding. Filled with the love for another man I seemed to become so much woman that all men were accessible to me. His fingertips touched the edge of my sleeve. Like a swimmer already past the breakers, and into the dangerous calm of the deep ocean, I thought of all the dangers between me and the shore. Excited by my daring, I enumerated all the crude subterranean habits of Lilos. He smoked opium. He was obsessed by his vile acts and beautiful sensations and was committed to seek varieties of physical contact even as he severed them from the intellect which might distinguish them. His breath near my cheek was green and transparent as the poison he drank. I hovered in a male landscape. I imagined an embrace by Lilos…. Just as he grabbed my arm and began pulling it hard… like a child. Shocked by my thoughts I lashed out at him.

"My god.. Lilos! I trusted you!"

Without letting go of my arm, he kept saying. "Yes. Trust me. You can trust me…trust me"

My calf muscles were shaking. I was pulling my arm away.. He dropped it and leaned back to the wall..knocking his head against the heavy frame of the old engraving, and twitched his shoulders as I'd seen him do sometimes. Was he epileptic or slowly ill in some way? Doomed people are fearless of death as he. There seemed to be tears in his eyes. Without conviction he said, "I ask your forgiveness, Zoe."

Equally insincere, I said, "It was nothing."

"May I come again?"

"When Ritter returns."

His head lolled strangely to one side as though something he had to listen for had come loose. I did not like him. What had possessed me?

"Forgive me. You must. Please."

I accepted this contrition. What is the use, now, of wondering why. I took it as homage. Perhaps. I overestimated his vision of the world. I told him- not unkindly- that he must leave and he asked, like a shy schoolboy, "May I come tomorrow?"

"When Ritter returns," I repeated.

"Good," he said. "But I would like to see you alone. We can do many things together."

I remarked, archly on his "activities".

"It doesn't matter," he said in all seriousness. "There is nothing I can't give up."

"Your life of sin?" I blurted out, feeling my face burn with shame.

He began laughing so loudly, I doubt that he saw my fist up to my mouth to close further stupidities.

"A lovelier confessor I couldn't imagine," he said in a voice still creased with his laugh.

I started towards the foyer, angrily straightening an antimacassar awry on the chaise longue, as I said, astonished at my words, "I'm not old enough for that."

"No. You are certainly not. A pity."

He bent over, and taking my hand, turned it so his mouth fell on my palm. When he looked up there were tears in his eyes. Then he was sliding out. Like sea animals move. I stopped him in the passage--- tapping his arm, not wishing to dismiss him so coldly if he would weep for me. He frowned and the door closed.

From the street I heard whistling, but did not look out. I was relieved that I did dismiss him and went into Ritter's study. He had torn off the calendar to reveal May 1. I tried to remember his kiss. Of that morning. I tried to bring it back.. Flakes sailed down, beyond the window glass and I reminded myself that under the snow of touch lies the hard spring of memory.

*

I can still remember that the stone building across the street, rendered octofoil through my iron balconette, had vacant windows. As I sat with my paints, with paper and pen, it sometimes occurred to me that someone there might see me, especially when the gas was lit for evening. I remember Aniko during those four month. I remembered being startled by a second's unfamiliarity as her hands, devoid of her, repaired a jug and sprouted hair at the wrists.

I walked on errands, a few times making a detour up Frederikgasse where, always,,Lilos's shutters were closed. I remember feeling that I should like to speak to him about many fallacies which had occurred to me in his decadent life, but I never encountered him as I strolled, often with packages, once with a gown from the dressmaker, up through the old city and back to the carpeted stairway to my door.

I slid across the threshold into a vegetative world past resignation. Errands each day, falling off to sleep calmed by the intricacies of Anna de Noailles, waking in the dark alone, militantly chaste, with my life slipping through the months.

A few letters arrived for Ritter, some from women correspondents, and only one came to me from him. He was unsettled, he wrote: he missed our home and was lonely, but he said, during loneliness we must seek the beauty in it as we would look into the root of a flower.... He ended the letter with the cry: 'Oh Zoe", when shall I be there with you again?'

There was no address to which I could send the words: "Come back.! Please!" And the first of May [assed with my waiting for the shadow of a Hackney to move across the building opposite.

Then in the second week everything happened at once. Lautreamont's 'Maldoror' arrived -without a card -addressed to me in a hand like that of Lilos. I decided to have some wine sent to him. It was a pleasant day. Windy. I decided to choose it myself then, further, to leave it with his concierge on my way home.

In the early afternoon, I held my package and paused, angry, humiliated, in the banal entrance to his building. On the rez-de-chauseea life unknown to me went on with some regard for conventions. It seemed to me that I was there as I might have gone to take the waters at a Kurbad---- because I recall using that phrase later to myself. I'd had no desire to see our mutual friends without Ritter. I was lonely. I pulled the bell over his name and as I looked at the patent leather toe shining out from my black skirt, remembered the close-fitting dress, and felt on my head the small crater of a hat enclosing it, I spoke as to those articles severed from another me which had been carried off like an object in baggage. "OH, how far I've come!"

Lilos answered the bell and called out for the visitor to mount. I did, accusing Ritter: "Why have you left me so alone?" No. I saw the traitor as that motor, that freedom-crazed inexplicable which moved my leg one step further up, and beat my heart against its skin-bound pilgrimage of veins. Only my decent white voice rebelled in tones which must have been learned over a picture book from a bearded governess.

When Lilos saw me in the doorway, he threw down a small unlit pipe, the clay stem of which was ground under my heel as he pulled me across the threshold.

"Please," I said. "I've come only to bring you something," and I drew back, offering my gift.

He put it down somewhere behind him and thanked me. He was wearing a chemise that left his forearms bare, discouraged, hanging at his sides. The room was shuttered and dark, but rather than opening some daylight, he lit two candles and soon I was able to see his lodgings which shocked me.

"Please don't bother," I told him. "I cannot stay." And added, irrelevantly that I hadn't expected to find him at home.

"I've just come in and was on my way out again"

"Well, then…" I said backing to the door when he asked me to sit awhile which I did. On a low settee he described as a 'Family heir-loom", with a laugh- denigrating his title. He asked if I were surprised to see what sort of place he lived in, but said it with a pride that showed me he had no idea I expected it to be not only different but better. That it was poor would not have bothered me as much as finding it cheap and gaudily furnished in crude taste. Like an icon behind the candles, flickered a famous saccharine print of Cleo de Merode. A table and a chair were turned over in the center of the room, their legs grotesquely pointing up and useless. On the walls were jumbled a poster from the Bal Bullier, an obscene print across which hung a saber, A large drawing of a nude woman with a heraldic crest---probably of Lilos' family- covering her face, a circus announcement framed with dead leaves. Nearly all the space in the room was covered with some bibelot which seemed in disgrace for having been chosen. There was, everywhere, an irony directed against those things which the rest of us simply ignored.

He handed me a glass of wine from an already opened bottler and asked what I thought of a hideous painting behind me. Even in the semi-darkness, I could see the garish color and reprehensible drawing.

"Wonderful, isn't it?" he asked me. "It is by a countryman of yours called Nolde."

"I see," was all I managed.

"And there..." he pointed to the disheveled poster on which a muscular acrobat held to a rope above the ground with both hands which, in the dimness, were severed by black wristlets he must have been wearing. In huge letters beneath his pointed toes was printed: "C. Agnelli". His first name had been blotted out, deliberately,unlike his wrists --leaving only a first initial and a large dot.

"There," Lilos repeated, "is the great Agnelli. Do you like him?"

I shrugged.

"He was a suicide. Did you know that people who kill themselves have no right to their names?"

Then as Lilos was silent, I remained silent also. Curious, I again hovered on the edges of him, but the sweetish smell of the room dizzied and repelled me, and in a crack of light from the shutters, his hands appeared old, like roots.

I said something about the darkness of the room, When I said, standing up, "I must go," my voice was deep and uncertain.

There was not a sound. It seemed to me that his eyes were closed. Just as his shutters always seemed to be. Twice darkened, I thought. To find what light? To find what, to remember what? The place of his birth? Still not a sound. The darkness was sister to his silence and it was very peaceful. It was one of those moments that fall out of daily life, when becoming nothing, you allow someone else a simple honesty of being. I stood there, wrapped in myself like a child in a greatcoat, not even waiting, when I felt his cold mouth touch my cheek..

"Zoe," he said. "let me take you now." Then a phrase never used to me, said deliberately, with a formality that made it doubly shock.

My arm came out of my sleeve, the coat fell on my shoes, the something of me which I trusted roused itself in a voice that kept repeating, "Oh no oh no" not to Lilos who took it for a woman's last modesty, but to my belief that this could happen.

He dragged me through a curtain which struck against my back and into a chamber so dark that my eyes fell into pockets of my skin. One arm pinned me like a rod and his fingers darted like starlings all over my flesh while I was dumbly saying "no no Oh no oh no," until like the primordial world pierced by a first black star, I was shocked out of my separateness.

Replacing with me the peace of the oily dream which smashed in the pipe, Lilos was wild and precise like a lunatic with a small plan. From an old source of purity, some tears ran out of the corners of my eyes, but he didn't see them. I had already been memorized and stored into a single portrait for that eternity of nowhere in which Lilos was alone with himself.

In the silence, in all that darkness, it came to me that he was nothing but an enobled reprobate who had injured my life on a whim. Who would not believe in chastity because it was the only instance where understanding required a lack. I asked him, "Now. Please let me go." But he refused. "No. You are as deserted as the future."

"Even in the dark, men are not interchangeable to me. Your kind of love is the lowest…"

"On the contrary, my ardor for you took place very high up… near the roof of a house of cards."

Fury like a magnet was drawing me away when suddenly his mouth over min had an odor that made me terribly cavernous. It fitted so tight over my own mouth I had the notion I could walk out of it and enter him. This fantastic possibility drove the blood to my head and---snapping my clear voice like the stem of a flower.---.rushing over it -- -came a whole crowd of myself to the call——-a call stronger than time or place or private agonies, asserting, like bird of prey, its aerial superiority and pure facelessness.

I lost the polarity of I and thou which keeps a woman safe as a stone in a river. Like a drug-take, the universe shifted to inside me and landscape was only a worldly expression on its damaged skin.

Hours or one hour later, I wondered how much time had passed. Feeling hurt, almost wounded, I dressed quietly and pushed through the curtain into the scuttling light of the main room. It wasn't surprising that I looked for a mirror to do up my hair, but there was none. Only the same clutter on the walls. I opened a hinged door. There was a lamp and in a holder beneath it, some matchsticks which I used. The glass smeared with black until an amber eye showed through. There was nothing in the room. Only a succession of deep grey cupboards which were all open and empty. In the bare whit=washed space above them there was no window. Nothing. Only higher, a green cravate dangled as a pull from the skylight. I heard a complicated noise beneath me and realized I had stepped on something. Heaven knew what. I bent and found a crushed box. Only half of it could be seen.. It had been a Dutch chocolate box on which there was part of a pretty girl's face with one white point of her ox=head hat, a damaged bit of red mouth, one blue eye wrinkling, tea colored lace half encircling an alabaster shard of neck. I recreated the lost part almost as though I had become a mirror, myself, giving back a whole. A fear rose against my strange situation and I could no longer understand what I was doing in that kitchen. I could almost hear Ritter saying, "You must give freedom to the inexplicable."

And not without difficulty but ---it seemed to me----- full of composure, I dragged myself back to the bedroom and let some light fall on Lilos. His beard blended away all but his sharp nose and the empty socket of its nostril. His eyelid was closed with a thin band of black.

I ran away from him, but as I closed the door, I felt he might fly after me, dark sheets trailing like a shroud.

Going down the Vogelallee, coming out into the Marktplatz, the shadowy statues held out bright arms under the street lamps. The streets were empty. I breathed in and out. Then, it came to me: the darkness; and I began to hurry.

All the signs added together; a leaf dropped on the stairs, a light under the door of the study, Aniko turning quickly away from the fire as I entered the "great"--- staring at me with rust-colored eyes and her mouth a black zero.

"He's home!" she said in such a horrified whisper, that I paused to think whether she had been, like a depraved duenna, some party to my faithlessness.

"Why does that frighten you," I asked coldly.

Then a glance at the pale clock told me it was eleven at night, and my finger in the warm water surrounding the cyclamen told me that Ritter had brought them much earlier. A tiny bud had already fallen like a drop of blood on the starched tablecloth.

"His arms was full of them. There's more, " Aniko said.

I thought of the melodramatic prints of the last decade.; the balustrade-shaped woman with her curls undone; two men----one in shirtsleeves--- staring over identical moustaches at each other. The matter of jokes. Why then as I stood there did I feel a dread, a horror, that I had tampered with those borders over which life crossed? Above the bouquet. my little pier glass cupped between its gilt arms a white oval. Two holes punctured it suddenly- startling me. It all trembled, dissolved like shapes on rainy windows, expiring through my eyes. The irrevocable circled me. The afternoon was past. Other days pass in both directions from two opposite points, but this one had stopped like a drum in a tomb. I was filled with such remorse that the shape of my foot in its strapped shoe, moving to his study, looked coldly unfamiliar.

I knocked and heard an unexpected scuffle from the room. He stood sideways behind the door, his face unrecognizable in the shadows. allowing me to pass as he says, "you knock like the concierge, darling.." and with one hand raised to approximate my fist, he blocks all the space through which I might have fallen into his arms.

He had expected my figure lambent in the doorway which melted his last months into the life he had set down. His flowers held up like a fragrant torch, and I smiling at his absence and his presence.

He lies down on the chaise longue, excusing his tiredness, and closes his eyes asking me to sit by him. Over his sentence, "I have been concerned about you," we haggle in polite voices for meaning. I touch the material of his shirt just below the ogive of his chest. A vague area where my touch is lost.

"You, are tired,' I said. "I will see you tomorrow…"

I was standing at the door, blowing him a kiss, when he sat up angry, abandoned like a child…." (my name was somewhere in there)…you always…..(something about leaving him in such an abrupt manner)…." It was incorrect and irrevocable. Yet I came back and approached him just as his hand was moving backwards through his hair and I stroked his forehead that was creased with worry or pain. On that pinpoint of care in which I had ceased to believe as soon as Lilos put his hands on me, I stopped myself.. Out of blankness there was developing a desire for confession or subterfuge To erase everything by hiding it, or to put it aside by being absolved. Caught between the two, I resolved into despair and began to swagger. I sat down and told gossipy news of friends, mentioned rumors. I avoided his eyes, looking at his thin hands as they struck fire for a cigarette. Perhaps I asked him about his trip because he began to say it had been ruined by the thought of his being called up, by the evidence of war everywhere. He said, in sorrowful tones that Rosalie Seguy had killed herself after Appolino fell at Flanders.

I was incapable of judging this news because my sensibilities had deranged themselves by sinking down past my understanding, and insane and irreverent, meaningless to myself if adhering like a wound plaster to some incoherent motion of the universe, I told him that people who kill themselves lose their names.

"Has something happened to you Chere?"

I looked at him, not knowing. A door closed in the building. I looked at the grain of his skin, and at his lips that appeared bronze in the candle-light. I wondered what ran in his blood—this man before whom walls broke down as they did for no one else. I went stiff with fright. Then his hand, like a compassionate friend, one trusted by his soul and unawed in the constellation of the poet, Ritter, came by itself to take mine.

"You are very dear to me, Zoe."

You are very dear to me,Zoe. I was very dear to him. In his eyes there were silver leaves that fluttered above a long avenue that I followed...until I reached the stairway to a house, into a spacious room I had seen in a dream and was called by a name I couldn't remember. I looked out of the window which I knew very well. But there was no view. Neither sky nor ground. For a moment I swung like a single star in daylight.

"You are very dear to me, Zoe"

A longing to be glad overpowered the horrible that blew like particles around me. I shook my head. "Nothing," I said. "Nothing happened to me."

He, of all people, would have understood. Absolved a woman. Admired her despair. I would have wished him to know what aberrations, possibilities were in me: what lives---over reaching fate. What melancholy pride in my taming of shock. But I wanted him to love me instead and feel I was a graspable core around which beauty spun.

I told him I was only worried at not hearing from him and he explained that his trip was prolonged because he hadn't found what he was seeking.

"I'm difficult, I know. I wait for rapture the way people wait for the poste. Isn't that what you think?"

"I've lost my thinking," I said, and then amending it with a burst, I began to talk about spring and the new plants, white as the day he left, sprouting in the courtyard.

In the unpollinated region behind my consciousness, too small for speech to enter, I found deceit enough to show him the truth: that I loved him. I told him I was torn between the beauty of the season and the emptiness without him. That I'd discovered that hell was not below heaven but that space was marbled.

He reached behind him and took from his desk an edition of the Zauberbuch, bound in leather with my initials stamped into the cover. We were together again and in the fiery ascension of being, I wanted him to be my way.

My love for him. In it I confronted myself. It was window, mirror, landscape. From a series of events, embraces, encounters, and memories, it was distilled into my blood until ---if I didn't hear his name in the world and hold something he had written—I could believe he was one of my selves, invented like the finest work of an artist who sees life as inchoate.

*

I nearly fainted the next morning when I heard Lilos announced at the door. At the end of the sienna hallway I see him, stranded by my memory, the faculty he contemned. I saw his outline, his arrogant head. I saw his figure, featureless, bow towards me without a word, and excited as I was, I spoke calmly and was cold. Uncaring and indiscreet, would he ruin my life with Ritter? I opened the door to the small salon, telling him he might wait there while I called Ritter.

"It's you I came to see. Why did you run away?"

"You must forget I visited you, "I whispered.

"I'll do nothing of the kind," he said. His voice was deep and aged – like an old man's -as though condemning past and future might have made him pass through all time at once. "I have no intention of letting you go, Zoe."

Yes! I remember! How angry he might be that a wretched old woman has closed him entire in her life and the only Lilos that remains is left in me.

"Do you hear? I have no intention of letting go of you."

"You must," I said spitting out the words. 'Because I hate you. Hate will make me smooth as a stone. You can't hold on to me."

He shook his head. "no. You don't hate me. You don't." and coming closer to me I saw he had a bandage over his nose and another crossed it---- the sign of the religious and the condemned. He rubbed at it, saying, "I fell----trying to follow you…" Lying.

"you see.." he went on in an unctuous tone, "I'm not afraid to follow the waking out of the dream."

I heard the door to the study close and whispered "Be quiet. I beg you."

"He'll leave you again. Come with me. Come to me." He spoke with his eyes half-closed, like a mesmerist.

I heard a noise. My heart thumped even in my fingers. "Go away. Oh, go away. Please. My life is here."

"it's an invention—your life.." he was standing almost against me. "You wear your innocence like a mask in a primitive play. Zoe, you wear it like an eternal quality. Have different forms.---Be everything" 'he said more excitedly.

"Who has come?" it was Ritter's voice from the hallway.

For a moment, Lilos looked at me from over the bandage, and his eyes devoured my heart like black dogs with a bone.

He said, loudly: "A visitor!" and I sighed gratefully, as he turned away to smooth his hair before the small mirror which was out of my sight. I could see the young stalk of his neck rising out of a creased collar and I felt a terrible warmth for him who had stirred in me things I had never known and which---by never naming them--- left open a part of my life if I wished to enter it there again.

I began to say.. "Lilos"—but he and Ritter were already shaking hands astride the narrow carpet on which the light threw down their joined shadows--- a breast-bone heaving, a bridge raised and lowered, a dark wing pinioned to the oriental flowers.

*

I brought in the tea and as I poured, the green shirt Lilos wore clung to his chest and I had a moment of bewilderment thinking I'd spilled the tea on him.

He looked up at me, smiling, in a very affectionate way, and as unworthy as I found him of my love, I wished to give him my protection somehow---- my thanks for showing me a death which was not skeletal, yet had been— unfrightening in his arms---like all death: a completion of the senses and annihilation of the light.

Ritter asked me to sit down with them, but I excused myself, as though they would always be there for me, and as I went out, I heard Ritter say something about man today facing murderous truths- as he had never been. I froze when Lilos said he "other" had told him the very same thing, but he meant 'his Roman'.

I didn't even follow Lilos to the door. I'd made my future by stuffing the past and present like a dead pet in the center of it. The real future was to be Ritter leaving me to become a moving symbol as well as Lilos walking away down the hall on those unsubstantial heron legs--- unusually exuberant, almost healthy, going wherever he was going. Perhaps knowing himself already released from the flesh of his hallucination, from all the women brought by some reversal back to bed. Yet what fate was there for Lilos or me? What destiny like Ritter's? What mortality that would last past the rotting of youth? There are forces that move us more than love or art and whose only failing is that move vertically—like spring—instead of forward ; and like moons must be constantly renewed.

*

Bald Ettore brought the news. It came from behind his smooth ordinary face with the masculine ardor of a voice which dwelt in him like a sinner in a bare retreat. Comfortingly neat and undistinguished in his dress, he wore the adornment of a ruby tie pin- almost as the insignia for heart in a parable.

His expression was unmoved by the trembling of his words. "I am afraid--- I have brought bad news with me."

It was the end of summer. The war was happening beyond the frontier and was brought to us by shreds of news without sound as we might have seen a photo of exploding shells. Only the imminent possibility of Ritter's having to go thrust it into our home and gave me excuses for our shifting relationship. I thought of us in terms of candles flickering and brightening only things within their radius; areas I knew to be there were thrown into darkness.

"Bad news?"

Ritter's mother had just left us. My daughter had been to see us. It could be no one close.

"Lilos is dead." On Ettore's white shirt, the red stone, lidless and beyond tears, stared into my eyes.

"You are mistaken!" I gasped. But Ritter put his hand on my arm and said: "I knew it already."

"But how?" Ettore asked.

"Because it was new," Ritter said, "and convulsively, everyone takes part in the new and terrible today." He went on talking…. hard to reach back and find.. -----but the new was everywhere… but tell me… go on Ettore…"

"They say---" his voice stopped and went on: "Well it is rather incredible. How do we know? I heard," Ettore went on: "It is said.--. that Lilos.--- that he –disappeared out of a plane over Vienna---" He went on……

The story was… well that no one knew whether he had just unfastened his belt or whether it had been an accident. The belt coming undone--- a turn of the aircraft---- the pilot could not be sure. Someone had suggested that Lilos was in one of his hashish dreams and had just stepped down, but how could one know?

"He was a very interesting fellow," Ettore added. "Perhaps a mystic without a faith."

He and Ritter talked about him. His ideas, his friends, one of whom -- Ettore reported --- the poet G.,- had said that Lilos spent his life trying to un live it.

While they talked, I looked across the room and saw myself, waiting, in a white lawn dress and flowers in my hair as though I had come to be in an improbable wedding.

"But," I finally interrupted them: "if he loved life,,?

"His dissatisfaction fed on that," Ettrore said.

They spoke of the abdication of the self, the conclusion of involuntary joy, the narcissist becoming the world. They haggled with memories, facts, suppositions, arbitrary decisions---- sitting like petitioners to the silence that follows a death.

'I have no intention of letting you go, Zoe'

Lilos stands up. Dark hair blowing against a background of irrelevant sky and irrelevant mechanical sounds. One last made laugh sweetened by shameful delicious odors. Denying the horizontal... down down--- his heart in flames. Straight pure light warm No Lilos! Stop Lilos! And over, diverting birds, the star-shaped form of black and small. Gone.

My love of one time, stopped now. The famished look, indecent gestures of those hands. Move side. In front of me lies something gray and cold. Broken bones in hieratic poses, opaque eyes----a set face maculate with earth. Dragged from its retreat in life. Your austerity makes me blush. Let me go. Please. I no longer have anything in common with you. At a respectful distance I mourn. Sepulcher of desires, marry the ground.

My fellow beings draw me back, approaching ill at ease, whispering, "I'm afraid it has upset her." "Prerogative of friends..." Ettore's head bends over my hand, the nape of his neck as clean of hairs as his thoughts of my secret.

"A fellow like that--- who knows? He may even reappear.!"

Watch out. A wave runs through me, a gentle vibration----- infallible signs---he advances---greedy lips----holding out his impious arms—nothing is sacred to him. "Come to me—come with me---" in God knows what miry swamp. What ornate palazzo of lust----. Beautifully proportioned soil, rest in me.

"I'll show you out."

"For you both—my dear, a vacation. I imagine our dear Maitre here will be of my opinion".

As Ritter turns, passing close beside me, something emanated from hi clothes. A warm breath. Familiar. Reassuring. I was already going on with our life. Making plans, working again- perhaps on Ritter's portrait. Occupied in what he called the "sensuous faculty of looking". But I would be wearing what Lilos called the "mask of my eternal quality" under which the dark impulse would thrive like a flower in a grave.

I ran to the mirror as though having lost my memory, I needed a visible accomplice to remember me and I saw a disorder of terrors behind a beauty as regular as a peacock's eye.

20 JUIN

Tonight holds no surprise for me. It is difficult to remember how a meeting could have hope in it or that a walk might change the direction of my life.

My dreams are albums now.

Once, I had no home, yet every window was a possibility. Once, when my love was falling, I went to a little shop the way that country girls might seek the old crone's hausle at the wood's edge, and knock for the surety that would bring back their lover, cause him to die, make them forget him. Do they ever know which? I would have trusted no old country-woman with love, with peace. I wanted only the strength to go on moving without the fear that life had dropped out of me. Although I knew it had. Ritter covered the world; he connected sky and flowers. He was my Venice, my concert. Birth and death came true, and like a work of art, it was finished. Was I not trying to find a corner of the world which might be new, in order to bring it back to him in me? Could I be finished too, like the last small poem----beautiful and full of love--- that he tucked away in his veined leather satchel two weeks before he set off for his long vacation with the Duchess Mandelsloh?

That evening on Eglantinestrasse, hope still walked with me. We found the shop easily. The door—a red door already described to me by Samontagne—was bolted with a curious bronze "S", and a grinning marmoset was placed above it, its tongue inviting me---no! rather preventing me from sounding the bell. I stood instead, looking in through the windowpanes. But I could hardly see further than the heavy articles of furniture which pressed forward and Oriental bowl, a set of handmirrors, a carved dolphin: all these enticing small offerts which could be carried out in the hand, but were meant to be taken with a home in mind for them. And I had no home now. Yet I stood irresistibly drawn; I wanted them all. How odd that I had never had a hunger for such things and do not want them now. Perhaps, feeling a vaster beauty of relationship slipping away, I yearned to surround myself with objects in a splendid boudoir. To arise each day and linger through rooms filled with glorious possessions. Only to dream of a man I loved finding me there. Taking me out of that cluttered place to a bare swept room with a few simple things all in use. No, no! This---not errand, but really pilgrimage—was not to seek out carvings or tiny blazoned cups. I was still looking for beauty in a human mold: my own--- through the eyes of someone who was expert in recognizing all its forms and would be prepared to pay its full value. Hadn't Samontagne seen beneath my varnish of sadness and believed that I could be restored to original perfection?

"There are three such shops," he had said. "I leave it to you to know which is mine."

I suppose that this was the last time I had hope in my relation with Ritter. Perhaps it's why I paused so long outside and thereafter associated those windows with a crucial turning in my life. I stood quietly gazing at the collection of antiques until only a spot of sunlight was left on the arched back of the china dolphin, like a circular promise of other days. I stood there assured that what I needed was inside and Samontagne would discover it for me. How our dreams remain intact from their resolutions! Each time I think of hope, I see again the simple shape of the little fish against the massive chairs and consoles behind it. I touch again the letter "S", and I feel the same surge or excitement. Old now and crooked, my skin as rippling as the fish, I stand again as I did then. "My name is Samontagne," he had said. "And here is my address. But when I saw you, both changed for me."

I would have gone wherever it led; my beating heart and my cold hand on the bell had told me that. And I remember that I was prepared to go even if it led me away from Ritter to a man who would cherish me. But I was scarcely twenty-seven and there was in me the same want as in other young women: an overwhelming desire to be possessed, totally and perpetually, by a man---any man---I could love. The marmoset, knowing and abandoned, invited me again: pull, pull, pull out my tongue; I'll sound the alarm but I'll say nothing. Safely pull out my tongue and my master will find you. As I reached up, my sleeve fell back. I saw my wrist and I knew I had no first words. They would be his. The tongue withdrew from my hand and a light musical note released it.

In the scant two hours since my pneumatique - letter, what had he done? Back there, behind the darkness, what personal arrangement of beauty must there be to allow such precious objects to lie unselected in the window? The fact that I could not guess at it proved once again that he was the discoverer, not I. I might have imagined to find a flower thrust into the bolt; any other man might have let that speak first for him, as lovers send out prescribed letters to the eternal mistress. But what had awakened me for him was his recognition of myself. He spoke of things I knew; he touched on small and lovely details: private and light affections of the sort that make a woman long to see herself in those gilded handmirrors rather than pass her image quickly in a café-glass. The human is not always profound. And still, the smaller loves can sometimes lead down to our deeper selves. Or even when they do not, our personal trivia—what is it but a way of naming ourselves? My love of pearls was my address that year. And so his approach to me the night before in the Seibert salon was an act of recognition. He spoke first of the pearls I was wearing--- the necklace which Ritter had carried in tissue from a shop beneath the Rialto bridge, and which he had clasped about my neck with the words: "You can never hide your soul from me. I will see it in each pearl."

That evening Ritter was not there to see me reflected in his gift. I had fallen into a chair, mute as a piece of music dropped by its player. Not even the Seiberts could coax me to speak. And that young man was suddenly by my side. Galanterie alive. Whatever. I had read or seen, he could speak about. He divined my sign at once and bound my Verseau to other facets of my life. We spoke of the pearl headdress in my favorite Pollaiuollo, the sheen of Meissen-sculpture I had ried to approximate in my eau-fortes, the early Trouvères who illuminated the song of the world which followed them. The face of Guillbert, The Fratellinis---and in all these things he found, as I did, what we called "l'essence". The recognition drew me to my feet and so we stood. Unadorned that year except with a glow which love strains through the skin, I stood before that face more light and perfect than my own, and I marveled that he could see my value. How many men had I passed through the street or in a salon who saw in me an unescorted woman in unfashionable clothes—"déclassé"—but hardly worth being bold with.

But how different had been his glance. It was when he moved away and reappeared with a thimbleful of brandy that I saw his eyes engaged. He had found the value of something he did not own, and his desire for possession was made more delicate by the wish to restore full beauty by a careful touch, in accord with its particular nature. Yes, it was this that drew me up—but not down into any depth of him. A pale beauty was anchored to his face by planes so sharp that all brilliance was held on the surface—not like shallow glass, but like pure crystal which needs no shadows—only light—to animate its being. I could feel his hair, bright as foil, blinding my very skin as though the sun had shone in a windowless room. (I who had held a head so dark, so loose, that each thread led my fingers on journeys into night.!) And I marveled at that golden hair because I could not see its roots.

"My eyes betray my life," were his next words to me. "What I have been searching for has already been accomplished."

When he said this I tried to turn away, but I could not. It was as though I had been a child again, staring trance-like for hours at the iridescence of a pool or the implacable sheen of the North sea on a winter night.

"You will understand," he said. "If you ever find the entrance to my home, you will see that only Della Francesca has caught the color of your lips."

Understand? I had no desire to understand.---only to surrender to his perfect charm.

That superior things are incomplete, I knew even then. Each of Ritter's poems, grown into unalterable form, sent out from within its exactitude the threads of groping toward a vision never reached. Each precise word carried within it those weeds of darkness in which we tangle for definitions. And more and more, as he saw the impossibility of knowing, he turned not to great images, but to small. His poem of the child's wagon, realized with unearthly simplicity, has uttered a monument to childhood by grasping a fragment of its complicity and leaving its mystery more awesome than before. I used to think, that year, that had Ritter been a sculptor, he would scarcely have finished a head; he would have climbed with exhausted hands across the bridge of the nose as though the distance covered eternity. The rest of the face, hardly delineated, would have had a reality beyond features merely by being placed around the mountain of miracle within it. I sought to remain part of this greatness in Ritter's life—a love forever tapped and, like those deep earth-streams whose source is hidden, never completely known. Because I wished to be always in Ritter's life, I was drawn to the perfection of the beautiful Samontagne who might have enabled me to equal his. Unlike Ritter's poem and the unfinished head---all those fragments over which he sobbed for want of Deity--- might I not appear to him at the Chateau of the Duchess, my cheeks touched with fire, my eyes cleared by the gallant alchemy of discovery and craft? I would be able to rest his heart.

So, without doubt, I had made my way to that door into which a stain had been rubbed by those hands which had given me a card to enter it. But would I have been there if I had been left standing with his card as white upon it as my glove? No. As we were about to part, I had seen his face rise up like a dream and vanish into touch on my palm which held his name. It was not the simple regard paid to woman—that touch. It was a nod which beauty gives to beauty as they pass between the world. And the act of recognition, it possessed me.

Could I guess what gesture he had made when the bell sounded? Had he glanced at himself or at some magical tableau which needed both our presences to spring it into life? Was there a certain wine--- --a wine I had never <u>known</u> I loved? Oh, what young woman has not gone through a street and stood with one hand on a door and thought: Now! Oh, now! And let it be the same for both of us!

At the moment the bell ceased, a light appeared through the massive shadows of the furniture, my fish leaped up as though to catch an ever-impure moon, and I could not see, but heard him coming toward the door.

Earlier that day, a button from my shirtwaist had threaded off into my hand; the door-knocker had been too muted to hear old Renaldt come and go away again with the little broetchen still warm in his basket; the console, on which in my sleep, I had seen a letter waiting, held only one from Brache; and the Kuhnle where I continued to take my coffee even without Ritter showed the placard which meant Closed. All small things had slipped a fraction from the ways, but the square card that read "Samontagne" appeared to me as a request. It fell on my hand when I shook out my dress; it dropped flat on the mantel as I wound the clock; and it appeared in my purse at the flower-market. Shouldn't I have believed it a talisman and not the envoi to that day?

The door opened. Samontagne stood in such sudden light, I could not see him all at once as he said, using my first name with alarm, "Zoë! Oh! Come in."

It was to his back that I said, "But--- why are you surprised?"

"Wait. Follow me. This way......" was all he said.

There was a scent of polish, perhaps soap. I had not noticed that his height caused his shoulders to pressed back as though some jealous altitude was forcing him to lower levels. I followed down a shadowy aisle as well as I could, but my hand touched something soft. An alien cry rang out; my own sound after it in a chocked gasp.

"It is only Sonah,' he said. "She startles people. Come. Ah, if only I had had more time."

It was a notation from whatever moves the fate of us who dream ahead. That way was lost to me that night. I knew, at the first howl of the cat, and although I continued to hope through the hours over that supper on thick porcelain plates from Gabriche, I knew. I could never bring anything new back to Ritter. There was nothing new that Ritter could find in me together. My choices lay between keeping him, saddened, by my side a little longer, or seeking my own way without him. And either route was a completed one. Had we not used up all the combinations in life we thought beautiful to use? In my hunger I had forgotten to leave some dream to Samontagne who walked in front of me on chamois slippers and, holding out both his arms to the jewel-like chamber, offered me a setting and bade me gather my black moiré dress---- shabby enough for lovers---- into a sateen-striped armchair as he took its mate. There was no intimate meal, no flowers. It had not been his dream. How often can dreams bed matched as those two chairs were matched, except by a master who restores both?

I believe that his kiss on my palm the night before had sealed his dream for him, and as he might have paused a moment, baring his head, before a window in the Sainte-Chapelle, he then went on his way---- his vision, a jewel in a vault. To an absolute longing, possibilities are leeches. I had to know with certainty something I was already quite sure of. "You did not expect me to come today," I said.

He gave me a glass, the rim of which was so supremely cut, I felt the craftsman touch my lip and I all but closed my eyes. Then he said, "Ah, no! How could I hope...... But I am so happy that you are here."

As though my look could give them one more life, he pointed out to me the treasures that surrounded us. Ownerless, he had found each piece like some lost breath of kings or dukes long dead, in vaults, deserted chateaux, ruins, shops which hid them under blatant china, impoverished chairs, sections of fabric parted from their frames. It was not only age but beauty that he bought. I regarded them all----- all his precious hoardings. I see them again now through eyes already three-quarters of a century old and which if Samontagne still lived, he would perhaps treasure not only as sapphires in an ancient setting, but those which also had reflected once the marvel's of Ritter's face. He offered me food, saying, "You must come another time. I will prepare a specialty....."

Disappointment is a sleep that clears more space for death. I sat stroking the Siamese cat whose tense body gave way to a terrifyingly anguished head. The stiff ears seemed like chips imbedded deeply enough to make the wide mouth open in sounds that tore my heart. Samontagne said that such was her way of speaking. I held the small face between my hands and felt for this creature more sorrow than I could say. Of course, was it not for myself I felt? Quivering with passion in the midst of perfect order, drawing in those beautiful nails to pad over the polished wood and slip down the smooth velour's---- could I not have found here some echo of my own need? What deceit, to close in an animal –form that ready soul I might have met! But didn't I know, when I loitered outside the door, that life could not exist without this yearning sound?

And what did Samontagne think of me--- sitting there in a sedate black dress, my hair hidden under a bonnet (to make it more resplendent when discovered)? Between the white tapered fingers and the point of my sleeve, his lips had whispered homage the night before----and now the hand was revealed as human in the fur of his animal. Could he still perceive and echo of the vision he had had? But no! This man of and for beauty---what would it grant him to crack open the little fish in his window to see what was within? Its value to him was delight to the eye--- to the visual sense which is released from bondage to pain.

As I go back again, I know that I put too much in that night; it might have saved my life with Ritter. Only as I sat in the tomb-perfect chamber with its appointments assembled out of the same taste of love was I aware of the need for a third. His love was for these objects, and in the embrace, not even death lay between. The animal pulsing to my hand was a deadly reminder that under the shadows of her flesh, there was a beat of blood, and only in wood do the veins lie quiet on the surface.

What I said that night, I hardly recall. I know only that I watched Samontagne with the resigned attention with which those proud ladies have gazed at the tumbrils stopping outside the gates. The details of a wheel… a broken slat…could occupy the heart. To whom could they make an appeal? It was not strange that I fixed upon his fingers as I might have looked into the eyes of another man, or at the slender joining of his lips to find the accent of himself. But,in constant graceful motion and silent, those hands carried silver to the porcelain dishes from Gabriche. I could not eat that food--- cooked and carried to the door by someone in an apron filled with coins. Another hunger made me sate. And Samontagne looked up and said, "Does beauty feed upon itself, then?"

Ah, yes, he spoke about my loveliness. He served me with a Sèvres cup of exquisite rareness, and said, with the great pleasure of having discovered an object of similar pattern: "It suits you as it would suit no other woman." I caught no scent of the coffee he had brewed for it, because a slight shift of the wine had stirred the unlit chimney: I caught instead the acrid-sweet smell of memory. As full, as light, as quickly-vanishing as smoke---- still it reappeared the same. I could not drink.

"It is rare," he said. "But you ought not to be afraid to use it. I should have supposed that you would like delicate things."

"I?" I said. "I do not know." And at that moment, I did not know. I only knew that when I lay flat against the earth, it always felt thin as a crust; and, hollow beneath, there was yet a vibration which was not my own. And even as he urged me to drink, I could not. Obsessed with my own beauty, I felt it intolerable that a cup should be used---- should hold something in it---- when I did not.

I was committed to the life of love. Its moeurs are inexorable as the form of a sonnet within which private visions can perform. Sitting in the striped armchair mated to his own, I knew that the window behind us might have been filled with stones if they had been gathered on some walk before or after love. A man gives a woman a necklace, for thousands of years. Unable to grow love with his hands, he works in the way of his flesh, by day and night---- a process which, like a low-banked fire, often lies under ashes, pitted by coals, without color, and---in miraculous conjunctions----flares up. But in the meantime he hands her flowers more perfect than themselves. Without shame. I knew only one way with a man. This man had kissed my hand and spoken my name too soon, and it distinguished me from the other treasures in his room just as it made me one of their kind. Completed. What I had foolishly desired.

And then I knew that love was even that: a poem; the impossibility of knowing; a fragment of it understood only by the heat of the flame which leaves the fire more mysterious, more awesome than before. And once I felt such a thing---guided to it by the cat's lonely howl, by the feeling of completion in the room---I was prepared to give up my dream of having something new. I would go at once into the rigid form which governed love. I told myself that Samontagne had not had enough warning for flowers---those tender-scented colors which soften the aftermath, the terror of losing oneself in the dark of the lover. There had not been enough time to plan a repast on plates so perfect that hands made clumsy by longing are struck by the senselessness of china.

I considered whether I might have been mistaken; whether his gallantry was hiding his hope like a maniac behind a cellar –door. I wondered if the velvet jacket, blue and soft, might draw its silk away from muscle and bone as ridged as earth. I could see nothing in his eyes, his mouth, and yet I wanted to make clear, at once, what his charm might prolong to a year of time.

"Samontagne!" It was the first time I had said his name. He looked at me in surprise, not as someone who has been called, but as one called away. I scarcely knew what I might say. When I leaned forward, my hand braced itself on the console which held the meal I had not tasted. The wood was cold.

"This table between us," I said. "It was made from a living tree." He must have thought me mad, for when I said, "Do you think it is better now?" he answered "What?" and then, "How can you---- you especially---say so? That tree....before.... That wood was crude... unformed. Now it is perfect."

While his sensuous fingers moved over the surface on inlaid wood, he talked about its workmanship and all the time I tried to deny: the button, the false dream, the closed café, the flowers nowhere; the cat having found rest upon my arm and broken from some sleep as I moved back started up --quivering. It voiced again inconsolable hurt through that blind mouth all pierced with pin-like teeth. It made my heart go white.

I saw entire that room in which he set me like a living treasure. I felt the grace with which hew honored art as someone who had never been in the cellar of its birth. No vase, no cup, not one bisque toe of any figurine was broken in that room. No imperfections; I could not see a stain on any of the fabric all around us. I had a moment of wondering if the purity--- as shadowless as stone-bottomed pools--- might not be another way of love. Another language which could dream me into a different life where no one suffered and so did never sing nor write of it. This accomplished man---- those marvelous fingers--- could he artfully disguise that stump where my life had come apart from Ritter's? Or would he cast me aside when he saw that I was disfigured?

I told him I must leave. I think he stood up then because I see him standing too and asking me--- his arms by his sides—to stay. Would he have been able to make me as beautiful, as calm as the other mute things he owned? But not if I could still feel. And feeling nothingness was pain. For if I stayed, he might truly rub out the scratches on my heart while leaving none of his own.

I stared at his hands again. Those long flat hands of remarkable delicacy which either had been drawn to touch those things like themselves, or had grown too much like them. Those hands to which long wrists held tight as women to their dreams, and almost more beautiful than any spoon or knife he had passed to me. Yet, in a sudden glow of rose on the palm, a tensing of the joints, a clasp together---- they had mortality in them. And I had a solemn desire to have them touch me---hardly sure that his wrists, those shoulders pinioned by the air, his breath or limbs would understand.

Suddenly he moved forward. My soul fluttered far away and pale as the reprieve one waits for on the block. He bent and kissed my hair at the parting of the bonnet strings and that kiss doomed me as his vacancy doomed the cat to listen only for its own cries of life.

I refused his offer to accompany me to a fiacre and I last saw his face hammered into darkness by the closing door. I touched the S-shaped bolt once, out of homage to the crooked spine which bent it into posture of a suppliant, and to poems which are prayers. Then

I paused for a long while by the little canal that separated the old city from my apartment, and -as though by rendezvous - a mallard appeared under the lamplight and walked past me on thin brown relic feet.

12 JULLIET

My heart pounds directly in the center of my throat today. Somewhere hidden in this bulk, I am. Like a little pigeon en cocotte. Ritter said that if the body remained the same we would not change.. That as we grow older, not only the people in our lives, but WE multiply. We had just arrived in Venice. Dynter had lent us his palazzo. If Dynter had owned three palazzi he would have lent them all to Ritter, and Ritter would have moved us from one to the next, seeking, through transience, to find the home in himself. But there was only one: cold, beautiful, sinking under the weight of stone convolvulus and seraphim with eagle wings. And it came with Flavio who had gold rings and an inhuman smile when he looked at me. Like the mouths of animals, his spread open by its tendons---not delight.

Ritter had once lived in Venice, but it was my first visit. We were standing on a small bridge near the house of Manzoni, and when he leaned over to look in the canal, I told him he was seeking old images of himself, while I was making new ones. "Not exactly, Zoë," he said. "There is a loose relationship of all our selves and they manage to pull together like a ruin." The word surprised me and I asked him why a ruin. He told me because so many parts of our lives become broken off and lost and it remains for us to discover what they might have formed to. I see us there on the bridge---my blue tailor-made with the lace fichu I later tried to bleach in the sun over the fondamenta and which---even as I watched from the balcony--- lifted up and sailed like foam---like my past—down the sparkled water of the canal. I see his tweed jacket stretched up to his shoulders when he leaned over the railing. I cannot see our faces, and although bent in the same attitude of looking into the water, I cannot see our needs. Like two figures in a bas-relief, our being cut into the same scene appears to be our only connection.

Lovers are aliens--- each of whom seeks in the other an ancient language of his homeland and ends by adopting the country of his dream. My life with Ritter had already been more than I had known of happiness. In Venice there was more glory and yet more danger in mingling with a beauty so lavish that it became less a setting than the form of our love, and I was afraid that to leave it would be, finally, to leave us.

The city enthralled us: its maze of alleys, secluded courtyards, bridges, archways, tortuous passages, quaysides, dead ends. Dark overhung back streets and sudden sunlit squares, At times when the city was glazed with light and I stood entranced before the castles, I could have believed that I was in the tales of my childhood, and that because I was young, beautiful, and in love, one of the fish streaming by would speak to me. No diamond would fall from my dark hair, but I would wish to have Ritter----forever after.

I did not tell him these fancies, yet because we shared an interest in the occult, we often spoke of strange happenings and he knew my passion for fortune-women, one of whom I was to find in an alley near Ca' Foscari. I remember Ritter's telling me that I confused the enchanted with the forbidden, but I was to forget that---or deny it—after the day I entered the light room behind a curtain and the bejeweled woman said in place of a greeting: "Here comes one who seeks more than human happiness." I remember that she had to repeat it slowly until I understood, She rested my hand, palm-up, on hers. Perhaps she knew I could not understand her well, she said only a few simple things: whatever could be gathered from my clothes, my tired radiant face. Things unimportant and banal. She offered me a talisman for an exorbitant price and ended the session with the words that I must not be afraid to go after what I wanted. I had already stood up and as she offered me the talisman again, the row of beads shook over her large bosom. "You will always... be saved," she said slowly. "....by recognition." And---I did not know why----- these words struck me to the heart. I went out, leaving some lire on the table, refusing her little medal, thinking her another charlatan who lived off fools like me.

I would race home from one of these escapades--- my eyes ringed from excitement and fatigue, my face thin. I see my feet, daringly bound by a few ankle straps. The soles already worn to the thinness of a beech leaf. I see my short voile skirts --- adopted after a few weeks--- my hair a la Greque with a gold band circling it and small curls slipping out over my ears. Ritter would tell me, "You are a wraith. You have suffered a sea-change!" But, in fact, I looked rather ill to myself. No one would have guessed easily at my happiness and for one of the few times in my life, other men hardly noticed me as I roamed the streets. I had never looked so undesirable as I was during that period when I was so desired.

Each morning I carried Ritter's coffee to the high cavelike room which gave onto the church towers he liked and I always tried to leave it quietly on a table by the door. But he would hear my steps on the marble stairway and his face was turned to me when I entered. More and more often he began to say, "What? Going walking again without me?" And he would leave his papers weighted by a book. Once he ran up behind me in the corto and he had his hat still in his hand. He said he wanted to write but he wanted much more to walk with me. We wandered the labyrinthine streets, past the bolted doors. Or we rocked in gondolas, gliding under bridges, listening to cries as though each one was made to us. We came to spend all our time together. He did not visit anyone he knew-----the great actress who lived in her poverty as in a tragic masquerade depressed his spirit---- and we moved alone in Venice, passionate and hushed, the way our voices moved in our words.

One day we came out into the empty piazzetta startling the pigeons in such an instant they seemed thrown against the sky. We sat down near the black-suited musicians who began, with calm nocturnal faces, to play Wagner with desperation in their arms. I see myself again…. Sitting next to him…. surrounded by empty chairs and tables…… only the two of us played to by that crazed orchestra. Ritter in his great emotional excitement, trembling to each chord of music as though it had been he sounded or drawn over with a bow. I remember him saying that the beauty or Venice and of me--- which had become linked--- had assaulted him and he was afraid for us if we stayed on. I took this less as warning than flattery; the dangers which my mind rejected, my heart desired. I did not know that pushing love past its usual boundaries was for me only touching the same furthermost limits I had set for my dream. I thought I was careening into the unknown and that my beauty was an amulet, a golden skin, a fair exchange for love, safe passage. Each day I brought his coffee, paused, waiting for him to follow me---- believing we were worthy substitute for the rigid forms of his art. My painting and his poetry flowered at the edge of our life like a garden at the foot of a forest.

As we walked to the Scuola San Rocco one day, a summer rain had begun and under the eaves sheltered pigeons emitted plaintive cries: higher, some gulls lifted their wings several times as though to struggle loose from the city, and triumphantly, sailing above all obstacles, shot towards the open sea. At that moment the storm broke and it seemed so beautiful I should like to have been as drenched by the Venetian rain as by its sun. But we took refuge inside and it was on this day that I saw the wonderful Tintoretto Adam and Eve on the ceiling---- an interpretation which, more than Cranach's or Michelangelo's, fixed for me the relation between a man and a woman: the powerful back of Adam restraining his greater strength to cup tenderly in his hand, the hand of Eve which holds the apple. Surely very woman in love feels, once, that she is Eve and shares in the culpability of drawing man into love which is her domain.

At first I took only casual notice of other people around us: the woman with her crucifix humped over a goiter who came from the laundry; the vitrier bent almost horizontal from the weight of his trade; the servant, Flavio, to whom I brought coffee before going upstairs with Ritter's Flavio would take his in one hand and bow, still holding the tall stick he used for cleaning. I could see his smile even as his head was facing the floor. Then he would stand on the open balcony where the cushions were airing and drink slowly from the small cup. Flaming hair, glittering fingers, Flavio yet moved in secret---keeping order, hiding his tools, his voice, the sack of rags he used for polishing, and, finally one day, himself. Serving dishes collected, his basket hung on the kitchen hook, and a sudden rain through windows I could not close ran along his polished floors. I asked the old woman who sorted peaches in the corto, and without looking up from her hands she said: "These things happen, Signora." One of the men at the fountain laughed.

During the days Flavio was gone something faint and lightly spreading began to appear like a stain around my image of him. I could not touch the little cup in which he had last had his coffee and it was Ritter who found it rattling on the balcony. This disappearance changed our lives, not only because I had to market alone--- thus drawing me out of our self-enclosed promenade--- but because on one of these errands something happened which sprung together all the diffuse excitement of my love, my baroque fatigue, and my "fortune".

Near the filthy district of San Polo I was in a water taxi around which the gulls cried and skimmed for food, when on a footbridge above, Flavio rose up against the landscape of shuttered sculpture like an image rusted by the timeless sun and damp. The boat stopped, everything was silent; then he called out to me----cantingly and loud---- a phrase which fell somewhere between the joy and malice of living, and lifting his arm high, he threw toward me an object which splashed into the water. The woman next to me bumped into my side and as I turned I saw that she was crossing herself. Then she spat on the floor. She intoned something repetitive, but although seeming to address me, I could understand nothing of what she said. Then she stood up and, still mumbling, descended at the Rialto.

As the boat cut through the water again, I thought of the shocked woman and wondered whether Flavio had been guilty of some obscenity. "These things happen, Signora." Looking ahead and then sliding behind us were the unharmonious stone carvings, the gargoyles, rooms hidden behind red curtains, pigeons clustering on the shoulders of battered saints. Back there, Flavio outraging the women veiled in black, caressing their rosaries. I saw him kneel in a cold church, his gold-ringed fingers clasped together to hide his impiety from the severe images. Flavio enjoying all the liberties forbidden to saints. Patron slave of fulfilled desires. But what had he thrown to me? A stone? A talisman? My fancies transformed him.

Did he recognize me as someone who would not refuse unnatural aid to fulfill all human wishes?

When at last I reached the Giudecca, I asked the driver what Flavio had called out. He was knotting the rope around a stanchion and without looking up he told me, slowly, that it had been a blasphemy. I was intrigued and I insisted to know the words. As though reciting a verse, he repeated carefully: "Oh how long the world takes to die!" Then he added what I took to be his belief that Flavio had been drunk. I rushed back to Ca' Mostra, eager to tell Ritter these incredible words, but as soon as I threw open the door, I saw Flavio there---his back to me--- polishing the floors as though he had not been away three weeks; as though he did not measure the hours as other people did; as though he knew the real passage of time which raced with mortal and insolent swiftness, or stood still like the centuries' old city lapped by sensuous water. Forever after..... forever after remains in the eternal present because it is unchanged. Flavio did not seem drunk, nor did he make any sign of having seen me, called to me, or thrown anything into the canal. Ritter was ready for our walk and we set out. As we walked down the fondamenta, I saw Flavio up on the balcony. His fists were on his hips and his slender legs –struck apart---threw a black chevron against the white stone. The formality of his shadow did not deceive me. His flaming hair, his glistening face with its animal smile had nothing of the austerity of things bounded by human will. For a dazed second I was transfixed. Then we began moving down the fondamenta. The sea was solemn and full, silver gulls flew overhead, every conceivable color massed together in the sunlight. It was exquisite, but I felt agitated and although telling Ritter nothing of what had passed earlier on the boat, I asked him if he believed in the devil.

He said he did not. "But if someone spoke of him," I asked. "What would that bring to your mind?" Rather vaguely he answered: "When one doesn't do enough."

We were coming into the piazzetta. He seemed already to have let the subject fall and was leading me to the Floriani. I felt unsatisfied, lightly piqued. I asked him to think of operas, other poets-----so many artists who had given the devil a voice: "What does his voice sound like? What would it sound like to you, if you wanted to personify it?"

"Retreating steps," he said, and was already pulling out my chair.

In my own life I knew I was guilty of "retreating steps". Was I, then, the devil because I had abandoned my child? I told him that I found his image facile. Weren't there moments, I asked, when one is incapable of "doing enough"----when one's duty seems too difficult and one's heart yearns elsewhere? He seemed interested, now, and said that this was something he tried to see clearly: that he often pondered on great men for examples. He though we must look for, even love, the "difficult"--- that we must seek its unyielding features among the more blissful ones. Only then, he said, would our vacillations unite in a group as solid as a funeral of peasants for whom Death wears, momentarily, the face of a friend.

I believe it was on that day that Ritter told me to be quieter, more patient, and to look around me as he had always seen me do---- like a beginner. To be overjoyed, as I had been, by the colored wheels of a cart, by the shape of an ear I found superb. As we spoke of the times we shared, I remembered going for a picnic in a jolting little carriage; we had talked to the men in shabby fishing boats; we had sat on the doorstep to gossip with the woman who delivered bread. How could it happen that these things began to seem banal? That the unexpected had become so fascinating? I told him that since I had come to Venice, I had found as much unknown in myself as in the streets. "Isn't it ever that way with you?" I asked. He said that he tried not to be with his feelings like a landlord who lets houses to strangers: he tried to live in them himself.

But I could not feel or desire this concord with myself. I had become more entrancing just by being different from the little girl and wife I once was. If I had "let my house to strangers", they were as mysterious as Royalty at a masked ball. I seemed to be flying through the dance, cutting my way with sharp slippers while outside someone was singing a simple tune, my windows closed and the world put away.

At the end of June Ritter marked his forty-second year. Shortly afterward came the news of the assassination of the Archduke at Sarejevo, and those two events brought him to a stop around which I continued to flap like rags in the wind. He began to look worn, consuming coffee after coffee, but eating very little until his face began to admit behind it, curious grey figures of bone. All through July he gasped half-way up to the tower room and could hardly write at all. His digestion failed him and from the dark of the bedchamber, he would grope at dawn to find, in the open salon, the first light. Once he said that he did not think he would ever finish the Stanzas and he spoke with an effort as though his voice were being pulled away from him. He told me that he would like to leave Venice, but I did not wish to agree. I pretended to form a working arrangement, and while I was supposed to paint, he would write----just as we had done in Basle. For several weeks I tried not to see him during the days. I had no desire to paint, but went on walks----finally passing the same doors, going through identical streets, my face and arms darkened by the harsh sun, my nose repelled by the putrid odors floating off the canals. I waited only for enough time to elapse until I could race home to him. I would look up and see him watching me from the window. He would slowly put down his pen, tidy the desk on which nothing except perhaps a letter had been written, and come to meet me.

We were relieved of the sham of work when our first visitor, Brache, arrived with presents. There was a bottle of Chambertin and when Flavio brought glasses, Ritter sent him away at once, saying, "Cher, I want only you to serve me."

We were in the grande salon and it hung dry and woody in the nostrils from being so long closed. My "domestic devil' had stealthily cleaned it, but it had not been aired. To this day, on the backs of old mirrors and inside the framework of darkened pictures, I can smell that day. Brache sat at the piano, playing from time to time, and Ritter was unusually animated. He talked happily of Venice and described the musicians swept off by their mad playing, past the poles and into the Canale Grande, still fiddling as they disappeared under water. He declared that if his soul were turned inside-out, we would find it jeweled, carved and dappled with the light of Venice. Brache looked at both of us with pleasure. Then Ritter stroked my arm and said that he had seen a different Venice through my eyes. They spoke about the precarious situation in the world. Brache said it would come to nothing. We laughed, drank wine, and sang around the piano.

But after Brache's departure, Ritter grew melancholy, and on one of my circuitous walks, I found a pair of tooled House-shoes to replace the ones he wore without latchets. On the marble floors they had sounded worse than in Basle. He turned them over in his hands and kissed me on the forehead. Because they didn't fit well, they made as much noise as the others and looked grotesque on his narrow feet. I wanted to take them back but realized I could never find the shop again. He said he would keep them and they would grow used to him as I did.

As I was beginning too much to do. In that small corner of the world, surrounded by water, I wanted to remain. I wanted each hour to pass overhead identical as the gulls. In myself I heard the incessant lapping of the tide, a chain of echoes on a bridge beneath which dark little boys clutched at fish as I did happiness. There was no way for Venice to expand. Insulated by its canals, it lived out its ancient past in the present like a story repeated through the ages; the form enclosed at its conception, embellished but impossible to change., it can only be perpetuated through a different voice and eyes.

One evening as Ritter and I sat facing each other at one end of the long dining-table on which the food, as always, had been magically laid under covers, I told him I wanted to have a child.

He stared at me. "How very odd!" he said. Then, appearing to address the mural on the wall, he mused, "I thought….I knew you so well." And again, looking at the wall, he shrugged just slightly and groped with his fingers until they found a spoon which he rested upright on the table, gripping it like a man waiting for soup.

So long away from my face, his look and smile when it came surprised me like someone entering the room. "Well." He still smiled, but in a bemused way as though the sudden unearthing of an unfamiliarity in me had buried its substance.

"Cher. Zo',,,,,," He reached across and laid his left hand on the cloth. I saw it lying there, next to a dish, and as I touched it lightly, it turned and closed on mine as though it had hit a spring. Our hands held one another and we sat over them watchful as duennas.

It was about this time that Germany declared war on France and Ritter grew even more depressed. He stood by the window, holding the newspaper, repeating "How can it be possible?" I tried to reassure him, reminding him of Brache's opinion that it would come to nothing, and I suggested dinner at our beloved Il Vapore. I dressed with great care and to my satisfaction, he was greatly cheered during the meal.. I felt carried away. I told him of my plans to paint the fortune-woman, wove stories around her--- whom I had, in truth, never seen again---- and with each detail I had his face as a fascinated gauge of my success. I saw that he was greatly interested in my impressions of this strange woman and, inventing as I spoke, I seized on old tales, on ancient stone-cutters who evoked on cathedrals squamous demons with horns and tails, winged rumps, clawed hands, taloned feet and reptiles writhing in and out of every orifice. I would have Ritter imagine her in a secluded palazzo with mysterious comings and goings, lanterns flickering among the trees and smoke billowing up at midnight. I was at the point of believing, myself, in these things when suddenly taking my hand, he kissed the palm and laughed.

"Thank you, Esmeralda," he said. He asked me, please, to go on; to tell another story. "But one which would have a kind presence," he said. A presence to which he could attach himself as to an older brother. With an unfathomable hurt, somewhere in myself, I tried, but could think of nothing fascinating. There was a sort of towering presence in my childhood: I told him, without knowing I remembered it, that when I was four years old, my grandfather died. "But before he had died," I recounted, "He hid a copper pfennig in his beard, and as it was the same color, I could not find it right away. So he took my hand and guided it to the coin. I still remember my joy......"

"Why?" Ritter asked very soberly.

"Because the pfennig felt simple and very much alive...... And more real than he has ever been for me."

"Yes, of course, "Ritter said. And then he added that he would like to have that story, but that I must keep it for myself..

We walked back, holding hands, yet I felt troubled and unaccountably disappointed.

September brought with it a clammy cold which the residents claimed was early that year. I forbore changing my usual garments because I had liked the way I felt in my light clothes. A cough I developed seemed to grow worse on the day I set out for the Lido to pass the day on the beaches. It was after this that I confined myself to the city again and ventured past my usual haunts---- one day walking almost the distance(taking only a few traghettos) to the lonely promontory where the Casino de gli Spiriti stood in the weeds of its ghostly legends. A drenching rain caught me until, on the way back, I hid under the arcades of San Marco My cough had become a presence in me and that, together with wet clothes, gave me a curious exhilaration as I watched the black slaves come out of the old clock and sound the hour for me alone in the deserted square. A gray cold had lowered like a canvas and the beauty of the city appeared to me behind it in a luminous glow. I lingered so long and came back so late that Ritter was waiting pale and anguished in the doorway. The more he begged me to take care of myself, the more some perverse wish pushed me to keep late hours, often drawing frenziedly until I marked hundreds of papers with careful delineations of the crumbling palazzi- each ultimately looking like the next and none of them yielding me anything beyond the stone exteriors. And although it was not my reason for pushing myself past endurance, I felt that my disregard of my health and the future fascinated him. My coughing, my feverish look even came to the attention of Flavio who often stood silently watching me as I curled up on the chaise-longue near the balcony.

I remembered that he had thrown me something and recalled the fortune-woman so that I began to link them in my mind. I wondered whether they knew one another and one day I set out to find her again.

All the flapping curtains of summer had been drawn in behind locked doors and it seemed useless to search. I went home ill and again Ritter told me we must leave for the sake of my health, but I knew that he felt led into a bizarre and inconclusive love which entranced him. I felt a need to know how far I could conquer him----- how deep I could venture into that solitary place he reserved in his heart. It is possible that I had fever at this time, because it seemed to me as I sat with Ritter by candlelight that night I saw Flavio nodding his head in the shadows--- one hand raised with rings that thieved the flame. But when I looked more closely, he was not there.

Then, finally, on the morning after this as I set out, Flavio followed me. At first he sat aloof, way back in the vaporetto, one arm trailing over the side. It was a mist-ridden day and cold, but my head was on fire and my eyes burned from the fever which made me weightless in my seat. At Zaccharia Flavio stood up, came forward, and when he caught my eye, his face seemed to stop like the stone. In his green eyes I saw the tide rise, break, fall, rise again, transfixing mine. He motioned with his head, moved his lip-----in silence--- unmistakably beckoning me with him. Welded in my seat, I watched him get off, leaping onto the docks, and then begin walking, his head down, his mouth set. I turned around and watched him as the boat moved on, and again he looked up. I saw the cresting in his eyes and again he motioned with his head and his lips, telling me: "Venga!" I turned away and yet I could see myself descending at the next stop---- running back as he came forward--- wondering whether there was time. I asked an old man facing me what the hour was. Minutes went by before he understood me, then looking up at the hidden sun, he gestured, estimated the time, and gazed at me perplexed. Under some spell, bewildered, I passed the next stop and the next, wondering where I had meant to go after all...... finally descending with my sketchbook. I stood, not knowing at once where I had got out. Then I began to walk back. I wandered, looking into alleys and courts and even trattoria all the way back to Zaccharia--- looking for the red hair, the balletic step, the green eyes I could have invented. Afraid those eyes might be watching me from a dank window. I went, noticing everywhere, that ineradicable odor of the city….. the primordial slime of ages.

"He could tell you nothing…..show you nothing," I was repeating to myself, and still I imagined walking with him through doors which were no longer bolted, into streets cut off from the casual walker--- his gold hand pulling me past a fretwork grill that opens magically…. showing me the secrets …..the true city …..the past which is only sleeping. Opening to me the terrible majesty of the forbidden which, in my heart I only simulated through the arrogance of my beauty. He knew where to find that pristine place kept sacrosanct even after the world was charted and fixed with names by men. "To have missed it……..to have missed it….." I kept peering into windows, seeing ahead of me Zaccharia and nowhere that russet hair.

"He is the devil…..He is the devil…." I was saying to myself, but when I came out into the Piazza, the throb of despair was suddenly gone from me. I laughed at myself. "You will see your 'devil' when you get home. Polishing the floors and flicking his rag over the little tables."

But he was not there. We waited a week, but he didn't come back. When a woman from the corto took over the care of the household, I tried to question her about Flavio, but she pretended not to understand. She said she did not know him. A man by the fountain said, "Ah, that one, Signora….." Ritter refused to discus him, saying I gave Flavio an importance from my generous imagination. I did not know. He brought out in me a Zoë, just as the sun brought out the darkness under my skin. She sprang from under my fearlessness, bolting right through, shattering it, making me vulnerable. I was afraid of myself. I could not find in me the understanding of why--- if I had wanted to follow him----I did not.

It was somewhere during this time that I received a telegram telling me that my father was very ill. With the end of summer weather, my own bad health, and the loss of our servant, this summons was used by Ritter as a signal to quit Venice at once. He even began to pack up his papers and spoke of taking a trip while I went to my parents in Munich.

I felt pioneered, as though invisibly, against his decision. I was conspired against and greatly feared leaving the beautiful city as much as being separated from my lover. The near future contained only the ordinary----- which I had already fled. Travel arrangements,, my sad reproachful mother, my sick father...... all of which turned my thoughts again and again to Venice and its mysteries which I had not plumbed. I became obsessed with the absent Flavio, that brazen fellow who stood like a conqueror, or moved like fire over the darkened city. Wherever he had gone to---if I had gone, would I have returned or would I have been lost in some fantastic violation of the days? Would I, in some city beyond the city, have become as golden as his rings?

Each detail of our departure induced in me a panic. The most lurid destruction of myself would have been preferable to studying a railway timetable. It was less superstition than the re-evocation of excitement which made me ask the housekeeper to direct me to a clairvoyante. but Ritter flatly refused to accompany me. He reminded me of my grandfather-story and lectured me on how natural things lead outwards, and how systems---no matter how much they purport to be occult---close us in internal prisons. I recalled to him the interest he had once taken in séances, but he told me that this "was not the time for gossiping furniture." When I pushed him further, he admitted that his concern had been a mistaken desire to refuse death; that one of his defects was to fear the transitory and he often needed assurances the way the way the half-blind require large print.

I pinned on my hat and went alone. Again, as during our dinner at Il Vapore, I felt unaccountably "deserted" by my lover. I made my way to the cool dampness under the Rialto bridge and found the address which matched the number on my paper was only a curtained shopfront with none of the usual crescents, gypsy ornaments, or placards announcing the future's clarity under a neatly-segmented drawing of an enormous bald head. As I peered through a slit in the curtain, the latch withdrew and the door opened as though my arrival had been observed by the tall old woman who faced me.. I say old for she was above sixty, but her crumpled face seemed to jut forward---the way cut-down plants produce a strong new shoot—a robust conquistador nose which was like a relic of youth. While I looked at her, she surveyed me from eyes like grey oysters overhung by reddish brows. Was this my clairvoyante? Unadorned by beads or colors, her head was bound up in a black scarf and her only jewel was one earring----the other earlobe forked open where its mate had once been.

I showed her the paper and her resonant voice startled me. "Entri!" she said imperiously. "Passi da questa parte," and she led the way through the empty shop. Her large torso was hidden in a sack of dark fabric which fell around her in great folds as she moved with a regality that intimidated me. We entered a small room where she obviously conducted her séances, and by the light of a smoking kerosene lamp, I saw a table covered in violet brocade---- a chair on either side of it--- and instead of astrological charts, I was amazed to find colored pictures of the Pope tacked with glittering pins to the smoke-stained walls. A further room was completely taken up with an ornate carved bed and the fabric which made up its coverlet astonished me by its richness in this miserable place. It seemed almost to be cloth of silver and it glistened in the poor light like thousands of fish……….. I was so hypnotized by its radiance and incongruity that I believe she must have said several times, "S'accomdi, la prega," before I sank down on the proferred chair.

Not recovered from the surprises of these unexpected details, I experienced still another when she continued to stand, studying me with a conoisseur's tilt to her head and intoned, "Bella. Bella brunetta," instead of the usual "Cross my palm….." Expecting to slip into the ritual, I offered my hands but she ignored them and sat down in silence and immobility across from me.

We remained thus for several minutes. I realized I hadn't uttered a single word and was about to speak when, with a ponderous movement of her swollen hands, she lifted a Tarot deck. My disappointment showed me the feeble structure of my skepticism. In my mind I was already leaving; already storing up her image to make a story for Ritter's delight, as she scattered the pictures like shipwrecked voyagers on the dark sea of brocade and moved a gouty finger over the cards. Suddenly the finger stopped in air and pointed towards my chin.

"But this is not what you came for," she said in a thrilling voice

Was it possible that she was genuine? I knew that people with extra-sensory powers existed. I spoke at last. Without understanding why, I asked whether it was possible to contact a living spirit. I meant, I said, the spirit of someone who was still alive and I did not feel that my request was absurd. Nor was I sure that she could enable me to do so with a potion or a waxen doll. Yet there was something so certain and knowing in her voice and mien--- none of the hesitance of things which live suspended--- that I think I would have been satisfied if she, as an older, wiser woman to a young one, were to share with me some of the knowledge she had gained in long years of dealing with people for whom the ordinary was not enough. Rising out of all that was formless and creased, I felt her authority and I fixed on that conquering nose whose very nostrils seemed to breathe out secrets like dark carnations.

"I understand. I know what you want......I KNOW you," she said, and my heart leaped as though ignited.

Her next words, "Faremo quanto potremo"----we will do all we can---- sounded so much like Ritter's admonition of "not doing enough", that I felt my need within me, heavy and vibrant, finished in every detail, like a child the moment before birth. Only its face was still unknown to me, but I knew I would recognize it. I leaned towards her, confiding that I was afraid of not being happy...... that I wanted to live....to live fully. Without warning, she touched my head, but withdrew her hand quickly as though something were alive in my hair. As I faced the silver coverlet, footsteps sounded in my ears.

The old woman was standing and beside her was a thin, languorous girl who appeared to bend from the weight of her complicated attire: a crimson dress figured with white spots, billowing, crisscrossed, and scarred with embroidery, was snatched in at the waist by a blue ribbon; a scarf of green knotted convulsively around her neck; and an antiquated. large-brimmed hat with a paper flower enclosed features which looked like the left-overs of things that have been: eyes like dried puddles, a flattened nose, and a mouth so pale its edges dissolved in her skin. Across these vestiges an arrogant expression was smeared like badly applied makeup.

The melted lips opened, she looked at me, repeating "Signorina---Signorina...." as though considering me as a possible addition to her decorations or asking me to admire those she already wore. She stretched out an arm, pinched up her skirt---- showing frilled knickers--- and turned around slowly, tauntingly, to show off her dress. When the old woman stopped her, she gave an abrupt laugh and proceeded to a eulogistic description of Guido's body which would have made me blush except that the speech was delivered with a business-like clarity that deprived it of significance. It might have been an appraisal of a shoat she'd bargained for at the market. She made me uneasy and I was relieved when the old woman, speaking to her as to an over-indulged daughter, requested her to come back later in the day. She seemed to ponder. Very, very slowly, a hand rose out of her sleeve until it was visible in its wretched dirtiness, and, displacing the scarf, scratched at a bad sore on her grey neck. This sore seemed to me like her destiny---- a nonchalant contract with humanity---- which I was called upon to witness. The old woman sped the girl's departure with a slight shove and the red train sliding behind her, she slipped out through the door.

As I watched her leave, I felt only constrained and embarrassed, because the ease with which the old woman took her seat and continued as though uninterrupted, weakened the lubricious nature of the scene and made it, for some minutes, only as eccentric as a hostess calmly leading me through a garden where she cultivated flowers with the heads trimmed off.

To her questions---was I married? Did I have children?---- I gave honest answers, polite as a guest observing the etiquette of the house, but my heart was fixed on the exit which had swallowed up the girl and my mind was freezing around details: the bed....the awful sore... my sense of being interviewed. Unhindered by any subtlety, the old woman posed a simple question: what was I planning to do for the rest of the day? Even while bracing my hand on the chair, levered to rise, saying I must leave, I was irresistibly drawn---- despite myself--- to find out what she wanted me to do. In the center of my fear and disgust was the distant shimmering and flickering of a scintillating tranquil flame ---- a glory that was promised me. My fear obscured it. I stood up, casting out the ransom that I would return the next day if she permitted, and reached into my pocketbook to pay. But she stayed my hand with a snaplike gesture and refused.

"Your must come back tomorrow," she insisted. "I can help you."

When I began to turn away, her massive bulk moved upwards like a black cloud against the luminous sea behind it.

"Aspetti un momento," she said, commanding me with her eyes. They were so formless, so without sharp pupils or light that rather than seeing myself in them, I felt I was being absorbed as by something I loved. She kept murmuring that she would help me to live, and although her touch was crawling repulsively on my arm, I was unable to withdraw it from the caress of her thick finger. There was no doubt of her intentions when she turned those ghastly eyes towards the silver coverlet, but I was still smiling politely when my pocketbook caught on the edge of the table and I gasped "Oh!" in panic.

She was calling "Domani, domani" as I fled the room. I was back in the street under the bridge, breathing deeply. Lifting my skirt above my knees to mount the stairway. I looked around, once, to see if I was being pursued. I fixed my attention on the glittering water of the canal; no, I looked at the faces of people who were going on ordinary errands. The picture of myself with Flavio on that glistening bed would not leave my mind. My skirts clutched like tangling weeds, I ran.

Ritter was still bent over his desk and it was to his blind back that I said, "No one was there.....It was certainly a..." but when he turned his face to me, it was shocked. He said I looked very ill. Assuring him I was alright, I set down my purse with a shaky hand, picked it up again, and burst into tears.

His pallor reminded me that this was the first time he had ever seen me weep. He was afflicted, anxious, awkward, and as impatient for my tears to cease as if I had willfully contracted an incurable malady before which he was powerless. He said he understood how terribly worried I must be, and it was only when he began speaking of the rapidity of covering the distance to Munich that I realized he was speaking of my father.

What schisms I felt between us. What scabrous plants I knew in the darkness of myself---growths not untouched by the splendid light of my passion for Ritter, but, rather, energized by it, as though through an open crack in my heart. Leaning against his shoulder, knowing his scent, my eyes isolated it, transformed, allied it to every anonymous muscle and bone of gondolieri, delivery men, Flavio. ....oh, why this defective bestowal of the senses? The faulty shedding of my desires appalled me. As though I were sticking pieces back onto myself. I looked up into his face. I looked at his familiar features as though they were thrusting stair out of stair on which I must climb to see him, also, whole.

After dinner, I began to pack, but with each garment I put into the valise, I thought I saw slivers of my happiness folded into irrevocably distorted shapes. Venice---and what else with it--- was slipping away from me, just as our effects disappeared from the palazzo

When Ritter embraced me on our last night in Venice, I wanted to chew him up, devour him so that he could pass down into my entrails. Become part of me, inside me, and I would never have to look for him, know always where he was, his pulse inside mine...... and I would be free. To be lost. The rhythmical language of the enchanted gave way before the cryptic word "forbidden". Did it mean a bed glistening with pleasure, a grey sore, something too tremendous to handle, or the too-accessible ? Enchanted and forbidden: I knew that Flavio was yoked to neither, but I also knew he was not the devil. He was only the apparition the devil took, and he never takes the same form because his crime through us is always different. When I next saw him, he was less beautiful. He moved slowly... bent double, his scarred face hidden...his sword dragging and striating the dust.

PIERRE

Seen from a distance, my single life appears to contract, and twenty years can be brought to memory tonight with a few phrases, joy springs up in the same few scenes, pain permanent as an old relative who exchanges board for silence.

I can see, unrepeated, the happiest day of my life. In spring, leaning against Ritter's arm, we stood before the home of Byron and I could imagine him going up and down the great stairwell inside, dragging his ruined foot. Everything was silent. Surrounded by the erasures of time, I felt eternity in each moment of my life as I touched the side of the man I loved with the sense that the world had just completed itself like a statue carving its fourth limb with two magnificent hands.

During the hours when everything is shadow and silence, my imagination constructs, as though by enchantment, what time has made disappear. Ouf; I have a dream that I am standing on a bridge over the little Seine in the Pre-aux-Clercs from where I see a golden church held up by columns of marble and I know it is built over the temple of Isis. There is a garden; the trees are always green and all the flowers are in blossom.... around the square tower is the sweet breath of Spring. I'm looking towards the city which has always been rich in tender mysteries and piquant love intrigues.... I can see the Palais Royal, the hill of Montfaucon where a monk is kissing the lips of a man cut from the gibbet. The boulevards, Saint Sulpice, and the statue of Leda that turns the rue de Regard; I see Saint Lazare, rues Lepic, Petrograd, Cassette.... distance has many prisms: I want to see my friends and neither they nor I can lose by it. "The absent are wrong," the proverb goes, but I say that the absent are wrong to return. One loves the dead better than the absent.

Someone finding these words may know that in 1921 a sturdy fellow of the Provence had inherited from his father or master, a chisel, the rights to a quarry, and the patience to carve an angel below which was engraved: Allevia- Brok Ritter. The rim of the sky had cracked like an egg-shell and the death of Ritter was within it. They put him under broken soil and I stood there knowing he still way, but no more for me; his presence had accumulated around his soul the way hours cover a lifetime--- inseparably cut down together. His death occurred not only in his life, but in mine.

Never again to have a moment of understanding the world through the touch of another human being! Yet, passion remained, dozing like a cat with blank eyes half-open. Passion doesn't create ideals; it follows, and without them it rots, although it seems to become more alive as apples smell sweetest when they lose their color and, finally, their shape.

Just as everything was perfection with Ritter, so everything with Pierre was five palms to the right of what should be. Pierre! Death didn't stiffen his soft finger-tips or open sensuous lips that smelled of mint. When his head was put down on that pillow, his hair was not the color of pollen dust…the arrow-shaped waist had pinioned… pinioned… and been buried finally in softer flesh. But that is the only and the last I knew of him. I must not allows hatreds to accumulate in me like age…. I can see past the rue des Saint-Peres to the rue du Bac. There was a Nun who would visit the floor below mine and each night she rushed off before darkness fell—perhaps to a refectory where food tasted good to her. In winter she disappeared by four in the evening: by August, Saint Thomas d'Aquin sounded eight as she slipped around the corner of rue de Varenne. The snow was giving way to rain one evening in February when I leaned forward to call her, and did not. Trudi was always there like the pink flowers, unattended, that grew out of thin films of moss..

I can see Les Halles in the distance. Walking across Pont Royal, there is not just one day, but many. I remember the details of Pierre on a quai… Beside me now I have some words on brittle paper, but the inked letters are now part of the paper and can't be lifted up to reveal anything below them. No hand, pink palm up. Orphaned sentences are signed: *Pierre.* Inappropriate, he stands in heaven: erect, triangular, his trouser legs too tight, a lacing half-undone on his black boot. His eyes assume the pain of love before the form of a dark angel and he says.... *Thy face is real...like something of the earth.* The front of his shirt lies open on the little forest of hair.

Pierre, come closer. I will bury thee.

I will collect all memory of thee as cleanly as in a sac and destroy it. Then thou canst die.

Never again to step down over and over from the opposite side of the street and look into my eyes.

That February day it was raining. My feet climbed horizontal trees and severed the branches that grew again behind me like quivering salamanders. Shadowy rafters halted over the street: short legs apart, a young man stood in my way against a sky the color of hiatus. Stocky, wearing an army field-coat, his light hair damp, he might have been a lost soldier- lad separated from time and his comrades.

As I walked nearer, his blue eyes widened into mine and I did not know whether the OH! was in them or in me. He moved. I turned quickly to the right and went on to the market. As I passed the flower stalls, I saw the fair face with its wide lips and dark brows. I moved into the next aisle, but everywhere--- at the end of a passage, behind a queue leading to a counter, and as I approached the gate at Montfaucon, the handsome head and immobile figure materialized as though borne by the lightening blue of his eyes. I didn't think to go around him. I stopped. Facing me, he said: *"Forgive me...."* with a country accent. Then he looked deep into my eyes and pronounced slowly: *"But...I might never...again....have seen you."*

His accent and languishing air wearied me: yet I could have carried off that charming head and kept it in the place of my mirror to judge my fading beauty in those struck eyes. There was something familiar about his face. Then, I recognized it as sensuality. A great innocence returned to me, and instead of passing through the market gate, I might have climbed a long flight, and in a room, inelegant and spare, found myself waiting for me with nothing to do.

When I consented to meet him on the following day at a café, he moved closer to thank me. Pleasure widened in his young face and I saw that his long white teeth were parted like pickets between which I might enter if I squeezed my heart quite small.

He was there on the next afternoon, leaning against the window when I arrived one hour early to test my destiny and his need. A cup of black coffee was in front of his hand. He sat up straighter when he saw me--- his stiff country shoulders straining in a blue dress shirt, a necktie dangling from the starched collar like a broken noose.

I can still see the knife-pleated cuff of my grey frock folding, unfolding, as my hand tapped the edge of my cup ; I remember the glint of my shoe buckle near the table leg, the details of his life which I could never imagine would interest me: he was training to be a masseur--- a métier of people one didn't know in the evenings when waiters and coachmen were still in uniform. The news of his recent twenty-fifth birthday pronounced in me the foolish waste of my afternoon. But even if I didn't intend to see this pretty child again, his yearning eyes had waked in me a femininity which was encouraged by my irresponsible presence there. I treated him by turns as a flirt, a provincial, as unhappy, as young, and he told me as seriously as possible how at twenty-one he had emancipated himself from the parental roof and joined the army four days before the Armistice was signed; how he had become blasé...cynical...wanted really nothing, ... and so on..... I was somewhat amused. ' If only, I thought, 'he knew who I was....and with whom...' But perhaps he had never heard of Ritter, or Mose, Yasha, Rodin....

"What do *you* do?" he finally thought to ask.

"Nothing. Nothing at all. I have been ill."

"How many times have you been in love?"

"Once."

"Oh."

"Perhaps....more."

"I would like," he said leaning towards me, "to be the more."

"Then you do ant something," I said, getting up.

He shrugged.

It is curious that I was finished. The little scene was over, and yet, when he suggested walking me to Janka's where I was expected, the same irresponsibility held me like an active vice. Besides, I seemed to see no character to reject in that unformed boy. I might have been strolling---- the rain had stopped: the air was sweet----- with a Frederic who had blown out of Flaubert and would soon flatten into a frontispiece torn off by the wind. Then, in Janka's lower entry which had never been paved or lit, all the banalities of our meeting whisked together like grey birds around a crust. Without a word he pulled me into a tight embrace as his lips moved to find my own.

"Not here, not here," I told him, furious—pulling away. Yes! That why I had lived alone! After Ritter there could only be encounters— like that.....

I heard the scratch of a stylo, and his hand moved around my sleeve, finally closing my fingers on a scrap of paper. He said, "Until next time. Please...say yes."

For an answer I turned and shoving the paper in my purse, mounted to Janka's door. I knew the whole situation was absurd and yet I felt a quickening and suspense that had been lacking in me for so long. I showed Janka a harmlessly pleased face and could not resist telling her the story. Finding that the paper contained the address of a café near Opera, the time and the date---two days hence--- we began to laugh. Her shrill "Oh my dear!" the very way she poured out the tea--- shaking her head and smiling as she pretended to wipe away a tear----- irritated me.

On the day of the rendezvous, I was in Rueil and knew I had looked forward to that meeting like a child who is missing a treat. Hirsch had arranged the negotiations for the portrait of Ritter, and yet, now that it was within reach, I had lost interest in the sale. Some of my pen and ink drawings were strewn on the table: people were only just arriving. I said I would be back in an hour, and I left, trusting myself to understand what I could not reason just at the moment.

So much to people decorate the reasons---- otherwise difficult to see---- attaching them to each other, that I did not know whether it was a small miracle that occurred at Opera. I arrived at the meeting-place three hours late, described "the very young blond gentleman" to three waiters--- only one of whom remembered seeing him--- and expecting to find nothing, yet borne, as we all are, by the momentum of a search, I moved, myself, looking, among the tables.

If he wished to, I reasoned, he could always find me by roaming my quartier….he could find his way to Janka's… still I had come so far. One last look! As I slowly revolved, putting on my spectacles, I saw in the mirror a woman with two birds of paradise fluttering over a toque, her white skin sinking down into grey fur like a keel in a cloudy sea….. I looked away.

It was just then that I saw the young man passing the windows. Soon I was out the door, running towards his back along a narrow street, unable to call a name which I did not know, until for no apparent reason --he turned around. I saw the flicker of his blue eyes. He said "OH!", ran to me, and we both began to explain at once---out of breath—exhilarated, as though we had been in an accident together and did not yet know if there was any damage.

He led the way back to the café and guided me to a table. He began by saying, "I might never have found you again."

"I don't even know your name or address."

"I cursed myself a dozen times," he said, "for not having given them to you." And so saying, he wrote it all on a small paper and then called with authority to the waiter. He had a marvelous deep voice which seemed to fill me inside as though I were hollow. He leaned towards me, took off the spectacles which I had forgotten, and tried to look through them. "We do not have the same vision," he said folding them up and gazing at me.

I knew I had no way of judging, as this young man spoke, whether what he said was mundane or poetic. He accompanied me all the way to the steam tram and took his leave by standing off, head to one said, to admire 'how well I looked ' in my furs. His confident air of knowing about such things made me smile, but I accepted his compliments. We were to meet the next day at the same café.

"What on earth have you been doing?" This with a wave towards the kitchen garden and Neuilly was my reception at Rueil, but since no answer was expected, I understood that my absence had been so rude, it had been explained by my hosts as something essential. I was grateful And I was moved when I walked in to see my painting surrounded by several of the guests, and my sketches still spread on the table. Just the day before I had made the splendid drawing being shown at the moment. I'd felt the complete sensual pleasure I always felt on seeing one line jut out from another to make a solid dimension.... a thrill that energized me. There, by the table, I found myself longing again for the kind which would instead...destroy me a little. During the interminable dinner, I heard the voices and saw the elegant faces floating at such a distance that my only grasp on the world was through my fingers holding to an ice-cold spoon.

On the next day, riding to Opera, I thought, Jesus Christ gets the left-overs, looking opposite at a quivering woman bent by the weight of three silver crosses and some half-dozen pompane ovals on chains hanging from her neck. A kerchief flattened brown hair that erupted on the top of a rectangular head—scarred on the front by features and over-burdened, like a heart by its sins, with a red nose. There was a stack of miniature volumes on her knee. Bound to one thick nine-centimeter book by a string of elastic was a small white bottle,, and between her eyes, as between so many on the Metro that day, was a grayish smudge which marked the beginning of Lent. I found them all cowards. Mourning the Great Death through which all smaller ones lost their unbearable repetition; it taught them, incorrectly, that death lay within and not—as I had seen it---- surrounding the dying like a terrible atmosphere.

I was discouraged when I arrived at Opèra—a section with many motor-cars that I did not like. The Café was without charm. The young man was hatless for the third time, his blazer of some sporting design, was dizzily mullioned, and under it his shirt flapped open. We had nothing to say to one another. I looked at his handsome face smiling at me: his mouth was beautiful and wide. His big hands lay open on the table. I blamed him for being the man who had drawn out my reaction which, like all things precious to me, I could not leave in the custody of a stranger. And as we stood up to find "a more tranquil place to talk", I was thinking----if only I could send off my body like a horse at the Gate and leave behind, inviolate as the startling-post, myself.

At the top of a bourgeois house on rue de Pétrograd, the paisley carpeting gives way to plank floors and the young man holds the knob of a glass door, warning me, "It is only a student room."

There is a chart of the dorsal musculature pinned to a wall, at the end of which, a window on a pole slides open to give a lover's view of the city. He must stand behind me to open it and I smell his soap near my ear. Now I turn and see that the room is a narrow rectangle--- the size of my scullery—with an aisle between desk and a cot hanging over which there is a photograph of a frantic cat on a rope. It made me think of Samontagne. I felt suddenly as old as fear and thought to leave, but.....it did not seem to be me there...... seriously. It was a room of youth that Ritter and I had locked years before: I was there as a guest and I sat down on the cot much as in another parlour, I might have waited for tea, and if with Russians, had it in a glass.

And meanwhile, I scanned his books: medical volumes..... a horoscope of the signs Poissons...he was speaking in my ear... something by Carco... a thick edition, probably uncut, of Baudelaire.

"....... You are going to make me wish to stay in Paris," he said.

I found that his cheerful banality left me calm; never could I have accepted the individual personality of another man. If this well-bound edition of the young provincial had revealed to me some handwriting passionately scribbled in a margin, I would have fled. The soft hand that dropped on my sleeve had no distinct history in it. For a moment I turned away from his eyes because I saw there tenderness...... tenderness like the messenger in a play whose function is to make the inevitable astonishing.

"It's true," he said, turning my face toward him, "that I was looking for a woman....but not many women. One woman."

I replied, "There has hardly been a young man who hasn't said the same thing."

Somehow, as calm as I had been, as little essence of self this fellow gave out to disturb me, yet as he moved in closer and closer to me, his features blurring and his shoulders blocking the horizon as though pieces of the sky had fallen, there was in me a fear I did not remember bringing along……..Moving…..beyond his own tenderness, menacing…….. and like all generalizations moving back to their truths….he was male.

Swaying in a fiacre late that afternoon to the rue de Bac, I was remembering the first kiss; the feeling was in me and yet was something I could not have felt alone. He had stroked my face, put his arms around my neck, covered my mouth with his breath…..I came out of a mist, clearheaded, recalling my state as guest, and his youth…….. as near in years to Trudi as to me. Then, the first touch of his body shocked me and my own age was cut down by amazement as by an axe.

A first kiss, the unique exchange of names, beginning gestures, are as they happen; those that follow after are revisions, contradictions, disappointments. I could still see us lying under the raw-edged shelf where his few books stood, and he named me "Caline", Shying away from a motor on the Pont Royal, the horses jumped and my cab rattled. Its red lantern showed, in the dusk ahead, that it was journeying slowly across the river where it did not belong. His name was Pierre. I turned away when he asked me: "What if you should have a little blonde?" The idea of a future------ the impossibility! My visit was only a short walk of pleasure between two blind alleys. Waiting, dreaming, suffering…… demanding a purity in which I could no longer believe, I had refound elation in an unquestioned interlacing of two bodies, and discovered in my own a fervid hospitality.

The sun was extinguished when I sat down to dinner and looked at my daughter. Two years of marriage, thirteen of separation, a child: that was my life. Eight years of loving one man: vacancy: that was also my life. If I had kept from childhood a patience, neat and useful as the clothes in my armoire, there remained to me as well the instinct for small rewards.

Trudi and I played at making each other's portraits. I was studying the round of her neck when I had the feeling of having spent a full day watching an engrossing spectacle which had left me nothing to think about. With Ritter I had never suffered the total privation that ends an embrace: the dream was forever, continuous, beyond us.

The next day I hungered for some confrontation: a raw laugh, a black revelation, and I told Pierre to descend. We walked, he with a worried look on his large blond face, to a café which had the name of a flower.

I began by saying : "Mon enfant, this cannot go on between us." I told him I was married, separated but not divorced, that I had been in love which had ceased only with the death of my lover........that it was not past. Then, surprised at the turn I had taken, depressed by my own story and bored by him, I was ready to leave.

His forehead, bending almost to the table-top, was thrown upwards with his fist as he faced me, perplexed. "Oh, why….. why," he said: "when one finds the woman one wants…… is she never free?"

He, too, he said, had been in love---the year before--- a woman older than he, with a child. He had nearly married her….. then realized that it would have been wrong… Was he comparing our stories? He talked on, of his village, of his small brother, of me…. But I really knew nothing of him. Only his lovely blue eyes, his handsome mouth…. But the eyes. In them was an admission of attachment which kept me from being alone with us and dignified my presence there. We climbed, that afternoon, with a gentle friendliness, to the Butte Montmartre; and as we stood in the cold overlooking the city, I felt a prick of guilt for taking seriously what I did not. I forced myself to look away from his loving eyes, and each time, my glance fell on his wrists and on the chest where I had, one day before, put my head. The world was moving below me. Far down, interior fires escaped from the houses in smoke; on the steep hillside, men were measuring the frozen earth for gardens. And from the belvedere where we stood, the legendary Saint had begun a descent whose direction was marked by his having taken it

The next day I went back to the rue de Petrograd. When the door opened and Pierre greeted me with one arm forward and pleasure in his face, I fell against him as against the wall which separates the world from nothing.

Our bodies trembling and dedicated carried on a search without us. No words, not even sighs distracted us from the slowly warm and numb unraveling. We never thought to call our names as we wrapped ourselves up again, one within the other, and accepted the gentle rhythm of an ecstatic journey by two travelers----one looking to left and one to right----- who hold the reins of the same cart.

That evening I did a splendid drawing of Trudi who nearly ruined it by insisting on a pose that didn't suit her at all. She sulked a good deal and would hardly look at the finished sketch.. Then, just when I wanted to be silent, she talked incessantly, demanding my responses. When I excused myself early to bathe, she put herself again into a bad humor. I felt impatient with her, yet guilty as well. Like a courtesan I spent two hours on my bath and toilette.

March was warmer than I remembered it. Pierre's quartier, the youngest of Paris and built up since the war, had a dim respectability of provincial towns: cafes occupied only at meal-times by near residents, dull shops, baroque boulangeries, straight avenues over which the sky was often the blue of vacations and a great distance away. There were pigeons and infrequent motor cars. It was clean, quiet, open, and the warm air felt cool on my eyelids like the breath of someone waking up.

Near his gate I smelled the earth in a garden patch and the first tulips offended me with their voluptie--- more chaste, which looked more innocent than mine.

The little cage would glide up past double doors clasped with stunning metal, spindling the serpentine carpet, and stop; so that on foot, over unswept wooden stairs, I continued not with love in my heart, but something which echoed far into my childhood and which I knew to be the static and reliable delight of forbidden games.

I could always expect to find him there because Pierre did not find the rest of the city more lovely than his street, and he spoke with a near desperation of lacking the country. Since his eyes, like the atmosphere, showed neither warm nor cold, this angry need was surprising in them. If at that time I had any confusion about him, it was his relation to the country. Understand me. I tried to imagine the Prussiasn stiff shoulders, the heavy feet with toes turned slightly in, the careful walk----- all flung out in the winds of a vast and unmown field. There was something unmoving in him, but something which I could move and which I knew to be the frantic energy of his youth.

For a few short hours each day, I simplified my life in that room. Always the same: I spent mornings in my studio, earning as it were my three hours with Pierre: evenings I passed at home--- atoning for them. Always I paused----- near to anger----at the door, saw, in the opening, Pierre's face for which I felt something like love: blond, blond, but stroked by the finger of some dark inconsistency over each blue eye. Then, close to him, I caught his scent----one of summer: a dry, out-of-doors smell, both reserved and blatant like the sexuality of a child.

A solitary, with no friends I ever saw, he studied and waited for me, as usual, one afternoon at the end of the month. I had been leaving my studio earlier the past few days. He greeted me with a kiss, the delight of which I had anticipated. I was becoming habituated to each caress, yoked to each response, and pleased by the game of ecstasies as any midinette who would dine at the same restaurant not through lack of imagination, but with the shrewdness of appreciating her appetites and her income. I had no more to say to Pierre than to the water I drank after a voyage and no more shame than when I touched my lips to the glass. Yet....something happened that day. I lazily traced my finger-tip along his eyebrow and said, "These are always a surprise to me." It was neither true nor interesting: only a few words tossed off to accompany a caress. But with a somewhat sinister laugh, he answered, "Thou hast found me out. I am not a true blond."

"Do you mean you have a dark soul?"

"As black as thy hair," he said without smiling.

Something twisted in me and sprung. As we stared at each other, his face changed, grew resentful and ill-tempered. My cheeks flushed and we did not speak. I felt it very powerfully, his desire. I felt its weight, self-supported, hanging over me like transparent eaves.

I had never done so before, but I fell asleep that afternoon to the sounds of Pierre arranging his small luncheon. Felling myself covered in red skin, my head quivering, eyeless and not knowing where to find a touch, I woke throbbing. Pierre was standing over me, and I tried to hide the candid love I had for his body. When his lips, so niggardly of words, pressed my lips, they gave forth the last drop of simple pleasure I had had in them------avowing my loss with a moan. Pinned where I had fluttered like a sphinx-moth under his strong hands, I emerged a beggar made arrogant by need.

I stayed far later than usual, not wishing to live out my days in that little room, not wishing to leave it. It was after seven when I returned home to find that dinner had passed without me and Trudi was waiting with the drawing materials. A few times she asked me, "Maman, what are you looking at?" and I would say, "The building across the street looks very nice....do you see? ..with the last light on the windows.." Or "what a deep color the sky is tonight. The marine of springtime." But trancelike, I found myself sitting-------for how long? ----my fingers tightening around the pen until sharply, I saw Trudi across from me, watching. I looked at her new breasts and flat stomach. Her black eyes in which was waking a privacy. I felt that if she had asked me, just then, questions about relations between a man and a woman, I could have answered her far more easily than ever I could have done in remembering Ritter.

At nine I was exhausted and so hungry that familiar shapes in my house were becoming indistinct horizontals and verticals on whose edges as I got up and walked toward my daughter, I bruised my legs. Further simplified through the occupations of my body, the world was reduced to a bed between whose taut sheets I was held and borne deceptively away as I fell into blackest sleep.

The next morning my painting went badly. My studio caused me great impatience with its whirl of colors, its chalky scents and flat light. Besides, it was lovely out-of-doors, for as April began, the city appeared to have snatched back some of its pre-war gaiety. Voile dresses swung above the ankles, crowds of young men with laughing faces began, everywhere to sport flat white straws banded in Petersham. But with the simpler clothes came a smaller realm of dream, and life seemed more immediate. Motor cars brought Montmartre closer to Montparnasse, and my heart popped open like the first lilacs at Parc Monceau and was green as all the head-high buds in the Luxembourg. I raced to that room near the pigeons and chaptered in my life as something which had fallen from its rightful place in time. It should have been at twenty that I looked over the roofs of Paris with that boy fresh as summer. There I was, an accomplished woman of thirty-five: I had borne a child to one man, given my heart to another. I was not--- although in the benevolent spirit of springtime I began to be mistaken for one---- a young girl. Yet I was circling back, mindless as a bird drawn to warm places by something impersonal as the stars.

One day in the first week of April, I arrived so early that Pierre was not ready. As he washed, he talked, but I didn't look for any soul in his words any more than I would have searched for one in the heavy mouth of the round short legs. I saw his eyes in their seriousness but more was I drawn to the coquet who smiled as he slapped his handsome thighs to dry them. Angry, passionate, with a small contempt, I watched him as he knotted a towel around his hips, prepared and ate, without ceremony, his omelette, a tin of beans, dipping into the liquid, brushing over the plate with a shaft of bread he broke off between his teeth...... and acknowledging me with a smile.

"I do not always have a lovely woman beside me when I eat," he said.

But that he had had many and lovely women before me, in other ways, near him, I had begun to know as he spoke of his celibate life. And when he leaned back in his chair saying, "Ah..... I wonder if I shall ever find a wife..." I was reminded again of the difference in our ages. Could I be angry with a boy? No. That was his charm. I was tired of indignant honesty. Our lives had nothing to do with each other; we came together in an ever- present and spoke of the next month as a generation.

Yet, I felt chagrin at his words about a future clearly seen without me.

"Thy face expresses every mood," he said. "What is wrong?"

He bent his shining head and avidly I watched him come closer. When he touched me everything became simple again. A dense numbness of every place but where his lips moved against my neck: I was a small throat for which he became a mouth. Gripped by hands and pulled to life like something not yet drowned, I felt my senses fill with desperate hurry and no memory of where to go. Then, thrown suddenly in space, my body was a tower from which the world hung scaffolding to walk. I looked into his eyes and saw that, wide-open, they were the remote eyes of someone assigned to kill a stranger. With some anguish, I breathed quietly.

The rays of the sun penetrated freely through the uncurtained window, illuminating the walls of grey stone and striking the chart of muscles which appeared, at that moment, to be newly stripped of their protective skin.

I felt disappointed in Pierre and tried to read something in his face. Then I sighed and said: "Oh…to be here so much! I must be mad."

"So much the better!" he said, and raising himself he looked into my face and said, "My rabbit..

you have beautiful eyes…… the most beautiful in the world." He had dropped the vernacular, using the formal "you".

I turned away from him. Caressingly, he threaded his fingers between mine and asked: "What if you should have a little blond?"

"I would love him, 'I said suddenly.

That day at the autobus, the warm sad look was missing from his eyes. Before the motor started up, he had already begun to move, his jacket becoming smaller and smaller until it slipped around the corner and was gone. I descended early and walked from the Quai, not to exercise my already leaden body, but to calm a mind which was depended over it like something from a bough that shook.

My days had been more and more simply arranged in paths of anticipation, pleasure, and the trance of remembered fragments:

his bent head, his eyes closing, his hand warm from the water and smelling of almond soap; his standing up nude as a flower dressed only in himself; his familiar shape disappearing on an unknown street. It occurred to me perhaps only at that moment of crossing the boulevard, hesitating in the space of the wide Carrefour, that I did not know what Pierre did in the time without me. As the street narrowed near my door, the light dimmed, and I saw that streaming down behind Neuilly, the sun had been fallen upon, as a carriage with highwaymen, by clouds. I had lingered too long and would be late for my party.

The last bolts of light wrapped and unwrapped my skin as I gazed at myself---- arms raised to secure my long hair. When I let drop over me a chiffon dress of shutter-green, my eyes looked the color of a deep sea. I could not help thinking, …… this year--- perhaps not even next---- he would…he must say ' Yes'. With my glistening shoes, my clinging tulle. I left the house feeling that I wanted to know if Pierre loved me as I would have needed a report of the weather if I were taking and open cab for the day.

For less than an hour I stood in a circle of people and smoke…. Troubled…..kept in motion by the heat of compliments and gyrating like a radiometer. At ten I slipped away to charm Pierre, and the long-absent Ritter appeared to me on the stairway and spoke with disappointment, saying, "Zoe--- this does you no honor," "And why not?" I was asking. "And please tell me whether all my life that you are dead I am to live up to a model of grandeur in which you did not, yourself, excel." It was the first time I had spoken resentfully to that dear great man…… and fading away he said softly "It is not love….. it is not love…."

"How can you know?" I said to the damp spring night.
Passing warehouses shuttered and smoked-white in the lights of the taxi, I dreaded Pierre's absence or the presence of someone else. The driver said without turning his head, "Going to meet your lover?" and coldly I said, "No. I am going home." I lost his rude answer- seeing ahead the rue de Petrograd buried in darkness. A chestnut tree, lit from a near building, displayed only the underside of its leaves and its

stiff trunk rigid in the glow. The night changed everything------ but I saw his door beyond.

The lift slid rattling up, and when I knocked at the high door, I was afraid until I heard, uncertainly, "Oui?"

"It's me!" I said as the door was already opening. "Zoe. Are you there?"

His surprise changed to pleasure as he drew me in, professing to be dazzled. "Oh how pretty you are!....How pretty!" he said. "But---- is anything the matter?"

I told him......" Nothing". That I had been at a party and left. "How silly of me to burst in here at night. Absurd!"

He pulled off my wrap and cupped my face between his hands. "It is never absurd for you to come here." His seriousness and admiring looks delighted me. There were a dozen epithets he invented as we sat side by side and I was blushing first with pleasure, then with the effort of controlling my happy laughter.

"You have a look of shining surprise that reminds me of someone...... an unknown woman in a grey cape I once saw, crossing the rue des Canettes."

"Do you like me as well ?"

"Oh yes."

A book lay still opened on his desk. The unique unsocial man, alone, who makes his own way. I marveled at him close beside me-----his warm body, the strong arms thrust out of his sleeves as he reached for something on the desk. All for me. We had no friends but his hands, my hips, and the senses that understood us better than we did ourselves. We had never wooed each other in restaurants There were no sad galas where we had waited, in each other's eyes, to be alone. Only the grey-blue silence of that room, and time which had broken off into afternoons. Suddenly we had a new friend: the night ; a mutual friend, we had never met together, who hovered discreetly behind the edges of a candle Pierre had put on the shelf.

"Tell me," I asked softly: "Do you miss that unknown woman?" and rather than forcing him to words, I accepted his lips as an answer. The night shared us, suddenly taking away the large strong fingers to make them all the more astonishing as they reappeared to thread mine. Hiding away all but my lips and Pierre's shoulder made us believe in them, and when I couldn't see, but only feel his arms, it made them more of a miracle. The semi-light mottled the walls, softened our voices, and inside the sensuality we had ripened by day, a kernel of love exploded.

I felt locked into a silence which I wanted to open to him that night, but I did not know how until he asked me why I had never had a child. Then I found myself telling him about Trudi-----even her age: ten years younger than his own.

"Why didst thee never tell me?" he asked with surprise, lapsing back into the vernacular.

"Because I knew it would not matter if you didn't love me and would not if you did."

"Thee shouldst have told me."

I twisted my head and searched for his face in which I saw an expression poised over me, then serene emptiness. I wanted to be just as I was a day ago----glowing with pleasure and ready to return home, but his weight held me.

About to cry out, "Do you love me?" I recovered myself and asked: "Are you not going to let me leave?"

We were fused when he answer, "Oh no!"

I had never before heard his voice within me and I hardly cared what words sheathed it. Yet I felt as a chatelaine must have felt on bowing before a conqueror from whom she had hidden all her jewels.

*

In the next weeks, my smiling shell sat across from Trudi at dinner, my real life----- how was that?----- had become less real than my days at rue de Petrograd. With a craftiness which sprang up like beggar –weeds in my new care, I had come to recognize Pierre's tastes and moods. I listened to stories of his childhood, questioned him about his parents, anticipated his pleasures and increased them.

Once I brought a bouquet of poppies because Pierre had picked them wild in his childhood. I catered to his love for Bruant by bringing him texts of songs, and knowing which of my dresses pleased him, I wore the same few that April while my dressmaker worked on copies.

My devotion to his pleasures was rewarded by tenderness and compliments made charming as poetry by his country idioms and accent. Of course I was not innocent and joyous. I had become so with Pierre, and for that dark harrow of time on which I dwelt with Ritter, I felt rancour. Oh, I knew that in the vacationing places of myself, brazen things of the city moved with the expansiveness of parvenus: old maps of love, open terraces, the love songs of shop people, marcelled hair and the Nina's and Mimi's with new full skirts that stroked the calves, shining mouths and buttoned garters...... All the songs said, "I love thee, I'm content." Small syllables like sighs.

Utterly attentive, Pierre listened as I drew faithful pictures of what I might have seen in the few hours away from him: a young man gaitered in mud who'd ridden thrice around on the ancient carrousel in the Luxembourg; my concierge replacing the ties of her apron with a heraldic button on the shape of a wolf---- found who knows where. When I told him that my dressmaker had been warned by a candle-woman against using needles and pins, we fell laughing into each other's arms.

I would return home to shed on little Trudi a happiness she believed to originate in her. And each time I left the rue de Petrograd, I felt that should a comrade come to fetch him out, Pierre might dress slowly before the tiny mirror.....carefully buttoning his shirt as though for life, and say, sadly, "I believe I am in love."

*

April flew over Paris like a green bird. The soft leaves trembled. The light of summer could be seen now far-off in the approaching sun, now in the warm haze that spread through the morning. The Chestnuts and the Lime trees were heavy under the heat of the blue sky, the earth quivered. The blaze of the Seine dizzied me as I made my way, with eyes half-closed, over the Pont Royal to Pierre. He had been more and more occupied with his training, but it was a lavishly warm Saturday----- the last day of the month---- and I wanted an outing: I was laden with fruit, with wine and cheese. As giddy as spring itself, I had ordered the cocher to stop on the rue de Buci just so I could leap out for another beautiful box of strawberries. The colors of the food, a quick passing whiff of Emeraude made me nearly cry out, and the powdery scent filled me, dreaming, back in the cab. I imagined Pierre and I resting somewhere on the grass...... our heads reeling under the sun, our ecstasy of having no thought but for the moment....... My eyes were blurred. I imagined Pierre going off to return with a first bouquet for me---- perhaps marguerites which I loved----- their black centers softened by the sweet white tears enclosing them.

I found him at his books.... He took the basket, saying, "You are much too good to me," and spread a cloth on the desk. Then saying... "Ah.." went to the shaving mirror and parted his hair with the clothing brush.

"Now," he said, "my little rabbit, I will open the wine."

He hummed as he knocked about for glasses. Hs bared arm plunged into the basket. I heard him say, "Ah, good. My preferred cheese......" and I saw his astonished face as I turned away with tears in my eyes.

"But......*why,* my rabbit?" he said behind me.

Warm and loosened from some spring deep within me, I felt the tears over my cheeks and my voice----- afraid of them---- I answered I can't explain... the weather. No! It's just that everything is so beautiful outside." Like the brush of a wing in the darkness, something alien touched my heart. "But it's not....... Really," I said.

"No," he said, touching me lightly. "it is not."

Light-headed and confused, I followed with my gaze to where his finger directed and saw that rain had begun to spatter his small closed window.

"It's not just that," I said, enigmatic even to myself. If something foreign to me, I thought, something apart from my happiness touches me, I must run from it. Weak, lost in space no wider than an alley, I pretended to seek pleasure rather than my way.

"I am afraid," I tried to say lightly, "I am disappointed because we never go out...."

He touched my cheek and said, somehow insinuatingly, "You have never complained."

"I'm afraid......I said, "that you want me only in bed."

He gasped. "Dost think I'm an animal?"

He was annoyed. Sat down heavily on the cot and tapped his fingers together. "Good, my rabbit," he said, "We shall go out."

We arrived at Robinson just as the rain gave way to a silvery grey light, and with near-formality we walked hand-in-hand, just like "New Marrieds" he said. The scent of flowers mingled with the smell of cheese and the odor of fish. Bewildering fields of hyacinths, sweet, erect, dissolving into open seas. I was elated and tensely excited. I wanted to walk and walk, but Pierre found a café under the Chestnuts where he told me the Vouvray would be superb and he ordered us some. He tucked a wet lock behind my ear. For a moment, I closed my eyes and said I was sorry the rain had stopped and I could hear his smile as he said, "Thou art a romantic."

A man in a blue tablier walked by us carrying, with great delicacy, a single red geranium growing from a ball of earth in his hands. Tears started to my eyes again. Through them I could see many people at the tables around us, an ancient Virgin in a niche with leaves, carved grapes, the little friends of Bacchus, and the words: *Le Vin et l'Amour.* The patron filled our glasses again, smiled, and returned to the bar— still smiling at us. Pierre's big hands rubbed mine on the table.

"My rabbit," he said. "To all of them....... We are The Lovers."

And nothing I had ever done before mattered. I had become part of a pair of lovers, with no more certain face than a bird.

I was so happy, but apprehensive, and I longed to remain with Pierre the rest of the day He told me that he had made an unbreakable appointment with a school friend...... if only he had known before.....
I wanted to tell him something, but he was already getting up.

It had begun to rain again. We ran toward the fiacre and suddenly pulling me to a stop, Pierre kissed me through the water falling on our lips. My heart went dark as a candle in the wind. If that had been my dream, the dream came true and when it did, I was wild as any animal. Without means..... I could have knocked my head against the building beside me. If I had a neck as long as that of a horse, I would have twisted it up, head at the end, if I could bellow..... But.... Because the senses go so far and then.... a wall. It was a wall in which longing buried itself. Long past longing is spent, the space is left.

Marbled with desire and disappointment, I sat up in the hack with my head jolting against the closed window, all the way home. I dragged myself, that evening, to see and acquaintance who never asked me where I had been the last year. She showed me a coat of old-blue Jacquard silk, and told me that white stockings were going to be a rage.

The next day, I bought some muguet de bois to carry with me. When I arrived, Pierre was already dressed in a grey suit and vest I had never seen. He looked stout as he bent forward and with one foot on the end of his cot, polished his black boot with a rage I had never seen. He smiled at me as he did this.

"I'm so glad you came early, my rabbit, Know why?" he said. And looking back at his foot, added, "I'm invited to my cousin for luncheon. The doctor......on the Champs Elysees I told thee about... .....I could not refuse."

His feet looked clumsy and ill-shod. I had nothing else to do that day. Any day. He applied himself to the other boot. He had never shined them for me.

"What can I do, my rabbit?" he asked. "Shall I see thee tomorrow?"

His profile looked heavy. I saw him, at forty, with jowls. He put his foot on the linoleum floor and examined his boots. I felt ill.

"It is nothing," I said.

He was in high spirits as we walked to the autobus where he left me at once so as not to be late. I had told him nothing. All the way to the rue de Bac, I realized that he had never once said he loved me.

He had never spoken my name. Taken me to see no one he knew. No flowers. He had never prepared a surprise. The list of what he had never done, came to me only on that ride, growing, each minute like the child in my body which..... Like all I had received from him---had in it more of flesh than love.

*

I came back from Geneva on a train that passed by firs, small lakes---as flat as tin—out into the mountainside, narrow white houses with blurred pink roofs, suddenly through tunnels. Stop at each station. A guard with a tiny red hat would come forward. Each town name was unfamiliar, the weather had a whitish haze, the ground was green and wet. Platane trees and Bridal wreath trimmed the wayside into the gradually flattening landscape that reached at last toward Paris. The bridge seemed very high, and in my fatigue, details took on importance and beauty. The bluish city I was entering seemed like exquisite embroidery stretched over a hole in the ground.

I slept that night as though I might never wake and got up simply, aware of coffee in the house. Breakfast, Trudi, my closet of clothes. I went slowly down the stairway. Like a blue square cut out in a black day, the doorway opened. Pierre was in the middle of the rue de Bac----- squat and sculptural, his mouth open, with terrified eyes, like some idol hacked from a primitive religion. As his hips turned slightly, he moved towards me.

"Yes," I said. "Yes. I want to speak to you." I walked toward a café.

"Where hast thou been?" he asked in the doorway. He looked startled. He was unshaven and his mouth, close to mine as we went inside, smelled of sleep.

"To hell," I said.

Closing his eyes, he bowed his head and shook it. He understood.

"You should have told me you were going," he said, throwing vernacular to the winds.

I smiled and asked, "Would you have gone with me?"

He looked broken, bent over the table. I almost believed at that moment it had been some part of him I had left in the serenity of Lake Geneva. The waiter was with us. A luncheon crowd had settled in. It was the same café where I had told Pierre, "I have a problem," to which he had answered, "Oh!" and whistled. He had told me that I was not alone, spoke of his cousin- doctor, but he did nothing. We spoke of it, we made love, we walked and then made love: we sat on the quais and spoke of making love. Too ashamed to face my own doctor, I wrote to the one who had cared for Ritter in Basle. Retired and discreet, he referred me to a colleague in Geneva. When at rue de Petrograd I told Pierre, he said, "Yes. That is the best way for thee," and I wept. He covered me with his soldier's coat. Then he sat down on the one chair and ate his omelette.

I wanted to tell Pierre everything, but for my fatigue, my anger, my story, I felt no care. I wondered whether, cut off too soon from my bloodstream, and carved away from my tissues, the unlived creature had drawn out with it some of my own life..

Pierre was looking at me-------his tenderness imprisoned in the sheer blue wall of his eyes. It tried to leap toward me but found an ally only in the big pink hands that reached for my fingers. How soft his palms were! I saw that the clear black dots of his irises were misting with tears. Hatred moved into me and, according to its nature, settled down unfurnished.

I asked him, "Why do you try to cry? It was you who told me to do it."

He shook his head. The tears, like most things he had and could not spare, didn't leave the birders of his eyes. I could not say the things which might ruin the image of my suffering. I was bored.

I told him, "Now there is no longer anything that connects us," and he groaned.

My tea was metallic and cold. I sipped it and thought of Ritter suddenly alive, bursting into that café as I sat with Pierre. Pain in Ritter's eyes(what a young man!). I had experienced all that a woman could and he would tell me: "Then you are lost, Zoe. It is only out of what is incomplete in us that we form an art. Or build a life." No.

That is not what I would have wanted him to say. I wanted Ritter to know what had become of me after him. Without my love for him.

I suddenly stood up to leave and Pierre held fast to my hands, saying, "I'm sorry thou did'st not keep the child…. I thought it was best for thee …to…… go.."

The café was nearly empty. A charwoman was moving some tables. Pierre said, "Poor rabbit," and I pulled away. "Pauvre Lapin. Poor rabbit, I hate Switzerland…." The surprising bass of his voice and the familiar banalities of his speech. "Little rabbit…….. my poor little rabbit……." His jacket was tightly buttoned across his waist, and as he stood up, he loosened it. The trouser legs were creased from sitting. I did not know where to go. I sat down again.

He said, "Go on…." He moved his head quickly, shaking loose a tear which he caught on the peak of his index knuckle. But in my mind I was telling Ritter, 'I went back to the country where we had loved.' I felt the Swiss spirit translated as though for the two men who linked me to it-----one German, one French. Along the dully beautiful shoreline of Geneva, I walked alone, lulled out of the horror I was entering. My pension was draped in crewel with azure flowers. The sun slashed at my window. I might have been on the Riviera. Alone, I walked the first few nights, past cafes where others were drinking. My hair was mounted in a plait across my head. I ate dinner outside, removing small kid gloves to hold my fork, I spoke to no one. I had no place in the world. Without honor, gain, or vice, placid as Geneva itself, I was in the plant limbo of reversing my womanhood.

In the morning I entered the clinic, terribly hungry. I swallowed some pills and water, then walked around the sunny room to keep awake. The nurse was kind but handled me roughly as though I was an object whose only quality was fear. Dizziness enveloped me. I studied one page in the volume of Ritter I had brought. I looked from my angled windows which gave onto a plot reserved for motor-cars and beyond it, the lake. Near shore, some swans, and further out, a sail. Alone. For nothing matched and everything belied my fading memory of something awful.

A young man in white up to his eyes slid me from his arms onto a high platform and wheeled me along a corridor, well kept. I remembered thinking: The walls are so bare because nothing can be hung of them. As doors swung away, the young man said: "You are not afraid are you?" I said—Yes. He said not to be and I began to tell him-----Stop this. Take me away and I will follow you and love you forever today until I die. But he had disappeared. An old woman with her head wrapped in bandages leaned over me and said in my ear: "N'as-tu pas sommeil?" And, wretchedly, before I answered "NO," she pierced the inside of my elbow and I woke in the sunny room on the lake.

I could not move. The nurse called from the door:" It is over. You are back." I said in German, happily, "You are very sweet. She blushed and vanished. I fell asleep. I slept until my eyes were clear. There was nothing to eat, so I slept again. I had some tea then, very pale and hot, and a biscuit which I could not chew. I remembered thinking, "What splendid care they take of me." I slept. I had a dream in which the old doctor, his face becoming mean and vengeful, asked me, again, and again, "Who is the *father?*"

The word woke me, sweating. No one else was in the room. What had that word to do with the blue sky over the sapphire lake spotted with sun? There were soft voices that entered my room, a charming bouquet of flowers in a baccarat bowl. It could not be true that an old man I had never known or seen had deftly, and without passion, handled what had been miracle and wrenched from my body the incredible idea of birth as though it was something as positive as a stone.

I was terribly hungry and I got out of bed. Horrified. On the white front of my gown, gorgeous roses burgeoned, spread out of shape and began falling in some garden murder on the fur rug under me. I began to scream and still was not sure I had screamed once. I was cold. I heard voices, the nurse who had been kind spoke to me severely about the doctor: "You must understand that he takes a terrible risk....."

She rubbed the palms of my hands with a pink cloth and between my fingers there were small red lines like glove-seams. The doctor looked down at me, displeased.

"Who is the *father?*"

My teeth kept clicking and my breasts ached.

"Who was the *father?*" A tiny flicker of feeling came through and like a tongue of flame in a five-level barn, it illuminated and meant disaster. The flowers did not cover the myopic eyes of the doctor. A nurse in filthy bedslippers pulled the blinds over the blue sky. My weakness heralded an important change in myself. What? I had not just been asleep in the sun on the Lake of Geneva?"

The nurses were leaving the room. They carried between them a small bundle and I tried to sit up, but the doctor pushed me and said, "Lie down." He was smiling.

Sometime afterwards, he came back with some papers and touched my breasts. One of the bills was for the laundry. The doctor said we were doing fine. He winked and said he hoped not to see me for at least another year…….. although I was strong, I was somewhat emotional. He said he was at my service and handed me a little neck-less bottle. "To have on hand just in the event------" he laughed: "that I might have any white rugs in my home."

I shook my head.

"Ahhh----- you do not? Well ……in any event….' You must keep it. I have already charged your bill."

But I could not stop shaking my head.

He was wearing a suit of some rough tweed with brown fibers that stood out delicately in the lamplight like insect's legs. His eyes behind his spectacles were the iridescent green of a fly's. Behind his soft kind voice I saw each corner of the barn. There were the filthy slippers and the hairy cheeks of the nurse, the sightless eyes, the blinds over the sunlit sky, my nightshirt flowering….. Dark spots on the back of the doctor's hand jumped toward me as his finger pointed to the sums of money I owed him. When he said that the rug was ruined, I felt something slowly burning into me. His voice went on, detached from the paper which was touching the tip of my nose. He winked one of those blind eyes at me and I said:

"Murderer......."

All stillness shook out in the corridors. I had never seen another patient. Only an old voice through the wall one night. It was 1923. Springtime. Through the unloving silence of the halls a terrible shout rattled even the paper before me and sunk into my heart very deeply. It stopped the burning flame the way a wagonful of sand would bury it.

After the shout came phrases struggling with it the way men might wrestle an animal, in gasps.......over and over....... "Pigalle... next time......next time........Pigalle......" He repeated some other words. Then he told me to get out. He shouted---"-Get Out"---- so often and so loudly that I knew outside people were sitting quietly without moving in chairs hearing it. Afraid to come in. Ashamed for me. All that waste of shame. I took in each word as though it were an object with nothing inside and unrelated to my life. The sort of thing one picks up at the Flea Market out of some one else's home. There was only the doctor bending over me: the thin wattled neck buttoned into a tieless collar, the head wagging, and from the old white face, pale and without lips, there erupted the last sound, soft: "Whore".

The next day I stopped at the station and bought a small bracelet for Trudi. But since I had killed the possibility of a child, it made Trudi less valuable. She was only a mistake that grew.

I sipped my tea in Paris and it was very cold. I looked across at Pierre---- into his flecked blue eyes are rimmed with lashes that were wet. I had an idea that his eyes were so much more human than the rest of him. Not that something tender was behind them, but that they, solely, were tender beings not responsible for his clay and fluid. Had it not been for them I might never have wasted the terrible on him.

As I stood up, telling him that everything was finished between us I did not really care. Nor was I sorry I had gone to Geneva. I wished only that none of it had happened. He stood up as well, that detestable jacket between what beat in him and the air. Yet how familiar that jacket was! And how familiar he was in a world where one's hand can look unreal, one's own repeated name become a word, like mine, like love. I glared at him.

"You have never once said my name," I told him. "I do not believe you know it."

He said, "Yes. I know thy name."

I wanted to pluck out those blue eyes like the eyes of a doll and see what made them move with love when nothing else about him did. From where did it grow, that tenderness? Or more? I told him he had never said he loved me and yet I had been through as much as if he had. It was the end.

What alarm when I saw that the bowed top of his head had the same expression and I need not pluck out the eyes. Possibly it was spreading through him like disease., this tenderness, and soon would reach his lips. I waited.

His mouth must have come apart for he said, "It will change. Thou wilt see. It will."

His voice was so low I could scarcely hear it. I moved closer and sat down because I was still not strong.

I told him I could not wait so long. It was too late. Warm and very familiar his hands fell flat on mine. He asked me to try. Please. "hou wilt see" he kept saying: and, once, he shook his head as though the invasion of this disease was ruining an unprepared but fatalistic land.

"I have never said these things to a woman before, but thou wilt see......it will come."

I told him I had never been with child by a lover before, but I felt that I lied.

He said: "Zoe"......." testing it carefully as if it were an exposed rock in a deep stream, and we walked out on the rue de Bac toward my door, where I parted from—hating-- him.

*

From that time, Pierre began to shrink before my eyes as though my hatred was a parasite body within his. I continued to see him in cafes and, always, on his cheeks and chin there were short hairs the color of un-dyed wool. The efforts of Janka or other friends to draw me into conversation or entice me back to painting, I met with the same vague depression and sense of defeat. I found myself more and more at home with the blankness of my life and the man linked to it.

One day we went to his room and, obsequiously, like an untrustworthy servant he opened the door and stood aside. At once I saw everything------the bed, his cup, the window open.

"Oh!" he said. "Oh Zoe!"

My name had an alien sound in his mouth. It might have been apple or lemons or flower. He sat me down and kissed my hands, repeating, "Zoe Zoe......." perhaps to ward off the serious implication which had come from my being nameless, being only woman. And laying his palm against my stomach, said, "I love thy poor wounded body."

I felt suddenly so terrible, so guilty and bewildered----- struggling with something I had no right to battle. Then the terrible shout in Geneva, floating, rang under the bridge of my bones

"Come into my arms," he said. "I have need of thee."

.............there were old slippers, a glass bowl, my blood laundered from a sheet used again the next day..... ...flowers, and I knew Pierre had lifted from me that sand-fall of horror so that I could breathe in those words, "Who is the *father?*' As the clear blue sky of his look lit up corners in myself, everything was there as if all the derelicts to whom I had given sous arrived to claim me as benefactor for their pocked lives. I looked closer, further, for some weapon I could use—knowing it could be used on me as well.

"My body is a clumsy fool," he said. "Let me touch thee."

Almost with violence he was covering my face and shoulders with kisses. I remembered love and began to sob, "Oh heaven forgive me! I'm a monster."

"Don't say that, please, "he begged." I'm as much to blame......... We'll have another child."

"That's past. That's past now," I said with horror. And I had a shameful memory of the rapture I had known in his bed. The grim joy of making love, the sacred blankness of begetting a child. "I'm a murderer," I whispered, "and there is nothing to forgive me." I put one of my hands to my mouth. "Because you are my accomplice."

His face still looked handsome and familiar but it was all the more terrible to me for that. I was all the more terrible to me for that.

"I recognize you," I said, holding his head by the thick hair. "I'm not afraid of you," I pulled his head down and almost with loathing I said to it in German, "And I love thee. Do you know that? I love thee."

In French he answered, "I also."

Stunned and hardly knowing where I was, I began sliding from the edge of the cot until he pulled me up towards his frightened face. I would have fallen on the floor if he hadn't held me.

"I also," he said. "I love thee."

My heart smashed like a blinded animal into his hands. I was terrified. I felt I was touching the spine of the world. I'll die, I thought. Only spirits roam......the body will die like this.....thin...hre.

"I love thee."

I moved closer and closer to him, hurriedly, with as kind of impatience. Before and behind us here was a vast expanse. I remembered thinking, which is life and which is the other? But I had no choice. And when he penetrated my body I screamed.

We remained very silent, like two people who had just received exactly the same news.

All the way home I leaned on him, strangely dizzy as though we were walking on something high and narrow. I was saying to myself, ' it can never be right now, now----but let me be happy.' And in the next few weeks I tried to be happy. Each time I thought of what I had done, something froze until I pushed the thought away. I tried to be calm. Pierre's eyes were full of love. He planned surprises------- a book of Old Master drawings which I tried to like, a luncheon at St Cloud, sketching paper---- and when we were out walking his hand never left mine.

But each night I had dreams. In frantic sleep I searched for what I had left in Geneva. "Where can I find it?" was the horror on which I awoke. It had not really ever been, I reasoned, so how could it be not? Pierre said sadly, "I have so often regretted it."

In one dream I hadn't yet gone and it was given to me to make the choice again. I woke, shivering, to find it was done. My forehead was drenched with sweat. I thought: 'How could I leave it in a strange country so far away from me?' And worse, ' What had they done with it?' Pierre told me we must stop thinking about it.

Where was it? Was it buried?

Afraid of nightmares I began to sleep badly and often could not eat. I knew that I was not mad and that there was no child, and yet here had been all the signs of one which I had to find.

In the gradually opening summer we spent more time in the parks, but I found myself despising the young women who wheeled prams. Pierre knew this and sought out secluded places like the Naumachie at Parc Monceau where we sat near the ruined columns and fed the birds. It was painful for both of us to see babies and small children who marked another direction from ours.

Toward the end of June, I read in a journal a sentence that caught like a claw in my brain. "At eight weeks," it said, "this creature already has a tiny beating heart." And a new desire came over me. I wanted to write to Geneva to ask if it had been a boy or a girl. Then I knew it was dead. I mourned like someone who would never be able to go mad.

I found Pierre in our spot by the little lake. He was staring ahead of him, at nothing, and when he heard my step, he reddened and stood up, taking my hand too tightly.

"Thou art very late," he said, and broke off.

In spite of my efforts to be calm, I knew that my lips were quivering. When we sat down together, he asked if I felt ill, and when I said 'No', he sighed and said he understood. I saw him pick a leaf from the seat, toss it onto the grass, then pat his jacket.

"I have some very good news," he said.

But I was scarcely listening. Somehow I wanted him to know how awful it was for me. There was no one else to understand. I stroked his fingers, but almost as though he wasn't aware of my hand, he kept brushing off the seat.

Down the path, coming towards us were two Nuns with the black wind in their garments and with sudden viciousness, I said, "They, too, will give birth to a ghost!"

"Again?" he snapped. "Always the same thing."

At the same moment we both began to say,"I'm sorry", and I smiled. Then, with the shy look of a child, he pulled a letter from his pocket and showed me it was a very good offer to work with a doctor in his village for half of each week. He did not take his eyes from me, watching how this struck me. I began to speak, but stopped.

Pierre seemed rather pale, and gratefully I saw that he understood how he had become my whole life-----how much this separation would affect me. I pressed his hand and told him it seemed like an excellent opportunity.

"Not only that," he said. "But my rabbit will have some time again...."

"Time? How do you mean?" I asked softly. I was calm but a nervousness in him alarmed me.

"Time for thy daughter.....for thy work,,,,,...." His voice sounded almost gay, but his lips were dry.

Suddenly I seemed to understand everything, but yet I did not wish to. I had thought of sending my daughter to her father. I wanted only to be with him. To go with him-----if he wished---- to his village.

"I want us....to be together...." I told him.

He turned white and looked very drowsy. Almost inaudibly he said, "But we are..."

I turned quickly, took his head in my hands, and looking long into his face, I held up my own and kissed his mouth and both his eyes. I felt dreadfully frightened.

He waited until I moved away. He did not lift his arms. To the suggestion that I needed some rest that day, he didn't offer his own room, and, in fact, urged me, tenderly, to my own.

"I must pack a few things," he said.

When I murmured, "So soon?" he laughed and in the deep lovely voice that was so much like him, he said, "So soon. And back so soon. In three days time."

Then, looking at my time- piece, he stood up hurriedly and took my hand. He kissed me lightly and smiled. There was something unimportant in his friendliness.

The next day, driven by some animal vision, I went to his room, took the immense key fro where he left it over the door, and walked in, straight to his desk. I the first drawer I opened there was a letter, which, for the trembling of my fingers, I read only a few lines. "One said, "But I love thee even so," and another had the scenic impact of a woman, waiting, one and one half hours for Pierre to come to her home, her room, her city or world. I could not finish.

For the night I stood musing by my window. I found myself sordid and longed, longed to hold in my arms not his body but the child I had made with it. With my eyes open I dreamed that I had ripped the blindness away from the green eyes and, behind it, found the reasons which made me go to Geneva, but suddenly I woke, frightened. Below, a long gendarme turned uncertainly on the rue de Varenne, and for a light second his face detached itself from the uniform in which he policed the night. I knew hatred was a strength I was losing. In seconds, the sidewalk and street were empty. Stripes of light cracked horizontally across the window facing mine.

Every clothed child I saw had become out of the thumb-length creature who had trusted in me. Pierre could make life with the force in his body, yet he threw it away in sensual pleasure. Like some pagan playing with God's toes. Except for the street lamps, all the house- fronts near my own were darkened now. A dog bayed several times. I had to think of where I was. The baying was cut by the silence. How does one survive the death of another life? By memory. I was so tired. In my own house, a sound came up which I could not distinguish. I heard it again, and stood up, frightened----- but for no reason: my door was locked. When I looked out into the dark and silent corridor-----even when I pressed the light and saw it was empty, I felt frightened. 'Everyone is sleeping now, I told myself. 'Even, somewhere, Pierre. And I must sleep too…..'

But I could not, and when morning came, the city seemed, in those first white hours of sun, more empty than in the darkness.

+

To desperate people, the world becomes so simplified that if they were looking in the right places they might find the great things of happiness and not the same adrenalin and lost hope that rushes them to people for whom that combination is life. So, a day passed, a second, a third, and I met no one wise but only painters, emigres, models, actors—all of whom had known me with Ritter, who----unmistakably through discretion--- didn't speak of him, and recognized that not yet filled with my own anguish I would have room to receive theirs. I listened to a Russian woman who had left youth, family, beauty and wealth in some distant parcel. We sat side by said, on a couch of bitten velvet, and with a stunning round arm on which the flesh was strangely glossy, she reached for my knee, for a dream caught up in the drapery cord, for the two silver-legged tea glasses by which the world could judge what heritage she'd lost. As we stood up in the little shop-front that was her anteroom, she clutched my hand against a spiny brooch at her neck, and hurt it, saying, "my dear my dear….. to grow old…is terrible."

And I ran to a once-beautiful model who spoke to me in a high-pitched chirping voice as she pulled her skirt constantly to her knees and looked from time to time, at a closed door in the flat. She had been young just a few years before and still kept the same round expression as though age, taking her by surprise, had written down quickly on her face some notes to remember later on. We spoke of Paris in early summer, and somewhere in the house I thought I heard a flute which made her say,"…… and there is no end. No end to it at all."

I sat at Janka's with a still-young tenor, a new playwright and his wife who had a mound of too-black hair set far front and not covering a very bald oval at her crown. This space of skin--- I did not know why---made me terribly sad. They all spoke with great familiarity, Janka laughed festively, and her exquisite enigmatic eyes roved over us all as she commended, to us, the wife for being the right mettle for Georges, To something which I was asked, I found myself looking into the dark-rimmed weary eyes of the woman as I heard Janka saying, "Ah...my Zoe.... She wanted to be a princess when she was small."

I walked down the long stairway, into the lift, and out the door almost to the rue de Dragon, but he was, I knew, near me all the way. So, I turned and faced the tenor and saw in his passionate eyes and small exhausted mouth, an expression of desire which had already torn past admiration. When he told me that he had just bought rooms in Montparnasse, I followed him, stumbling------he was long-legged and in a great hurry------- my thoughts on Ritter, on Yasha, on love, on the sunlight and myself surprised. If it was strange to go through something mortal and feel nothing in Geneva, it was strange to go through nothingness------ the senses dead, the heart unwound, a dense numbness that fostered stone-------- and feel, rising out, a horror like dark air too near the sea.

I felt my body clean as though dipped in cool water, and inside it everything stricken. This with a voice I would take to Pierre that day: the day of his return. The market was open on the rue de Buci and I saw the man who had once sold me the strawberries. He was wearing a brown cap and shouting behind the fruit. I knew I would have been surprised if he had legs. For a moment I couldn't recall where I had been. Then I remembered. I felt that my eyes were white. A vague sound whispered in my mind but I lost it. 'It's Pierre's fault,' I told myself grimly all the way to his Carrefour. It must have been that way the Devil built up hell ----- looking off with a blond smile somewhere while others did the work. How well I could imagine the writhings from Dore' drawings I'd seen: rich, complex, full of life. Paolo and Francesca......... and who had written, "Nous irons en enfer ensemble.'? Yes! Hell was peopled, purgatory is rich.........

Pierre was standing at his door, his arms out of rolled blue sleeves stretched toward me as though nothing had happened. Beyond his lovely head I looked to see the room lit with memories------- silent, unobtrusive, impersonal as torturers waiting in a cell. But it was empty. No executioner had hung my heart on that mirror where I had so often done up my hair. I struggled to speak but could not. He dropped his arms, moved back, and I saw him standing in the middle of his empty room. He frowned a little.

"What is wrong?" he asked me. And then he said, "Thou has been with someone?"

"And I said, "Yes.""

How badly I wanted him to suffer! I thought of the rue de Bac after Geneva. I wanted to say, again, "I've been to hell." I could have said, "I'm leaving you!" I struggled to speak but I could not: everything was taken away from me but the desire to be beautiful again in his eyes and I was glad that my stomach was flat and didn't point up under the white frock. He looked at me ; then, still without speaking, he came closer. I had a memory of snow falling in Basle, something scratched my hand: I saw the Russian brooch with its white and blue stones, smelling slightly. We embraced as though we were pounding on opposite sides of a door that wouldn't open, and his body seemed arrogant, gone mad, a hatchet hacking out my life.

I heard the sounds of his rising. His abrupt step across the room. It was nothing. The act of conception....nothing. One thing cannot be important if another is not because all the things of life are threaded by the same hand. I tried to think. The light was turned lower, then without looking up, he settled himself in his usual chair by the desk, picked up a pencil and began tapping it. From under my closed lids it sounded like steps slowly pursuing me.

Against my foot were two valises, beaten, with brown leather straps, open, neatly packed with underclothing on the top. I was thinking----' He left nothing, nothing.'

"Are you going away?" I asked trembling, going up to him.

In the pale light of the lamp I saw coldness in his face and a start forward of his hands as though he were ready for conflict. When he told me he was going away for four-----perhaps five---- months with a comrade from his village, I heard the flute, the model saying, "There is no end.......". My ears were cold, my feet and hands.

He was not able to explain he said, looking up at me from under his dark brows, but he was obliged to go.

"Oh why do you lie?" I pleaded. "Why do you never tell the truth?"

"I never lie," he said. His eyes lifted up now, obstinate and cool. After a moment he held his hand out across the desk and said in a tempter's voice, "Zoe…. Thou believest that people do exactly as they wish. But it is not true."

"It is! It is!" I said growing more excited. He closed his hand and pulled it back. I felt terribly alone with shame. I moved toward him. "Are you a coward?" I asked, pointing to his chest.

He said he did not know.

I spoke deliberately, some light fear constantly falling between each word as I said, "Why did you tell me that you loved me?"

"Because," he said, "I believed it to be true."

"Oh but you are depraved!" I shouted in his face. "Depraved!"

"Zoe!" He was out of his chair. "Stop! It's too much----" There were two spots of anger just below his eyes, like quartz.

"Depraved!" I cried out again. "You…do not…care. You are nothing…."

The menace in his half-closed eyes remained, although he held my arm. "If anyone but thee," he said, "had said such things to me----- I would hit them. But---" he bit the inside of his cheek, "I could never hit thee."

A deep motion within me which I never felt before, For anything. Any man. Nothing. Something freed, extending way beyond me, caused me to cry out "Do!"

Even as I stood, I felt myself falling. I could not be alone. Love or hate, some meaning that could scar the silence. I cried out, crazily: "DO!"

His stony face kept shifting in front of me. I backed away and shouted: "Gigolo!"

Thinking-------'How hateful,' I went out of the room. The stairs passed under my feet and I was saying to myself: "It is awful. Crude and without love. Without….love". In the entryway I tried to think of the child. I thought of the woman, or more than one. I could not… But how not? I wondered. I was moving quickly along the street, but

I did not remember at once to where, listening to his steps behind me as I got to the taxi station I heard his voice call out "Wait!" as I flung myself into the motor-cab. His face in the square of moving window had that first instant of bewilderment which gives way, in a wounded animal, to rage.

All night in the kitchen I held a volume of Ritter. I dozed upright in a chair, taking special pains to value my life. At dawn I fund Pierre at a closed café across from his room. He stared at me. On his lips were black ridges which to my sleepless eyes looked like the rim of dirt around an old cut.

"I walked all night," he said for a greeting. "I thought I would never see thee again."

I thought 'It can never be good now,' and I said: "I had to see thee again....or all that has happened to me would be nothing."

He did not move. His breath and clothes smelled stale. There were green hollows beneath his eyes and in each eye there was something mobile and blind as a worm. Instead of finding a quiet place to rest, I was taking in each detail of his face, then I looked at the dirty shoes and large behinds of people doing late-night errands in a part of the city dedicated to day. I took in everything like someone bending down gathering stones to forget the emptiness of the day.

"Look there," I said. "Do you see?" The caryatid. Between bent arms the bulb-like head from which no flower sprung. It touched the parapet, resigned.

"Ah yes, "he said.

"That mysterious smile of the face. It looks like my mother."

"What art thou looking for?"

"My spectacles," I said.

"Dost not see well without spectacles?"

"Yes. But I want to see better at a distance."

I smiled at that young man ten years younger than myself and I felt that the smiles could be picked off my face like flies from a rock that seeped decay.

"Pierre," I said. "I love thee."

I said it as something quite new. After months of making love, giving him my heart, my soul, my body of which he used the parts that came quickly to his attention.

"I love thee, "I told him. "I love everything about thee. I think that the last thing I see before I die will be that jacket you wear.

That jacket with its great orange squares and its great brown squares separated like bizarre pasture lands by black ditches........ He too stocky to wear it. The short marching legs in the too-narrow trousers and the chemise always open one button, and even when closed there was the mat of light brown hair that made me from a placid woman into a fanatic to sleep with him.

The café doors opened. "Yes. I love thee." I envied the people walking outside and inside, who were looking for love or had just been disappointed while I sat there in the center of it. He listened, looking pleased, but I was certain that if I touched his hand, it would be wet and two places of his chemise near his shoulders would be wet. And I continued speaking as though I had been reeling in a fish with an umbilical cord attached to my spine.

"Who is the *father?*"

Each time I said "I love thee," the sheet unrolled before my eyes, still wet. I said, "I love thee. I wanted to be free of thee, but I love thee....even so." And he pointed to his chest, saying, "I, also.... ....but thou art part of my life."

Admitting to that pleased uneasy man that I loved him no matter what, even reaching a point where I did not believe in that love: beginning to see like worms in holes around the flowers, the way the doctor leaned against my pillow, the heavy eyes of the tenor, the way Pierre really walked------- stiff and cold, rhythm –less, a mundane walk; the nurse said in my ear----"He takes a terrible risk....." I felt a deep exhaustion at having pulled in the great fish and found that the cord was wound with everything I had slapped dead on the way to it.

"Look," Pierre said, "the Romance bar is open. The sky is beginning to be blue…"

"What things have happened in the world since we've been here."

The handsome, too-fleshy young man with a tendency to jowls, smiled. A free smile. Ritter had lied and there was no reason behind life. I saw Trudi with a bald spot on her pretty head and a tall man was removing her clothes.

Suddenly ill, I went into the little café and bumped between a dirty man working and one drinking against the bar. 'It's like that between the world, 'I thought. 'Love is both and nothing. It's like digging a hole to the stars. That is love.' The stairs were steep. The light went on in the stone room as the door clicked. You had to lock yourself in to have light. To the swollen face in the mirror I said with contempt: "Don't worry. I'll stay with you."

When I came out, Pierre was speaking to a pretty, young prostitute and when I asked him if he wanted to go with her, he put on a very shocked expression and stood up. I remember his words because they seemed to stand for nothing between us.

"Come this way," he said, and put his arm around my waist.

I followed him gladly. The stocky young man whose body I knew as well as a small unfurnished tomb I had painted white within the hour.

He said, "I cannot throw away a part of myself."

He said this, looking off to one side as though the sentence had come to me without his voice.

The streets were empty and grey. I thought I had been happy walking in such streets but I could not remember why. A paper skidded lightly along the pavement and fell into the gutter. I'd once laughed in hose streets, but why? The whole lie that people told about the beauty of Paris was all at once clear to me: it was a lot of dirty buildings which smelled of history and old lives. It was only to take up the time that people lived in them, fearing.

He halted me at a stop of the motor bus and I asked, "Where do you take me?"

"In my bed," he answered without a smile. I felt a complete panic about staying in the foul streets or going into one of the buildings---even my own.

"We should go to a park," I said softly. "One last time…"

His arm raised and blue cuff popped out of his sleeve. "Don't speak like that," he said, and unhooked the twined cord. We leaned on the rim of the platform. Past the streets ugly with waking and people who were hurrying off to nothing. The children out of school with grimy stockings. A man mounted beside us. His black suit shiny, his hair thin and flaked; it had been silken under his mother's hand and she put him to sleep early when he was ill. He inserted a finger into his nose and turned it. Even that monstrous creature had thought himself loved. Ritter's clothes had never been neglected. He dressed and lived like a prince which is what he wished he had been. Love with him had been madly passionate and cerebral ; it was never consummated after it was consummated. Somewhere I had had a husband. All past. I was left with less and less. Too much to keep. Ritter had said, "possessions are the tears of memory."

When we walked toward the Buttes Chaumont, Pierre took my hand with the hand he had put against some woman's back and I thought, all the way up the slope, 'How could he?' until we were in the park. It was very green and ill-kept, with a foul smelling chair lady who flicked her tickets at me and winked as though to say, "It's not a seat thee would desire."

I was unmoved by the bridge from which men dropped like wingless birds. Or the nearby place where others had hung fowl-like, their graceful toes pointing in the wind. I was looking down at a small, mud-green lake, a boat, some trees, three swans which seen close to—just moments before--- had wet necks and flat uncomprehending eyes. I had stroked one. Just looking at all that, I put my head on Pierre's shoulder and began to cry like someone deranged. An unhinged door which opens by moving up and down.

The truth meant nothing, "I ..am ...ill, "I... I...I...I ..am expecting... a child."

His eyes were full of love or weakness, tears or fear. "That is very complicated," he said.

The letter from some woman who had waited for him to come to her seemed to be waving near the tip of my nose and it obscured my view of the muddy lake, the birds, the little boy who had been slapped and stood sobbing on the path. Just a black hole between some brownish hair and a tiny shirtwaist. He belonged to no one. When he cried he was all alone. I was extended forever.: the child which had been Pierre's before Geneva had become mine and I was alone with it, alone, alone with it -dead.

There was no father.

On the rocky slope as I passed some laughing children, they became quiet: one boy said something to another and they laughed again. I knew they spoke some viciousness of me. Below the thick neck of the taxi driver, I seemed to see again their opened little faces like pastel flowers around a burnt tree. The reek of his tobacco clung to my clothes even out of the taxicab. Behind the varnished doors lunch was being prepared. I heard it. Smelled the cheap entrails disguised with a dry wine, the chairs scraping up to the table, one child sent back to clean its filthy hands before they all sat down again to eat, to fill their bodies with some other. Pierre's mouth had been greasy once with sardine oil.

There was the kind animal look of the maid coming toward me as I took off my gloves. "I shall be dining in tonight," I told her, and as I saw the basket swinging on her arm go around the door, I thought, 'None of that matters. No one really has anything to do.'

When I let down my hair it seemed less full, and my feet were narrow: my youth had had to thin out to cover too long a period of time. In the water I saw myself on a last stroll during the War, wearing a long grey skirt with a matching hat that covered my hair, shaded my eyes, and left the long tip of my nose white to the air. By my side, Ritter was walking in an apprehensive daze, afraid of being called-up, translating objects into friends he'd lost. With his Swiss black suit and high-domed hat, he looked like a banker with a haunted past. "Zoe," he said with rippling eyes, "Nothing is ever lost. The lover rests forever in the body of his love." But who? Ritter? Pierre? An unfinished son whose small blood once mixed with mine? Between everything wonderful was the thought of how awful life was.….. I was very careful, but when I broke the skin I was surprised.

The darkened water jumped around. Grown tall my daughter stood over me and vanished into the cold.

*

The weather had alternated between heat and rain, and once, after taking the sun at some shore, there were imprecise lines on my face. One day, in fall, the lease ran out on my studio at Place Blanche. Trudi spoke of visiting her father, but we decided to remain together. Then, the school term began.

Every morning on the rue de Bac, my concierge would sweep water with a red straw broom. One day, behind her, there stood a man wearing rope-soled shoes of torn canvas on his feet, and a gray suit which he adjusted in front of the café window. Janka said something about the odd combination. Slowly the man in gray turned around : full-face I had the shock of his blue eyes.

"Oh! at last!" he said. "It is thee Zoe."

I was gliding closer, drawn forward by my hand. "Madame Janka Hagan," I said. "Monsieur….Pierre Belloy."

Pierre took her hand as well. Janka looked from him to me and began to say, "He is…" with an unusual tactlessness that showed me how unimportant she considered my love affair. "Very handsome," she said to me in German. "He looks Teutonic." I remember hearing the two of them talk. I recall everything they said about Rimini, his village---- and I could not speak: standing timidly as a child who is afraid to be noticed. I could not prepare myself. By his shoes I saw how much time had passed. He had bought them new, he had worn them out with the same peasant disregard and devotion he had for all that he owned. They had walked beaches and had been untied by his bed and other beds.

"How far," heard Janka asking, "Is Bracieux from Chateauroux?"

"Not far," he said. "One could almost walk it."

"You perhaps," she said. And turning to me, "But not us….."

Not then, perhaps, at that moment, but afterwards, I knew that there had been too much to pass through for Pierre and I to meet in the open. Empty days, Trudi's arms, the lake of Geneva, the numbness, the hatred, the moment of love and the cold plunge... We should never have met again at all, because if we had met---- as I sometimes imagined it--- running toward the other as tables and chairs fell aside, to be forgiven, as papers scattered, in each other's arms, it would have been the end just the same. There was nothing more for us.

They were looking at me—Janka un-benevolently—with a curiosity in her deep eyes. "Forgive me, but I find it amusing, "she said, 'that with your distaste for the country you have found in this city a lad from the Tourraine."

Pierre blushed. Janka looked at him as though he might have been a picture.

"You exaggerate----" I managed to say. I knew that her callousness was just her loving anger at thinking I had undeservedly thrown myself away. She said she must be on her way and told Pierre, "I thought to see Zoe before she leaves. Well! It's a good idea I had to get myself up early as it happens. With all the people she has to take leave of----"

"Leave?" Pierre repeated.

"My husband," I began,….." passed away. I'm taking my daughter to Germany this evening. You are leaving?" I asked Janka stupidly.

"Of course," And she kissed me, offering her hand to Pierre. "Monsieur Belloy, delighted. No, stay here." And I watched her, trembling, until she turned the corner.

I looked at Pierre. On his lower lips there was a blister covered with white powder. Like his shoes, it released me from knowing him too well. From under his dark brows, captive within the immaterial color of his eyes, I saw tenderness. I recognized in each perfect sphere the delicately crooked flaw which had almost cost me my life. I drew back into myself thinking, 'But his eyes have not changed. They and I have not changed."

"Your eyes are the same."

"How shall they not be when they are directed on thee?"

He lies, I thought. He lies he lies he lies.

"Well......? He said. He seemed shy and serious. We couldn't stand there in front of my building, we couldn't go to his, nor sit down in a café. What place is left for people like us who have run their course? A small spot in the center of a carpet in a high room where all around us people are talking or singing to a piano. We look at each other, say a few words, smile, both turning at the same time, and quickly, for many days afterwards we have someone speak ceaselessly of detailed things.

We walked to a side street in the middle of a crowded quartier--- a narrow street with the name of an ancient word--- and sat down on the stone sill of an old barred door. He told me he had just come to say goodbye. He was going to Africa.

"I have already said goodbye to thee," I told him.

"Please listen," he said with tears coming into his eyes. "I want to tell thee. I do not know how, somehow..... but I regret nothing. I'm glad it happened between us," he said hurriedly.

I turned to him and looked at him very carefully as though I knew I would never see him again. I looked at his hair, bleached nearly white by the sun. The sides of his neck had slippery patches of new skin and I imagined him lying alone Italian beaches, buried in sand. One beautiful arm flung out across some dark shoulder, turned away. Under the white powder a trickle of blood came out on his lips. I wanted to touch it and did not. A stout man marched down the street and passed in front of us. I smiled at him and drew in my legs. I looked at Pierre's black lashes and as he opened his mouth I looked at his teeth.

"All for nothing," I said. "For nothing."

"But no!" he said, reaching toward my hair. "But no!"

I wanted neither to go nor to stay. I noticed it was only ten in the morning and my train didn't leave until midnight. There was nothing I wanted to do, but I would eventually do something. I 've had wonderful success with my painting, but my best work might be my portrait of Ritter. Maybe all that would matter about my life was to have been the mistress of a great poet and-----with how many others--- to carry the candles over his life.

"Goodbye Pierre," I said, standing up.

He put his arm around me and said, "Until we meet again."

"Why are you trying to cry?" I asked him.

"Because I do not believe it," he said. "Less…..do I understand myself."

We stood apart.

"I understand nothing," I told him and kissed his cheek quickly.

"One day," he said, "Thou will look out the window and I will be there…. Standing outside…. As always."

With a small pain, I said, "All right."

That was all.

I had a letter from Africa where he was doing work in a hospital. He said very little----as always--- about himself, except that he missed walking in the snowflakes in France. It was a tender letter. There were two others---the second one more loving than the one before. I have them here with me now. I was regretful and justified to see that he wrote rather well. In the last letter he wrote that he naturally thought of me less often, "But when the memory of thee is present, I care for it as for a small fire before which it is good to warm oneself."

I never heard from him again, but that is no matter. Pierre will die locked inside me like a rainbow in its color finally and only when I die.

10 AOUT

As the train moved in, I saw the empty platform on which no one waited.

I came out and, after me, the small valise was dropped to the quais. It lay, far too-carefully strapped, by my feet, and as I took hold of the handles, I saw a carriage with dust flying ahead of it on the road. Four unfamiliar people descending, two by two, talked as they walked forward, and the last woman was looking into my eyes as she passed me, nodding her head "No." This stranger's face, detached from my life, entered it for that moment----in a transposition of planes--- like a messenger, and I sat down in the shelter without the dignity of choice. Although I was nearly twenty-eight years old, this was the first time I had felt abandoned by rejecting my past. Now, when the days roll over like heavy repetitive wheels ---too high to see any vehicle--- I am awed by the total entry of being which youth, with ecstasy or fear, puts into the phrase, "I don't know what's happening!"

By four o'clock the lonely place had surrounded and overgrown its unfamiliar look. I, the half-timbered shelter with its raw wood settee, the high loose stone steps---all seemed like trophies carried off from enemies that did not try to battle. There was a victorious vitality in the rough ground, the thick dust, the vigorous green plants which shattered the view, and the earth-smell which struck into my attention like an oddly-clothed person on the road..

I was thrown back to my hand-mirror in which I looked beautiful. The clefts, curves and shadows over a white ground: the dark fringe around light eyes behind which I stood in a room I had all but cleared. I still could not admit that love was adhesive only on the inside of the lover. I heard the sound of a motor before I saw the open coupe glistening toward me, and I remember my first view of the Duchess and Tino, her son, because Ritter was not with them. She recognized me only because there was no other woman there, but she addressed me without my name as "Liebe," and Tino, bending down for my valise, was examining me from that oblique angle as she was saying: "My boy....collect the lady's things.....my dear....have you had a wait?"

Answering the formula with one more alien to me than hers to them, I told her that my wait was rewarded by being at last able to make her acquaintance. As I said this, she paused to look at me -gratified. I knew I did admire the strong figure she presented; she was hardly out of place on that wretched clot of wood any more than in a salon, since she appeared utterly unconvinced that anything surrounded her. Tall and broad, her head was a fine pinnacle in which small clear eyes were set over a nose, long and cleft like a halberd. The skirt of her linen dress was caught up for walking over a stiff arm that seemed to wait on her, and at her open neck there fluttered as she spoke------ like banners---her splendid fingers, overbrown from sun.

As we drove along I said nothing to her that was not true, yet her absolute command relieved me of groping or qualification and caused me to draw out as from an invisible reticule the phrases required of each visitor to the castle of her presence. And because I wished to make myself agreeable to her---not only because of her influence on Ritter, but because he cared so much for her---I found myself parroting words like a child who learns their emotional equivalents later. No one had mentioned the reason for my presence or the absence of Ritter until Tino---who had been glancing at me from time to time--- looked off at the road and said, "Our San'Angeliko has bustled off to Fribourg to see someone, you know. You will have to suffer my humble substitute, Madame." Still looking at the road ahead, he added "....if you need a guide."

It was the mention of Ritter than made me stumble for the first time. I had no learned response to him. I reacted first to the name I know the Duchess had given him: Saint and Angel. When I knew him to be neither and yet I loved him very well. I lingered so long on this reflection that when it came, the shock of his not being there for my arrival seemed to send all my breath into my head. Just then, in a merciful fulfillment of charity, the Duchess said, "We assured him that you would be cared for until he returned."

In the Schloss to which they brought me there was a muffled opulence, complete in its past, and my spare being went through it with the shrillness of a religious cry.

I slept alone and soundly that night, and as I was up and out walking at six in the morning about the quiet grounds, I saw the majestic figure of the Duchess moving slowly toward me. We exchanged greetings and spoke pleasantly about the day. Suddenly, to my astonishment, she began questioning me about my relationship with HER San'Angeliko. When had we met...how long ago...what I did. I did not know whether to be grateful or perplexed that Ritter had never mentioned me to her except in the vaguest terms of---as she put it---"someone sharing his solitude."

"I am a painter," I told her as we walked into the rose garden. "I have been working for nearly a year, in fact, on a portrait of him."

"Ah, we must see it. We must see it....." She thrust into my hand a pink rose which she had clipped with a golden scissors that hung from her belt. "Ach, so, well.....we must certainly see it soon." And then in a lower, but not unkind voice, "He seems happy enough. But he is not working. Sometimes .....he becomes entangled...." I recall that she used that word. "....And he does not....work well."

Never before had I reflected on my position. In the presence of Brache or our other friends, our life seemed natural and magnificent. The sophistication of this great lady to whom nothing in the world was supposed to be shocking made her speak to me as to a woman of the world. She caused to be wrapped about me as a rigid disguise the word, common and complete, "liaison".

We halted near a bower seat. I grasped a piece of latticework and she went on in the same pleasant tones. "You are a fortunate young woman, you know...but you must be prepared. He has a tendency..... to flee from his liaisons. But with great men....." and I do not recall the rest.

Although Ritter spoke of her rich soul, the Duchess had seen too much of society, and as though this soul preserved itself by keen departures, I found a strange thing taking place while she was speaking to me On her long aristocratic face, the physical attributes seemed stripped as though the soul had been pulled away from the inside as a picture might have been removed under its glass. I feared her influence over Ritter if she did not approve of our "liaison". She continued speaking to me, this great lady for whom silence was either rapport or rudeness. She explained to me why we were both awakened by the dawn; we were women physically connected to the world--- she to its ageing, I to its awakening. And all the while she looked at my respectful face without envy or malice, but simply as though she had found the ground for our meeting. As though this ground would change no more than the foundation of the family castle.

"If I have forgotten the forms of young love," she was saying, "I am constantly reminded by my younger acquaintances...." The Comtesse de G....she told me, rose at dawn to be certain of time to make her toilette before her lover waked. For me, who waked slowly, drawing my first sigh from the breath of the sleeper at my side, this was shocking frivolity. There was a beauty and solemnity in the Duchess' voice, but her meaning and her words surprised me with a ring of coarseness. A once-handsome woman, did she despair of the face she saw in her mirror? Did she resist the knowledge that Ritter, bewitched by beauty, might sing the richness of her soul and not her self? And did she not love more than just the soul of her San'Angeliko?

No. There was neither envy nor malice in her initial approach to me. I saw her whole attitude as one that a cultured lady might adopt in the delighted assumption of camaraderie with music hall singers or streetwalkers. She would never see me but as a hammered rung in the hierarchical ladder that her rank had built. She knew all about the despair of the lower classes, but believed it to be a despair that could not furnish them with dreams. I could not speak to her about Ritter's work, about Basle, Venice, people we knew, art..... I waited only for a decent opportunity to return to my room as soon as she was done speaking what she took to be my language: how boring life in high circles…how dreary the teas and concerts compared with the 'artist's life'…… How free were those who were not afraid to move through life as they moved through the streets of great cities…… A queasy discomfort unsettled me, not so much from the stream of words I had not directly heeded, as from the confidential tone that she---- heavily veiled--- might have adopted to the porter of an opium den. I feared a terrible embarrassment and was about to take leave. She was pointing to the rose curled in my hand and she repeated several times some question. I put my hand to my forehead. I prepared to feign a headache when her hand fell on my shoulder, making my knees bend and my hips slide against the stone seat. In a brief silence I looked pleadingly at her, but the only expression on her face came from a smile so fixed it seemed like a motto on her skin. An exquisite long finger, nearly umber at the knuckles, touched the center of the rose I held. Her low voice could have been an insinuating croak near my ear, the voile head-dress brushed my nose.

",,,,Comte de Seguy…." And a laugh.

"I do not know him," I whispered idiotically. I gripped the gritty stone at my sides.

"Hah!" She laughed again. "I did not mean HIM specifically. But don't you agree….." She repeated a phrase several times like a tattoo in the air.

"I----I don't understand…." I stammered.

"Perhaps in French….." she went on and I said "No!"- surprised at my violence and a childish pitch in my voice that sounded like Trudi's.

With scarcely room at the top of her narrowing forehead for eyebrows, she raised her eyes to the fringe of the small head-dress and stared at me.

"Please. No." I spoke more quietly, humiliated.

She drew herself up as though I had insulted her. "How delicate we are….little painter. Or is it…..innocence?"

Her laugh was an abrupt bark. I had an absurd idea that the very heart of this woman was a family possession augmented and guarded through the centuries by one of those fossilized beasts on ancestral tombs.

I stood up, my cheeks hot and throbbing, my voice catching as though on hooks at the back of my throat. "I may have seemed innocent, but….. I assure you Madame…I.." I did not know what to say. I did not know what I meant.

She also stood up. She leaned back elegantly and opened those un-stained hands as though to receive the sky. "Please, please. Do not affect such things with me. Innocence Liebe, is a charming idea. We have it about our children. But---" she looked deep in my eyes, bitter as a child whose game has been broken. "But it does not exist. Even for children. They have simply not put together what they know. Their knowledge is simply disorganized…….. But you know all that. Hmmm?"

I saw only that I had spoiled her delight in a conspiratorial tête-a- tête with a woman who ought to have made no secret of her vices. I shook my head. It was a surrender to the knowledge that we would never speak except on her terms.

"Please!" Her tones were peremptory now. "You are a married woman. And with a child, I believe? Yes? Your experience makes it….."

I closed my eyes. I thought of lying, time after time, in Ritter's arms. I felt his body imbedded in my memory as though he had left it as a parting gift.

"The things….one does in love," I said in the darkness. "They do not give one…experience."

When I opened my eyes, her wide back was facing me. Then it moved quickly down the path. Through my stockings, the stiff yellow grass pricked my legs, and I had to assure myself that my dislike of the country lay not in its maliciousness, but in its disregard.

I slipped away from the chateau and stood on a dirt path. My hostess despised me. I could not take a tram-car and leave. Ritter---although he knew I would be arriving---was not there, nor had he left any message. I tried to gather my courage and I sat under the portico of a little summer-house wondering how many generations of Duchesses had met their lovers secretly, half-mechanically in the rooms within. Yet wasn't this the world where "love" had to be forbidden fruit else it be graceless?

The plants were as green as vegetables and I was separated from the chateau and the landscape only by the linen awning which calmed the reaching sun. I would have done a drawing. There were no flowers, not even buds, and really, on the countryside where details can be lost, one cannot even sketch without at least two colors. A yellow and green. And one could make the brown from those to accent the boles of trees and branches. In the silent morning, the sound came just after I felt the fear. It was a flat hollow sound and it crisped. And then began again.

A step unrelated to it, came close to the house. A little maid came bringing me a tray with a silver coffee- pot and paper-thin cup which she clattered down beside me.

"It's so quiet here," I said surprised. "I did not hear you."

"City people," she answered, "aren't accustomed to country noises. Noises in the country are separated. The country don't make any sound itself."

I detained her. She told me that the rustling was not the trees but the wind. And how city people jumped when they heard a noise and could see only quiet sky and earth.

"And what is that?" The hollow bang had commenced again and the linen drape flew up like my hands.

"Ah! Madame meant the old tree." She fixed me with her small pale eyes, the eyes she might have washed out with javel. Even the tip of her nose was white from it.

"Dead!" she said. "Two hundred years old. And now....." She made a chopping motion with her hand and the crisping sound came slicing through the air.

I looked beside me as though she were a dream and only a piece of it was visible to me. Why did she smile so?

"Two hundred years old. But still, you know.....more luck than we have, that tree." And she turned to go back to the chateau looking so bent that I wondered whether she might have seen the tree in its young growing. For a moment she stopped with just her head in my direction. "The Duchess is weeping for it, Madame."

Everything echoed a premonition for me. "The Duchess is weeping." I was alone and unwelcome. Just as sounds could be shocking because they were separated from the ground and sky, so one looked for a harmony of purpose in that ground. It seemed an evil sign that just when all the other growing things had worn to yellow threads and the last roses were brown at the edges, the tree should die as well.

Another step, light as an animal's, came up beside me and I threw myself to my feet to see Ritter rushing up the path as though to go past the portico. Impatient and polite, he greeted me as though expecting to find me, but he gave no explanations. He kissed both my cheeks quickly and appeared eager to go to the schloss. Happy and miserable at once, I followed him. Keeping my voice casual and pleasant, I said, "Ah....you had forgotten I was arriving so soon."

"Not at all," he said. "I knew you were here. It is why I hurried back."

He explained that the Duchess was much upset about the tree that had so long shaded the terrace of the castle. And he told me that Karmer, his editor, and Karmer's wife had driven down with him. In fact, the whole party was waiting for us at the scene of devastation. The great tree covered the lawn like a forest on its side, but the exposed core of the trunk was soft and damp with rot. Preoccupied, but gallant as always, Ritter made the introductions. His face was very tanned and his moustache had threads of auburn I had never noticed before. When we all walked to the terrace, he spoke of business details with Karmer, and from time to time he looked over at me and smiled. Or he gestured me closer, as though to say, "Soon, Zoë. As soon as I finish with these necessary things, cher..."

We had been separated for two months. Soon we would be alone together. My patience assumed a reverie which must have approached trance, because within minutes I woke to bewildering activity. The Duchess had disappeared. Ritter, wearing his reading glasses, was tugging my arm in the direction of the Karmers' moving figures. He was saying, "….to see the lake" and then something about an hour before luncheon. The laurels at the entrance to the great garden had almost closed behind the Karmers when I realized that disappointment as palpable as lead weight prevented my moving with them. I had neither time nor resource to free myself.

"Oh! Now?" I asked.

We said nothing else. I recall that without further questions or explanations, he was leading me into the chateau--- a silent walk except for my heels tapping the marble floor of the foyer until I said, "Were you surprised to have my telegram?"

His profile answered "no." And after a while, "well…. A little."

Hadn't he, however--- before he left Basle---- suggested that I join him here? He asked this, turning toward me a familiar lower face and his covered eyes.

"It was so long ago….." I began uncomfortably.

"Long?" he repeated, trying a door knob. "Long? But it was just a few weeks."

A final twist of impatience and the heavy door gave way to the library. It was an immense and silent room, cold, inhospitable. We were surrounded by multi-tiered shelves of books, varnished portraits, heavy paneled walls with thick mullioned windows which reluctantly admitted grey shafts of light. This alternative was less attractive than the social walk to the lake, but as I sat down in a straight leather chair, trying to imagine what should have happened, he came up to me and I smelled an unfamiliar cologne or shaving soap. He leaned against me and cradled my head against his jacket, twining his fingers in my hair. A button pressed into my cheek. There was an unusual awkwardness in his nearness and in my response. His caresses were like separate words which didn't form a phrase. I stood up, but I realized that his glasses bothered me. They shielded his eyes and they gave a temporariness to our time there because he needed them only for going over papers and always removed them quickly when he was through. As he embraced me, the light flashing off the lenses made our embrace surreal. I moved my face closer but he did not touch me with his lips. His head flung back, he kneaded my body as though his hands were frantically, impotently, searching it----perhaps for his own feeling which he had once placed there.

Then without a word, he pulled away and walked to the window through which it would have been impossible to see.

"You would have preferred to have gone with them," I said.

"Yes." He answered without turning around. "But you knew that, Zoë."

Yes, I knew that. Just as I had known that his invitation to the schloss had been no more than a parting gallantry.

"But….I had to know….something," I said. What? What I didn't dare to know. I went on in a voice so sad it surprised me. "I had… somehow…to follow everything….to the end."

And I felt for the chair. I sat in it, looking at the chevrons of wood which separated the small carpets: thick pegged floorboards stripped from ancestral forests, but which lay impartially under all feet. On which I did not belong. I saw his legs in front of me. He tried to raise my face, but I refused to show him my expression---- my chin childishly down against his knuckles as though our bones, without the cushioning falsity of skin, would finally meet. So clumsily that my hope jumped, he began stroking my hair. I longed to let it down over his arms and hands when small clear words came as precisely as beads and together they formed to: "I am afraid that I am meant to live alone, Zoë,"

And as though this had blocked off his feeling, the next sentence was warm and faltering: "It's ……an illness, an illness….of mine….I know…an illness…."

"No!" I broke in. I looked at his shoes which I had often put away and taken out for him. "No. It's not an illness."

Yet I thought it was, and my pity gave me strength to look at him. I reached up, and gently removed his spectacles and held them closed in my fist until he handed me the case. As I had done many times before, I folded them inside and slid them into his breast pocket, patting it. He caught my hand. He kissed the fingers before I could withdraw them. I thought him about to cry. He was looking at me with the expression we show on seeing someone after a long time, or about to take leave of them for longer.

"You have..... .....a great importance in my life," he said.

"Yes," I answered, standing up. He put his arm around me and the embrace seemed strong because his suede sleeve caught against the light embroidery of my frock. Even an accidental attachment of our clothes could move me.

"You are lovely," he said. "No. More than that...even more."

Happy and sad, I had grown used to the constant failures, interruptions, re-attachments with pain which make up the relation between a woman and her opposite. After fruitless searching in dark houses and silent hallways, she unexpectedly meets love again on the stairs. She is left new.

But not that time. His words had been a summation, not a discovery. He continued, musing aloud on my effect upon others: how people often misunderstood me because of my flamboyant beauty..... that they did not realize there was so much more to me..... That I could be-----what was it?--- more spirit than woman."

Had everything been ruined then by that possessive patroness, that greedy muse who could supply him with aristocratic ghosts and a legendary terrain for his poetry?

"Are you speaking of the Duchess?" I asked.

"The Duchess?" he echoed. I tried to visualize the scene which preceded Ritter's finding me in the summer –house. What had she thought of me as she turned her back and walked away with the malicious gold scissors slapping her side?

"No...... The Duchess thought you charming," he said.

"She thought me....." I felt my anger when I remembered her tone with me. "She thought me far more woman than spirit," I said. I looked pleadingly at him. "But I wish...that you would too."

It was the first time that we dared admit there had been very little passion for me in Ritter.........long before this last trip. When I saw his face, I knew I had admitted irreparable harm. Frantically I burst out: "What irony! Every other man I meet....!"

"It's.......it's...... I have so much tenderness for you, Zoë." Ritter spoke with an expression of such pain that it burnt my heart.

We stood looking at each other like two people who had committed a terrible act and who would have to divide it with themselves in order to bear its weight. In the broken silence I was suggesting that we not see one another for a while and he was shattering the air with "Don't make it too long."

As though we were planning a dinner, we discussed details in a banal way. He asked me what I planned to do and as though I had planned it before that moment, I said that I was going to the South of France. He arranged to meet me back at Basle before I left, but I reckoned that my departure would not permit the delay. He assured me that he would write in care of the Poste Restante when I decided on a town. It was all quickly accomplished.

The gong sounded on the terrace. He smiled. I smiled too. To spare myself shame. It was a time when nothing was possible. Neither to fall on my knees or to do something grand. Even without a mirror I saw myself stripped to the unattractive core of honesty which nature does not love. Nature favors the winning, the growing, the splendor of everything strong to the point of hallucination. I would like to have commanded a carriage. Thrown my valise to the driver and rushed off with speed as my destination. Instead, I walked out brazu brazu with Ritter and we crossed the spiky lawn to the terrace. I kept his pace, watching my silk shoes----vain and unnoticed tributes to our reunion---become ruined by the scratching of the stiff grass. "More spirit than woman." A sterile pain like a fruit dropped into my arms, finished growing, unattached. How would I not now become fatigued with the effort of being beautiful? I knew I had not yet felt the full blow of this and I listened carefully to myself as I might have bent over a well to fathom the depth of a drop. I knew clearly that physical rejection was unendurable, that it was a first cousin to death. Whatever sensibility would direct me to a new life would preserve this blow.

He was still walking beside me, his arm threaded though mine, yet it was over. I paid a visit to my turmoil so that it would not rise up and surprise me, and we approached the others who had again paused around the felled tree. I searched all their faces----- now turned toward us---- for signs of the dreamlike effect I often had on others. Like all physical things, expression needs constant renewal. If my face caught in a pair of eyes, I would have something as practical as a hook to sustain the rest of the day. But they all looked at me.... then looked away, as though I were not quite right.

The Duchess. Tall and formidable, a silver cane in her hand, stood straight as though planting herself in lieu of the tree. Three blue-smocked workmen surrounded her and an argument was in process----- Tino, the Karmers, looking on as the Duchess tapped her cane against an axe which lay at her feet. A workman, abject and bent over, was examining the shank of the handle. Tino's voice, strident and petulant, screamed something in a language I did not know. The tree looked frightful---utterly out of order on its side.; the huge trunk having inadvertently smashed its own branches as it fell on them; black earth clinging to the complex of roots which had sprung like gorgon's hair from the first seed. I had no understanding of the argument and less desire to comprehend it. I was waiting for each event of the day to pass. I saw the workman, crumpling a cap in his hand as he talked, set one filthy boot on the tree trunk, and in a swish of air near my face, the Duchess' cane flew by like a glittering bird and slashed against the man's leg- bone. His groan covered mine as though we had been lovers at the same time.

I concentrated on the man. Down on his knees. His legs covered by green and yellow leaves. Ritter moved in front of me. He took the Duchess' arm and they walked to the terrace. The others began to move also and I turned, almost bumping against Frau Karmer. I saw how much older she was than I, but traces of her beauty remained around her nostrils and eyes. I stared at her ruined face with the curiosity I might have about a house I might one day live in. I realized she had changed her clothes or I had not noticed before that she was all dressed in red. Her shoes, her tailleur, her pocketbook, the small woolen tam on the back of her head. Another woman might have looked bizarre and dramatic in all this flame, but she was so faded that she looked poignant and forlornly childless. She might have been saying: "No one to inherit my youth? Very well, then. I'll go out all at once like a summer sun." As I stared at her, could have sworn that----unlike the stranger who had nodded "No" to me as I descended from the train---- she moved her head in a quick vertical gesture like a small escalier of two steps. In an unspoken accord, we walked together to the terrace. I had a fantastic notion that I had suddenly aged and that my face was covered with lines. I looked at my reflection in the glass doors, yet the feeling persisted as soon as I turned away.

Luncheon was endless while I was sitting there, but it seemed to have passed in the blink of an eye when Ritter and I stood up to take our leave. He had talked about my talent, my portrait of him, my sensitivity.........but no one paid much heed to any of it. He was too voluble and they all knew that love is struck dumb by awe of itself. I could not feel that I was the chosen woman of this poet so revered by his distinguished friends. As he talked of me, Tino was bent over a dusty bottle of Lunel and Karmer was severing an éclair with the side of his fork. I had sat there with my throat tightened like a cold lock on a loose door, and I waited. We were assembled around a world which had no inside. I saw with blind surety what Ritter saw when he worked: all the unnecessary gestures and acts of days, all the occupations stripped of private terrors. I was the only one at that moment to see it clearly.

It was late in the afternoon. We were standing by the table and I looked at thee people I would probably never see again. Each of them would undergo some new loss---- something they believed they could not bear: a tree, a mother, a lover, a child, a dream of greatness. And I could have wept for them all. I could have climbed with the Duchess to her room where she would mourn her family past. Flung myself on my knees and told her: "Don't bother to please me: I'm a whore. You are right. Let every grief and confusion slide over your soul like rain down an impermeable. Be hard. Rest."

But instead I mounted the stairs in front of Ritter and at the landing to my room we paused. "Would you like to see the tower room where I stay?" he asked. I wanted to say "No." I had that choice. But I felt the power of my will crush my judgment like a blindman's foot.

"Yes, For a moment," I said carelessly. "I should like to see the room where you wrote the second Stanza."

"It's not grand," he said, going ahead of me up the last narrow winding flight to the top of the schloss. "It is really very simple....."

There were roses scattered on the walls. Out of the center of one rose and leaf sprouted the gold neck of a gas lamp which he did not light. He lay down on the bed and waved his arm at the small round room. "It's very monkish.....I work well here."

He did not move. I knew he wanted to be alone. I stood by the wall for some minutes. Then I quickly unpeeled all my clothes until I stood incredibly nude. He looked startled and sat up, leaning on an elbow. An odd rush made me afraid. Dizzy as though I had drunk the wine through my eyes. How could it happen that the face of someone, lying at a distance away could mean so much? There must have been an unexplained plot from where I had taken that leap. Everything had already happened. I had gone through a complete story and only the feeling was left. I responded with the background of something no longer remembered.

"Come here, liebe......you're shivering," he whispered.

I sat beside him and he drew the end of the counterpane around me. Worlds apart: native land, age, métier, sexe----different for each of us. He, directed for freedom and I toward immersion. I knew it was the last time I saw all those roses repeating repeating repeating as the same pattern would have repeated again and again in our life.

"Come closer, liebe....." he said. But I pulled away. I felt no desire. It was behind me and had not yet entered my body.

For one more minute I wanted to look out at him through my love. As I felt before Tintoretto in Venice, the first time I saw Prague early in the morning, my newborn daughter held up by her toes----endless endless. Mute. We are drawn to beauty without knowing what to ask of it.

A hard palm on my shoulder. I understood sexual passion. A frustrate anxiety---almost a rage--- to change from one state to another. A motion-reaction to stasis. The body wedges itself forward horizontally. No! I waited. I delayed and I waited. The consummation would be incomplete because it would center on special parts with the mind abandoned like a mutual friend who has made the introduction.

It was the last time. He kissed me. Then the great poet who had become a man tore off his jacket and threw it on the floor. I saw us face to face, moving from two points along the same parallel, slowly, toward each other. We would meet head-on with no place to go, no freedom of movement and no direction but the inexorable. No history, no fund. I knew that the making of a child would have opened the direction, upward. They were sad---my old dreams: they trailed around the present like cloth scarves around a dummy on an iron pole.

I had to shut out love the way the curtains had closed out all but a thin glow strained through the linen. Then, like a Magellan of the senses, I set off with the vessel which contained Ritter. I was thinking that I could never again love him as I had. I could see the knife-point axiom of my singular own self: dark, small, clean, unfindable, unfound except by him who had sharpened his dreams with it for the span of two years.

There was a surprised look on his face. He didn't utter my name or even a sound. It was a ride on our incomprehension; a harnessing of who one was and for once---- riding astride the mystery until one is no longer rider but passenger and at the formidable point: "Why?"----to fall into the physical and be lost together. Resigned to the unknown of the other's body. I closed my eyes and in the lids I saw the stranger's face again nodding "No" No. Then it came clear in Ritter's voice, "No. No." I wanted another word. A sigh, a name, but I heard only a gasp. I saw the roses repeating repeating the same pattern repeating repeating itself low in my entrails---- a pressure unendurable as though I was about to give birth to fear----which is never born.

I felt no love. I had become it, the way a gull becomes a cry over the ocean. My voice was like a light in the dark room when I said "I love you." I said it in German, the first language I knew. There was no answer.

I fell into a doze and in that state there came to me the realization that there must always be a white gown underneath life.

When I awoke Ritter was sleeping in my arms. I held his sleep in my arms. In his sleep was all that he was: his ancestors, his father, the long long people who belonged to the Sudetenland, his poetry, and his death. I studied his face----all its lines made simple again by the penombre, and I felt the pang of accomplishment.

I heard steps, a sob I think, and I imagined the implacable Duchess wandering her ancient corridors seeking an heir to the loss she had to ignore. I agreed. I began to cry silently. I cried for Frau Karmer when she would put aside her red. For the old tree of the past, for its torn-up roots in which disparate things had combined to make one magnificent flower. For the rose which stood for the perishable, the voluptuous, the corpse of beauty cut down before it rots. Everything in my life would die, wear out, pass away, leaving a few blades of necessity as colorless as autumn grass, and I cried at the age of twenty-eight without believing it to be true. Because of this I did not understand the sounds at first: what I took to be someone knocking impatiently at the door came clear as the rattling of loose panes in the old tower window exposed to the fields. A high wine had risen in the twilight outside the schloss. A dry wind to blow in the month of November. A wind without tears which was sweeping the countryside, ruffling the dry corn and the tops of wheat stalks I had passed on my train ride. The irregular tapping on the window awakened Ritter.

"It's the wind," I said.

He answered, "Perhaps not."

He said that the country people, when they heard it, believed it to be the tap of an old lover of the Queen whose heart she had carried in a casket beneath her skirt: and without it he could not find eternal rest. That he went from house to house before the Festival of All

Saints to see if perhaps some lovers within the house could find his heart or give him one of theirs.

For a moment the tapping ceased as though someone were waiting. On our first night together three years before in Basle, Ritter and I had dined out in the city and an old voleur had sold him three roses tied with a metallic riband. They were over-ripe, tired, fragrant and velvety, like me, he said. And later in his room—the semi-conscious climbing floating moments at the black heart of the night when I was woven into his arms. The roses somewhere nearby: a small package of garden sending out breath in place of roots.

I felt that all my limbs had gone to sleep while my organs continued to work like deaf slaves of a finished tomb. The wind sighed and again shook the window panes.

I agreed. Legend, poetry, love----all the same thing---open a gate in the life we know and the believer is invited into Memory as though it were the private home of the world.

1940
6 RUE ANDRE ANTOINE

Thirty-two years, and Yasha, are gone. The shuttered Cirque Medrano empty as Cluny. Time has elevated me six floors above the streets of Montmartre where pain and loss were once only personal.

Opposite my balcony the Tour Eiffel waves a Swastika. Young men who could be sons of my Bremen school mates, wear green uniforms. Their boots hammer on my heart on the cobblestones below and up the stairs of anyone who dares oppose them.

The poetry of my native language is charred by dark threats. Familiar words are tricked into breaking apart around demeaning meaning. Prayers are torn open and hacked into pieces. And the sound! Was this language always hurled like stones?

Through a crack in the black-out curtains in my bedroom window there is the Basilica of Sacre Coeur and Place du Tertre where the soldiers play tourist.

The last three tormenting months I've been as though in a foreign place. Rest, peace, goodness, understanding, have been fixed like prehistoric bits locked in amber.

On May 15, a call by the Gouverneur General de Paris, put me at the Vel D' Hiv as an undesirable enemy of France. All Foreign -born women and children...Germans Austrians Jews.... A suitcase of 30 kilos. Some clothes, my drawing pads and water colors, brushes... all on the long train ride to Oleron. Then a truck to Gurs, a shabby camp of mud and windowless cabins roofed in tar paper, at the foot of the Pyrenees. Twenty nine of us underfed, and unwashed -because there was neither sanitation nor running water.

I, the young activist Hanne Arendt, Gerda Groth, the lover of Soutine, the painter Herta Hausmann, a famous film actress– we all slept on sacks of straw. We all reeked of sweat, mold and worse.

My usual hypnotism: drawing. Every day I sketched my camp-mates. On the 22 of June France was defeated. Armistice. German occupation. Merciful chaos over who was in charge. Papers were burned..... Two hundred of us got liberation papers signed. I took my hat, my drawings and a toothbrush. And out...To stay risked German camps.

There was no transportation. We walked, hiked, starved, and by July 5th were at Montauban.: the center for "enemy aliens." I went on, back to Paris. I made a detour at Moissac to rest and see the sculptures. The train station at Cahors was open, but stopped at Brive when Stukas began bombing and strafing the roads. Going the wrong way against a tide of men women children, carts, cars, even soldiers and tanks all fleeing South. Scenes from Goya's war etchings: blown-apart luggage, clothing hanging from trees, abandoned corpses on the road.

A motor car, returning North, took me between two children and one on my lap, from Limosges to Chateauroux. On foot to Vierzon, I slept in a field. Morning. and- far off, the main road- a Relais Routier. Water. Bread. A functioning telephone. Six hours later Victor came in a stolen Deux Chevaux.

"Fancy you coming north," he said. "Tu ne fait jamais comme les autres."

At dawn, he half-carried me to my elevator cage at Raspail.

Young Aimee Maeght who prints my lithos, made me "new" documents.

Suitable for the cousine and heir to the music agent Gosnier who left the apartment in Montmartre. My brown and gray hair was stripped and replaced by blonde.

Jean Francois, Victor and I loaded all my paintings and some furniture on a van destined for the basement of the Conservatoire at Boulogne where J F also hid his piano. My apartment will be looted and occupied by les haricots verts. It was too near the Lutetia,and the prison at Cherche-Midi.

I agreed to meetings although. the apartment had only one exit..- and never on weekends when soldiers visited Pigalle, and Blanche.. At first it was jeunes combattants, from Lycee Rollin. to whom. I, ostensively, gave art lessons. I slipped out always just after the

Concierge left at eight a.m. to do her marketing(black marketing?) Marguerite D. was already there for my 9:00 coffee on le Pic. I gave her the key to my little atelier on bis rue Bardinet.

No one for a week. Then, downstairs, in my box a Gaz de France notice of rendezvous next morning at eight-twenty. An elderly man shoes-less and breathless at my door. 5 knocks rhythm: song: "Commed'habitude." Guy in Gaz de Framce overalls. Guest in a second pair. Down the stairs. I never knew who he was.

A lot of what passed for coffee. But no one all month. Then Victor. Three Kisses "Bye darling. Going Maquis."

Dear "Mundy" Schlesinger broadcasting for France on Avenue Trudaine at top of Hitler's do-list as "most wanted saboteur" may have escaped already in May on the Jamaique- the last boat. There is no sign of him here. But many disappear. Demonstration on the Camps Elysees.

Braque underground. Diego, Nelly and Alberto still here. Almost no traffic. Sudden sound of gunshot. Sounds of hobnailed boots. Rationing. Curfew. Black outs. Michel Leiris bartered some drawings for food. I can not sign with my name.

December 31, 1941

Very cold. Walked to Hippolyte-Maindron. Alberto's permit would have run out. He left today for Switzerland. Diego and Nelly stay on. D is earning a little making patinas and working bronze,

The three of them tried to get to Bordeaux and follow Jean-Michel to America, After days on the roads, they turned back. No sign of Diego's cat or Nelly's baby. Alberto dug a hole in a corner of his atelier and buried his newest tiny sculptures. I'll miss him.

Depressing walk back. Streets festooned with swastikas on blood-red flags..

MARCH 1942. Gestapo engaged. Leon Blum deported to Dachau. French police put 'commies" and Jews, on train to Drancy.

April 20, 1942 6:00 mass. Pigalle just opening her eyes. Slog up stairs to Abbesses. At Saint -Jean.-de- Montmartre Marguerite dressed in black. Kneeling." Pregnant Commie". Papers so fake they would never pass 2nd look. Jeanne List evaded roundup. Walked the streets. Safe house not. Reseau betrayed. Lover executed. Sixth month gone. Rest one &one/half hour. I am outside eyes.

Concierge is walking, lavender basket on her arm, rue des Abbesses direction rue des Martyrs. Quickly down my stairs. Up to my chambre de bonne. Barbara, - from Jeanne's group.- jumped from a window as police came up the stairs. Jeanne - Jewish, Polish, communiste, resistante, enceinte---will stay three days.

Jews to last car on the Metro. French police have become deadly. Sweet lyceene Anis Vinay of Jeunes Catholics Combattants arrested. Sent to Ravensbruck. Germaine Tillion also.

19 May LAW: all Jews must wear yellow star of David. Implementation in 6 weeks: June 7.

Michel's Gallery visit. One of my drawings from Gurs up. Unsigned.. Message from Madeleine La Grange asks that I store my watercolor of her before she leaves. Michel lends me his bicycle. To Quai Malaquais.

Wife of a minister, she'd been untroubled but now to wear the Star! "Mon amie!" she chirps at me in her little high voice, "Bien sur Je n'avais pas été assez sotte pour me declarer, moi, Mme La Grange." Plans involve two doctors; Laporte for advice and train tickets; another, friend of Clara, who will meet her in Dijon. Then on to join Clara and little Flo in Toulouse… from there to Montauban…

"..Et toi, mon amie…. Pouquoi t'es toujours ici?"

Pouquoi indeed. To play a deadly game of hide- and -seek.

New watercolors: some of view across the street; a few of old women at the market on le Pic. Signed with "Mel". taken to the framer on rue Veron. Plastered to the shop wall on a poster of the recently-executed is the name of my lawyer and good friend," Georges Pitard; Communist"

JULY 15-16 1942 GRAND RAFLE. Two days of busses. Two days roundup of Jewish parents and CHILDREN ages 2-16. From 4:00 a.m. to Vel D'Hiv to Drancy. To AUSCHWITZ. To death.

Cruel winter. Shock of barbarism. Of cold. Of hunger. But celebrated my November birthday working on 130x100 canvas of Circus from old sketches. Using the beautiful cherished remaining oils,the joy of spreading them, the smell of the medium, a lovely present to myself in this time of disaster.

January 15. 1943 Camus came back. He is on rue de la Chaise. Very near the Lutetia Abwehr. Publishing "COMBAT". Eluard's poem, "Nush j'écris ton nom..." is changed to "Liberte j'écris ton nom" He is in the Dordogne.

Walk by Concierge's window. She is reading *Je suis Partout* the anti semitic rag. I wave. I go carefully..

Friday at dusk, deep as woods. Doors slam.. Shouting. Wordless shouts. Down below, two shadowy figures pushed into a black car.

I stay in. Five watercolors of my geranium plant.

May 30 1943 Convoys leaving from Drancy. To Auschwitz.. The resistant groups: Communists, Gaullists, Independent Patriots, Catholics, Protestants—have been unified. But many have been shot in reprisals. Young blond soldiers replaced by graying older men who might have been my schoolmates in Metz or Bremen.

November 10,1944 my 59th birthday. Only water colors left.

December 13, 1944 A walk to Place Clichy. Au Comptoir. Threat of the Milice. Lay low. They know the city. They know hiding places. They go in disguise. Beware of Priests, We are occupied by police now. On every corner a calabo.

March. 8, 1944. Dreaded knock. Victor killed. February. A month ago.

All that I never told him, showed him. None of what goes on now matters to him.

Thirty-five young men massacred in the once beautiful Bois de Boulogne. My horror has an aftertaste of shame.

July 14, 1944 Celebration Bastlle. Allowed somehow. La Marseillaise sung in the street. Sung out of fear? Convoys still leave every day for Auschwitz in fear there won't be enough to kill.

July 31, 1944 Three hundred children taken from Drancy to Auchwitz.

AUGUST barricades of trees cobblestones benches. The FFI against German tanks. Fighting, killing go on in the streets..

August 25th. Liberation of Paris.

On August 26, German planes on their way home, bombed the Buttes Chaumont, Gambetta, near Nation. I could see the flames from my balcony.

In my liberated Paris, summer hangs like a cluster of marionettes, unattended, done in.

But ghosts awakened. The accused exposed. The sword of vengeance unsheathed, Not for accommodaters like Coco Chanel with her General, or poor little Cocteau, and Chevalier was only cheering us up like Colette. There were enough who fell into the wound of fester. My concierge was small fry: the young milice, the Vichy traitors, the women who were in love with colorless eyes and bright blond hair, the grocers who starved us for profit......

The Lutetia- stripped of German- has become living quarters to living-dead travelers over the broken bridge to humanity.

I am not able to sketch them. Only a survivor has the right.

I'm a kite torn from a string, but I'll go to ground, find if my apartment has survived. Go to Vavin for colors. To quote the poet: Denn Bleiben ist nirgends. Because staying is nowhere. Painting is my life. For the rest..if drinking is now too bitter I'll become wine.

Janka

It was a slippery descent which led to the bed under the vaulted white ceiling in Janka's studio. For two months I'd been ill, wondering whether I was really ill, shocked to find that I was, glad I was ill, eager to get well. I lay the days long, looking at a single etching of Madame de Staël that hung on the far wall. Her face dignified by self-acceptance: the cabbage –shaped turban, the ugly features, invited to join in. And I thought off the line: *Mein leben ist das Zogern vor der geburt,* without knowing why.

Madame de Staël—hung in an abandoned synagogue by a music-hall artiste who rushed home each night to nurse and feed a thirty-year old woman who had lost her energy. On the fringes of a kind of lunacy, I hid under the coverlet when I heard her steps in the studio. From there I would watch her enter the room—her long dancing legs and sensuous body, blank patches of winter on each side of her cropped black hair, and her hands carrying some dish to tempt my appetite. I would watch her, thinking: "She has me at last. After five years….. But I will escape."

"Come, my darling," she would say. "This will help you to get better."

"I am better already," I said, hardly turning my head on her embroidered pillow. "Today I got up and lay on the divan."

And setting down the tray, she might say, "But you shouldn't……Your fever…!"

And bolting up like an operatic madwoman, I would accuse: "There! You see…You want me to stay ill!" Which would throw her arms around my wrinkled gown; her convex body beat like my own; her high bitter scent surrounded me as the only breath of living in my life. She would murmur that she loved me, remind me of my talent, the things I would do, the people we would meet, and as she pushed back my hair--- fascinated always by its abundance, holding some ends in her hand---I could hear the tears ripening in her voice

And lay back, satisfied.

It was a world where nothing could hurt me, yet I often thought I was no longer alive and that the illness had hurtled backwards like a rock thrown by an explosion. Still, this was acceptable in a life ungoverned by all that I had learned or read. Perversion was as domestic as tableware and I might as well have looked for immodesty in grass. Yet my instinct mourned the woman's embrace in which breasts met like blind sisters in a hell of light.

But how lovely they were, those breasts which rejected the downward impulse of life and broke free from the vertical of spine and limbs, attempting the shape of continuity: the sun, the full moon, the egg, the womb, the zero point of perpetual origin. Mysterious,

Unnourished, I felt in mine a stirring of life as transparent as an angels breath on the day that Janka handed me a telegram from Munich and sat by my bed as I read it. My husband was bringing my daughter to live with me. I immediately saw the small white face pressed over my heart, but, suddenly, it changed to the dark head of Ritter.

"How old is she now?" Janka asked quietly, putting down the paper.

I saw the little girl who had visited me in Basel five years before. Just beginning school and with auburn hair to the back of her waist.

"Eleven," I said without meaning it. "Your mother ill arriving Trudi...." Mother child, mother child, the shape of continuity, the full moon, the egg, the womb of perpetual origin. Different faces distract the world's ennui.

"It's impossible, "I said. I lay back, exhausted, but Janka was holding my hand, explaining what we were going to do, what sort of apartment I would have, where the child would be schooled. Her splendid nose blocked away the room's confusion and the etched gaze of de Staël who had seen her parents picked in brine and survived it and other humiliations to form a life as naturally bizarre ugly beautiful and unique as the cloth crown that sprouted jewels.

"You would not mind?" I said, very relieved and partly hurt.

And as Janka answered, I realized I had known the single person in my life who loved me enough to trust me with my happiness. In one week we had to make me well and so I was moved to the chaise longue in the salon. There, I looked into the alien life of the street outside, saw the cast-iron bridge that saved the Ile St. Louis from isolation, and I went over the meager attempts I had made in the past five years to connect myself to something meaningful. I had tried. From the beginning, it was slippery down. I looked for work, I pined. Without knowing it, I longed and longed, and if there had been any direction to take me to a fulfillment of these longings, it was lost to me---willing as I was to follow.

Everything in Paris reminded me that I had been there before the war, but there was no overlay of times: I saw the past evacuated. The Rotonde where Ritter had given me violets was empty of me on the banquette At age twenty-eight, twenty-nine, thirty, I passed or stood before the hotel from which he had taken me and I saw outside glass and stone. The twenty-five-year-old who carried drawings up the stairway had fallen into my head from the hand of a year which passed above like an impatient God. Paralyzed into the mechanics of a toy, she marched up and down the stairs, unspeaking, absolutely incapable of seeing me. As good as gone.

.......We were the desperate vertical. Because each moment with him was a blow struck on the mouth of an hour. Hermetic. Crazed. Yet he kept his forward waiting like a carriage at the turn of the night.

I said, "I love you," I said, "I will die without you." It was just the decorative voice of my pain.

What was it all, those granite times? But they led not even to age as natural things do. I had a carnal guide to the absolute. Transferring destruction into end. And remember when the first night in Basle, surrounded by the flowers and the dim-lit unfamiliar room, I sat with my hands folded in my lap. What a terrible passion I felt for him the moment he closed his arms around me, his dark head halved by my neck.

But we were *more* ...like nature that dies upward. We were transcribed. My parents and my child, they were all moving forward-and I, too.

What fantastic transparency when the past strips itself of time! In a scene that protrudes from my childhood, (I am always alone because I never knew the feelings of the others),I see myself sitting by a table in a sea-side house, as though I were looking at the sunlight through torn black paper. But like a princess buried with hieroglyphs, the young sorrow I had is gone.

Everything rushing forward in life moves back suddenly to *but.* Like bees swarming home to drop the nectar from their legs.

The Château of Lassay deep-settled in August. Feudal. Massive. Grown into the earth which had begun to climb its towers with hands of orange moss. Monosyllabic, curt as Bruno who stood beside me with the hairs of his Norman ancestors growing out of his nostrils. His bass voice and the *patois* of the concierge. I saw his blue coat and yellow shirt beside me, his hand on my arm as though to hold me in place, to show me...

But I had already seen everything. Ritter's face with its expression of love kept moving into my sight like a moon over changing landscapes. By his dark coat I knew it to be the season of late love, and when I saw his tweed jacket stretching towards me, we sat in an open calèche without speaking, the sun trembling on his lips as the leaves passed by on heavy trees.

History—for me, the dated details of the forgotten—belonged to Bruno. I left my name on Ritter's mouth and I moved into the lives of Jasha, Bruno, Janka, Jerome, Mose, the mother, his sister---illumined like a candle in the night around her scene, guests who met and forgot me, the voices in whose timbre I floated. They were all lights in a corner of my sleep. Through them I saw my illness advancing like a private storm. To tear away my fragile presence. To leave everything as dark as my origin.

"You can rest here," Jasha said. He sat down by the table and pushed forward a dish of white grapes with a skin on each like frost. There was paint crusted around his fingernails. A streak of yellow gouache on his forehead. Like Lassay, grown into his work, his work climbing over his skin. His tenuous resistance in life marked by colors. Next to me sat his new woman, myopic and badly-combed. While I shined a grape with my finger, I could see him, standing, pressed to her lips, his eyes closed, as though he were drinking.

"Í love you. I love you". Ritter and I were standing close together in our coats. Dressed in cloth like ordinary people, we were getting ready to leave the house in Basle, The sky was falling past the window in rain. I watched his lips moving and when the sound ceased, I studied the shape of his lips. With wonder that out of two animal bodies that has joined was left a miracle as white as the stop in infinity.

I slid my cold wet shoes beside my feet and Mose's sister brought me a grog of Calvados. She had a gold tooth between her pale lips and the permanent radiance made her seem more delicate than I.

Apart from these voyages I made to locations of someone else's life, my own was imprinted, like a primordial leaf,on a dream.

I was looking at the back of Mose's neck where his hair was cut straight across. I watched his mother as she leaned over a jug to fish the prunes from their syrup. When she put some in my coffee cup, her eyes dissolved on my face. It was raining over the quiet suburb. It was raining without me. I knew Ritter in the rain, in the snow, in the sunshine. Mose brushed sugar from my dark wool sleeve, to touch it. Janka said, "You must be sensible. You must believe in the mystery of tomorrow. In destiny." I had been staring at something on the wall as she spoke, thinking. "You have to take care of yourself, Zoë," Mose said, touching my sleeve. Destiny was never ahead for me. It was all the grains of white powder that fell from my sleeve under the brush of his hand.It was the shadow behind the trees joined to the trunk. The way summer recurred. And was marooned in the year, suddenly.

In all the time I knew Janka, that was the only time I had seen her face hardened against me. Through the steam of the dinner. Minutes later she said, "That explains nothing." That was before or after she asked me to live with her. But it was all the same evening, and before that, I had expected it. I was speaking with great insistence and each turn I took was right, but there was no conducting road. The wine was boiling in my cheeks and when I coughed everyone looked at me. Each face moved together into a wall.

The night I put my ear against Ritter's chest-----bared in the opening of his robe, I could hear time dashing up against our isolation and I knew there was no safe way down for me. He held me by a hand against my head and I told him, "I will die without you."

Into my body poured the food and the wine. His touch on my hair was annihilated. I carried the plates after Janka and I leaned against the wall staring at nothing. What I could have said would have made a shape like the streak of yellow on Jasha's face. I could have said-clearly---- Oh! I could even hear the sound in my head and the room became immobile and there was no way forward or back—I saying, "I will die without him." Very simply. She would have understood, but I might have died. She was talking, but all the diurnal arrangements were wheels to move a life from one hour to the next. I walked back up to the small room at the top of the pension in St, Moritz. It was cold in the hallway, but I stood outside the door. Inside, Ritter and I lay together under the feather- quite. Inside it was silent. I was lying awake with wonder, watching his face closed up in sleep next to mine. I pressed my forehead against the thick oak door. Alone. Senses abandoned. Thinking the earth took its hair-like rests by going back to the memory of rock.

"Dors Zoë. Sleep Zoë." Moving wherever he went, insensibly, concentrated like the point of the wind.

I leaned against him as we looked up at the blank windows in the house of Byron I felt so fragile to contain such a fantastic growth of love. It was replacing me. Clothed in my name.

"I would like you to meet my mother," Mose said in the small room occupied with furniture and so many cups. One button missing from her blood-colored sweater, she put out her hand and the space opened like a blank eye. The eye of my mother. Locked up in my past like a childhood madness.

"You are no longer my daughter if you do this," she said. If I cried out so many years ago, now past, when Ritter took me into his arms. Into myself where ecstasy stuttered like a maladroit tongue.

"The mystery of tomorrow. The mystery of tomorrow." Janka kept repeating the phrase as she let the grains of coffee slide from a stiff paper into the pot. There were nights of joy that slid into fear: love inside and love outside and our two selves pierced like reeds in between. Tomorrow moved in place, like waves.

When I came back from Lausanne, he came forward, putting on his jacket as he moved to me, a point of white shirt collar sticking up hurriedly. His arm fit around my shoulders like the first stroke of clay on a complicated sculpture. "I'm happy to see you," he said. "I need you. I cannot part from you. We will never separate."

My flesh found windows in a word. *Love.* As broken-surfaced as the last cathedrals and as vulnerable to ruin.

"I loved you," Bruno said to me wearily. He was wiping his feet on the mat outside the door. He was bending over and the bones of his hips dashed against his trousers when his feet moved. He always used the *vous* with a curious combination of courtesy and peasantry,. In my hand I carried a piece of moss I had torn from the wall. The family maid was washing the outside door. A few kilometers away the sea drew back and the sheep grazed on the short wet grass and left clumps of wool on the fences. Gray wads like smoke. He went in before me and said, "The air here does you good." Inside I looked at the copper over the chimney and I sat down and entered that quiet place where Ritter was waiting for me. It was like two rooms next to each other, the doors opening on to the same hallway; Ritter and I in one, I and Bruno and the maid in the other.

Ritter and I took Trudi on a carriage ride and he sat on the seat next to her. He put his arm around her little shoulders. He said something about her small bones. A tiny ivory cathedral.... And something about perfection. What was it? I saw only my lover, across from me, with my child. An illuminated cameo as we drove through countryside on the click-clack of hooves and the whine of a back wheel.

"I love you. I will die without you,"

"We can no longer leave each other," he said. "It's too late."

In Janka's flat I was left alone all day. I examined my body as it lay outlined under the thin shift. Like something lent to me. A borrowed possibility. Despair has a hand as large as the weather, yet when it closes, there is not even room for surprise.

"I will miss you Zoë," he said at the train station. I was leaning out the window and the window began to move away from his black coat, from his unshaven face under the black hat. "I will miss you, Zoë." "I can get out!" I shouted, still standing by the window as a post, a watery building sunk in colors moved by.

From the openings of each day, the sleepless face of extremity looked out at me. I lay in Janka's bed and dressed tomorrow in beautiful costumes. "The mystery of tomorrow" legitimized by dreams. I was wheeling a high pram in which there was a baby and Ritter was walking beside me, his fingers on the metal bar. Trudi was with us and there was sun on the lake. We walked endlessly there in the sun. I took the baby out in a room and held it in my arms and the other two stood near me, Ritter bending to me. No one spoke. Nothing moved.

In the world outside there was patchouli and lilacs and small wild flowers unaccompanied by names. Roofs with red tiles and thousands of windows. Thousands. Some with gauze curtains shut in by *volets.* Somewhere buried in the wood of a small room was the sound of his step and my cry. He put his arm around Trudi's shoulders and she moved away slightly, but she smiled. He had bought her a doll with a Dresden head and large brown eyes that stared straight ahead. At a sheltered Inn we all descended and we left the doll in the carriage as we walked in, he between us, holding our hands. At the table he kept on his scarf and threw one end across his shoulder, giving him a boyish look. Trudi's lips were shining from the butter she had eaten. We drank cold Alsatian wine and he laughed for no reason at all.

The lovely smile and the small spaced teeth tore into my heart like reflections on a knife.

The darkness came as quickly to Janka's studio as it comes to me here. Poor old woman of thirty-two, I was young enough to want to die. To die and yet lay patiently while expectancy glided towards me as white and voiceless as a swan on a belled lake.

Canet Plage 23 Septembre 1963

The sun. I am curved into my bed like the moon and as silently gone. Space stares around me. No. No, it's these cries that wake the stillness in my heart. The same poignant echoes come in winter through a thin sleep. Is it only the human voice broken into separate births? Calling me? Call me. Call me. Let this pillow be the hard assigned place between shoulder and neck.......protective discomfort of love: a resting ledge. Time is become a narrow crack through which I can see. A voice shudders in the chest tones: ".......I am lay-ed, am lay-ed in earth." The staccato of a coming foot, the opening of a door, slowly, with the awful leisure of the over-rehearsed; and I am a wretched spectator who haunts the dead. Janka said "You must believe in the mystery of tomorrow," but her image wears the same silk dress and a blurred familiar face. The door closes the room like a seal and She sits on the floor with her dancer legs tucked under her, her chest raised and only her head bent down as though her neck had snapped like a stem.

Listening to her own voice pleading back to her... "Remember me, remember me..."

My affection is magnified by echoes. "It's morning," the young waiter tells me. "A beautiful morning, his Languedoc-French rolling into Spanish. He will bring Madame's breakfast to the terrace.

"You are very kind," I say, and he is kind. Yet, the simple act of laying his hand upon my arm without need or attachment opens my isolation again. Under the cover of age I am not ashamed to complain. "There is someone singing...who woke me..."

"If Madame is disturbed..." but suddenly there is nothing, I'm alone. If only love had been so permanent. This economy of mercy makes me think of angels small as bees and as self-absorbed.

My privacy is not even large enough for despair. If I hold the tip of Janka's skirt, it can slide out of my hand. If I am woven into Ritter's arms in a fragrant night, I can breathe again. Let death be something metallic and I can split it open like a flute some time after the music has ceased. Why am I so alone? Am I just the larceny of other people's hearts? A piece of nature ruining, formally, like plants? Each of my selves seems linked to a disappearing other person like two eyes closing in the same coffin.: and the small world of graves is as open, without estimate, as the sky, if I am searching for loss.

I can identify the lovely woman by three violets unfading over her ear. She died while still alive, struck down by such a boneless thing as time. At the moment of her death she stepped from the iron rung of a carriage and was looking to and rushing towards the phantasmagoric rocks at twilight near Rimini, From the other side of the carriage Ritter came, and close-to I saw his shoulder like a night cloud passing mine. "Are you in such a hurry to leave me?" he said with a face so huge it blocked all but the darkness that followed.

Colin's face, as delicate as cobwebs in the sun, forms and shudders in a long-gone breath of August. From the old dust of a voice he whispers: "He's a good fellow and he likes violets." And Ritter said, "I give you a violet for everyone who loves you."

Did they all love me? What bleak ecstasy can I take from that iron past ? It's over.

They died as punctually as punctually as flowers repealed by frost. And all I hadn't said to them became the words I used to others who had hardly touched my life. But I--- I hold their identities. And clip austere titles--- Friend, Lover, Mother, Father, Cousin---- to the browned stems.

Ritter said that death was more carnal than love. I don't want to know that rudimentary possession. Without the devil's stake, let me just go, eyes open, silent, like a fish.

What is worse than an empty grave? The sand without even a bird's shadow.

Over the wall of my terrace, her voice annuls the silence. "When I am lay---ed am lay-ed in earth...." If the waiter told her the old woman in the next room was disturbed, she must have answered, "Tant pis." I'm as glad she did. But why this again? I can do no more with Janka; her realm is fogged in sadness. Her face was already bloated and moist with the disease I didn't suspect, and I thought her ugly and crazed when she turned to me, saying, "Music, Zoe. Music, I think, is the missing body of God."

Even though she sang badly. Badly, yes. But always hoping, like so many failures do.

Believing in tomorrow, dancing, singing her ascendancy over illness and disappointment.

She sat beside the green cloth-covered ogive of the old phonograph while Mozart's Requiem or the jumpy voice of Galli-Curci crowded into her ears. Or when a desolate contralto sang---better than she---- her own beloved "Dido's Lament": "Remember me.....remember me........but, ah, ah. forget my fate...." I beside her on the floor, sketching the song-sunk profile that disappears when she turns----- distorted, radiant, fanatic ---telling me: "Music.......I think...is the missing body of God."

Or Ritter saying that it was the only communion. So long ago, holding his arm about my waist in the darkness near the convent as he------terrifying, sacrilegious---moved his hand to my breast and chanted over the music: Wachet auf! Ruft unz die stimme...."

Wake up! The voice calls us. Wake up. Wake up to your own death. Participate in it.

Isn't that what he meant? Wake up to your accomplished life, to the space which will have no sound.

Into my bodice he put a rose. For remembrance. And on my arms he had lay-ed a violet for everyone who was to die.

There is a blankness where my grandmother's voice used to be. She's already faded under her severe blue hat. Her edges are curled like scorched leaves. Her thin gray hair is all gone. Where have I put her worn-out image----- the soft-skinned face whose momentum skyward pushed it out of a woman's shape? It watched way past my childhood, observing as though from an invisible hole in the sky with all the restraint and simplicity of the endlessly dead.

"I only hope I live to see your marriage," she said to me from her bed in Colmar, the week before she died. In unbleached muslin, immense under the feather- quilt, she rested like a winter-harbored barge. Her hand with its crushed lilac leaves lay open like a fallen nest.

"I'm too little to marry," I told her.

"But you will grow up. Like me," she said.

Oh no! no no no no…….. I touched the long thin braid that frayed and faded in the cruel light of my eyes. To her own wedding she had worn boots and one got lost in the snow on the way to the Synagogue. The laughing people, wrapped in scarves and winter mantles, who accompanied her pulled it wet and shining out of the dark hole.

"I was so afraid," she said.

"Was your dress long?" I asked.

"I was so afraid. Caught by each arm," she said, "while everyone was dancing, and they led me away."

Why was she so afraid?

"I was fifteen, darling. Only fifteen and he had a big beard. My friends laughed at me.."

"Did you have your teeth then?"

"But I loved him. I loved him, darling. And when I lost him, I looked at the wall.

I love you I will die without you.

Her helpless big-bosomed body asked pardon for existing and they prodded her into a dress she'd never worn. That love which was like the simple furnishings she died in brought her no thanks. I'd rather have had rings. My child's scared face let her go a pauper's way and at the end she seemed not to know me. A disappointment in her grey eyes covered her setting- out like mist.

"You are very kind," I say to the young waiter. The butter has drops of dew. The strawberries are like miniature hearts with green roots. He is kind and she was mine. There is no distance enough for words in love.

Would she have known me when Ritter slowly unwrapped the fur cloak and carefully unbuttoned the round blue knobs that fastened my dress? "How beautiful you are!"

Turning away, she would spit against the evil eye. Kissing my eyelids.. ...".I will die without you," I said to him.

Up here, as the sand flies into my coffee, I reach in and claim my soft warm body.

On the right side of the neck there is a spot of his kiss. On the left wrist, a bracelet of fingers which only I could recognize.

The violent smash of the high tide rushes against the voice of my neighbor-contralto. Like an immense audience begging for silence. Yes, let us have something else. We don't like these Lieder. The will of God is as vague as our water. Let his body be precise. The great magic of HIS sorrowing face never hid from Mozart and HE dies---like us---- after every *Jubilo*.

I don't remember me as the small girl whose eyes have the sepia abandonment of an Atget. But I see myself held in an assigned and protected place on an arm near features set into pride under the square blue hat. After that, there were many 'me's' each one following attachments down a narrow road to desolation: "Zoe!" "Zoe!" "Zoe!"---- my name springing up like identical cities along the way.

A small girl, nourished on change. I grew larger in every new house, the three of us knowing that whatever we took hold of---street, towns, walls, bits of furniture---- bound us to father's rancor..

My mother in flowered voile, like gardens expanding under my head, my father leaning over, ready to pick me up, to carry me---- a little stump of a bride half-planted in dreams---into the new home. A lantern brings him close to. The beak-like nose, the opaque eyes, the moustache and beard----like a bird eating black grass. Wavering metal shutters, the soiled drippings of rain, and complex horizons where I saw futures as high and mysterious as the dark-eyed windows covering the town.

Early in the morning, father knots the flat silk cravat and punctures it like a butterfly with a spot of radiance: his own father's life reduced to its diamond shape winked through my childhood and made me think of the long-dead as jewels.

"Business" was always his answer. It was all the scuttled shops and sheets of paper over which he dangled his spectacles like a silver scowl. It was the dry street turning to ocean. My mother raises her arms in front of my window and breathes. Then, by the flight of a hooded candle, she reads me a flickering tale of Perrault and my day pinches shut like a flower. But my father walks the beach and perforates our life with plans. Multiplying footsteps, his calculations lead us to a frowsy shop-front where I sobbed to think of our little white cottage behind us in the sand like a sea-shell. I had to go to school, learning a new language which would lead me later into love. Mother put up curtains around my bed and cut my frocks to match. "It take very little to make me happy," she said----- which was the way she always began her examination of my father. And I, the traitor-dwarf, in a child's dress, began to disgorge his faults.

It was summer, it was winter, it was on the other side of the sun that I last awoke,

Grandmother visited us in her best hat which fit snugly over her eyebrows and made her head that impressive blue square. We showed her the day ending in Colmar behind the mountains, but she sighed and said, "My darlings, when the sun is so red it means that people are at war somewhere." Catching our fever for removals, she stayed only three weeks and left impressively forever. My screams altered nothing but my mother's face: it began to change over her like the protective case in which we moved our clock.

She longed to have a small plot of ground where we could put out tables and invite people. Where the child could have friends and space to run.

But a ferocious bitterness against his wandering fate kept father's mind awake all night in Utrecht until we found him nearly dead at eight with laudanum, his disappointed eyes just crescents in his dark-dreaming face.

As each new house receded from the heavy carriage, I felt filled as the family armoire with their joint possession. Until Bremen where we settled near the frozen port and father kindled the night for warmth.

I was seventeen when I saw Manes at a desk welded into place by books. His blond face and smile might have been the summer lining of my father. I felt that I held the sun on my arm. I became the cause of happiness. Even Father's. Dazzled by the implacable embrace that would change his life again, he astonished even himself and sang a Schumann Lied at the wedding supper. His beard was turning to dust in the sallow face, but he was almost jovial in the rented room where everything----- those thin un numbered chairs and white dishes----- even the unknown guests----- smelled of transience. He could walk out----perhaps even fall asleep----his head on the new telephone, dreaming of Munich where I was going.

And Munich which I was going to leave. Without them. Finally. Passing on, after five years, to take my chariot-seat behind maturity, a small girl, a new beginning.

"My daughter is dead to me," my father said to Manes. "If you have a wife I do not know her."

I was very brave then. Bravery wore the face of rejection and it occupied the body of love. It occupied *my* body of love. Waked-up. Come of ages I never knew but as the outsides of the castles in Perrault. And in what turning stairway, rushing down archaic stone that smelled of centuries, did I dash against that surprising self of mine which broke into the simple form of wonder. *You are no longer my daughter if you do this.* If, unable to think, not understanding, pulled from the center like a calm animal on a madman's leash, I fled to Ritter. Neither daughter, nor wife, nor mother, nor myself on the ledge of grandmother's arm, snapped empty like those streets in Atget. But spilled into roiling colored bodies out of Brueghels. Enchanted by bewilderment and the urgency of my body strained toward conscious death, I and I, facing each other like bones watching veins.

"Go back!" said my mother. "Can't you care for anyone?"

Having changed his countries, his businesses, his interests, unceasingly walking the house, the street, the beach at night, my father was moved into position to die and his face was small with concentration as though he had become a student of the inexorable.

He was old. He was worn. His beard was like the chipped plaster on a mausoleum effigy.

"Why did you come? To say goodbye?"

The pointlessness of his death and the pointlessness of my life were like the reverse sides of an ancient coin that buys nothing. On those boney arms in their wide hospital sleeves, he raises himself. He scents the freshness, the sacrilege of love--making which has taken the place of my history.

"You have caused me a lot of trouble Zoe. A lot of trouble."

"Go back," said my mother. "He's your father. It's as strong as love."

As strong as love. As strong as incomprehension. I went back. Death was awake in him.

The anguished face like an open eye between the white linen. Father who always had difficulty in sleeping. How often I woke out of dreams to hear the scuff of his leather house-shoes on ever -uncarpeted floors. So always awake he would never hear an outside call but my small voice-----enchanted to find the world continued after my first sleep. Stripped of his diamond pin and his brushed coat, he grips his robe together like a sheaf of pain. I call: "Father…." To which he answers, furious: "Go to sleep at once!"

It was quiet. His closed curtains refused the day---- pale, distinguished, thin as a hair--- -which was waiting for him. Then the old door----the Munich door it was then---sunk into an agonized square and my mother stood framed like and Egyptian mourner broken off from a longer frieze. There was red dust in her eyes and she held before her a small basket of hands from which her marriage ring shone like the single ecstasy in a short life. We were together again, our family, the three of us, scabbarded in a last moment, but heretic in the tableau. I thought of my lover. Suddenly my mother tapped my arm and whispered, very calmly, the way she used to announce the plan for the day: "I'll go with him."

I love you I will die without you.

She loved him then. To die with. To die without. Perhaps she never looked up as I had with Ritter and seen an awesome night, spider-shaped through his arms and my knees, but like settlers in each bare room, they had sat on opposite sides and rocked the same disappointment to short sleeps. And did I love only one person or did I love my parents? If I had said, "Father, I love you." would the phrase have been preserved in some small tracing on the heart, held up one last time to the light? Where does feeling go? Does it reappear depersonalized, like flame?

Our past moved toward me like a one-wheeled caravan and rutted in my love-bound life. The sound of many doors slammed. The houses replaced one another like long or short days. The grape arbor in Colmar, the cold sand sighing under the waves in Bremen, the square room in Utrecht when my mother, in the pitchless voice she used for calming catastrophes, explained my rupture with childhood and I was terrified that my father knew I was now a woman.. Oh that dour man I was left alone with in the Vosges as he took me to friend's house, cursing under the weight of my packages, his trouser legs wolfing up water in the snow. "You would come here, in days like these. You would. You give me so much trouble." And left me at the door. Had he ever kisses me? Wouldn't I have remembered the touch of that beard behind which his lips hid like fugitives. He left me at the door and I saw his shadow thrown like a black knife across the white path.

No. I loved him no more than usual. I leaned over the bed saying, "Father...." In my old voice, but a hand shoved me violently backwards.

"Trouble trouble trouble!" The words were like a mumbled prophecy out of that smashed white beard.

"Touble Trouble Trouble!" I was clutched by a tension in my breast as though something ready for flight had been weighted down with stone., when my mother's voice rose out of her dark dress into light light laughter. She brushed his nose, his eyes, his beard, with an immaculate housewife's hand. Above me the laughter, below me the nightmare muttering, and I fell between them like a roof-high wind haunted by vertigo, across the bed. Frozen, done-for, a shell of clicking teeth. The bed smelled stale. My mother's nervous laugh had descended into sobs and whispering complaints. "Why must you….why….now…." She said how terrible it all was and he recited, "Trouble trouble" as though this was the word he'd had to remember all his life. Pushing us both away with hands and arms stripped of nearly all their flesh, and stronger than we, it came to me that we had always been this way. Always. Hiding in the shadows of Perrault, I looked for turrets through the curtains of my bed, but our life was built of deserted shops with rubbish left in piles and dreams that separated from anguish only as the carriage took us off again to assemble the same drear life. This was the right end for our pretty story. Then the thrashing yellow arm flew past my eyes and without understanding why, I grabbed it and pushed it against my face. It stayed quite still. The fingers closed like ice around my hand and pulled it, fingers tangled, to his mouth.

I heard his torn voice wrapping itself carefully around some different words. My eyes closed. I heard him saying, "….meet some day….another place…." I felt his beard, his breath, like a hot summer breeze, his lips------ all at once as they joined together in a kiss.

Then my mind went out like a candle. It was like meeting God on the stairs. That's all. That was the end of that family of mine. It was the end. It was the end. I didn't like it. I wanted better for myself. But it was mine and I could weep. Why couldn't they====like me--- have found glory in the world of being alive? Isn't it given to everyone? They used to bury kings with beautiful objects and flowers to deny the perishable, but all we could have put beside my father was the small painted chest filled with insomnia medicines that he used to keep beside his bed, Saying: "Wake up! Wake up, Father, and go to sleep."

Unrelenting, the sun squats overhead in a chaos of dizzy heat. Passionate, unsensual in a streaming sky. The young waiter saves me from such terrors with a parasol and a change of plate. As though I care for peace. As though I care for single-shaded vision.. I'd rather be a member of disorder. I'd rather look up----and seem to cry. Janka cried with her voice: the tears washed up from her deep chest and broke over the shuddering, untrained voice, drowning in sorrow, while her enigmatic eyes looked on, uncommitted, above the cormorant nose. Mother cried with her hands: twisted, sighed with them; thin fingers dropped the weeping into her book and braided it into my long hair. And Ritter still cries in his poems----stoic as his Venitian heroine who meets Donna Miseria and takes her in to share a Princess' bed..

The sea is calm, now. But my driving wind whips at the sky and I drink in memories like an old graveyard choking on its tears.

.... My father's hand comes to me like a dry twig in flames. Do you remember me, Pierre? Pierre--- and my anguish at liberty again. Back to the point of beginnings, Pierre approaches me like streaming August fronting the bay......Ritter's mouth breathes against mine and my father's lips reveal themselves on my hand. Kisses are all lost. Touches cannot live in minds or hearts. They die apart from flesh.

The young man is asking me, "Madame, would you like anything else?" and I answer, "No.'

Once at night Ritter's arms curved like Roman arches over the he had drowned in me.

"No. Nothing more, now." The old woman has simpler pleasures than he. A well-brewed tea with sugar in melting cubes. A tarte with cinnamon. That's all she needs now. Her sex has dissolved somehow like moisture on the skin of awe.

"If I cannot live even with you," Ritter said with sadness, "no other woman will ever be able to move me...... I shall always live alone, Zoe." I traced my pretty finger along a crease in his neck, and said, "If only I had been this line I would have been able to remain with you forever."

Forever. Forever is hope, fatuous and young, with its hair gummed back and its pockets rattling with days.

I was young. My heart was touched, madly, inside the green mystery of my being.

Every gesture was like thunder. Numbers were dissolved.. I was a verb: I loved. I remember. It was to me he dedicated his only poem of Venice: *The Princess and Donna Miseria..* She is a good teacher.

Fills the notes with trembling leaves. Shoots the voice to the pitch of the wind, listens over graves for the sob of the earth....... Before the contralto just began again, it was silent. Then the music rested like seeds with everything inside until her voice swelled them open. Now up up they go and out they flower. Old Donna standing beside me.... directing with a black-draped sleeve, fingerless and full....only now as her voice goes down do I hear the words.....the music fails me.... Janka with her head bent down as though the neck had snapped like a stem.... "Remember me....remember me....but ah ah.. forget my fate...."

Old woman sitting on the hot terrace waits for evening, waits for dinner. All the surprises of life are contained under silver covers until the last tea pot reflects a whiter sun. The sigh of the tide, the shouts and cries down on the beach......the eerie borrowing of song by another singer.......the human voice broken into separate births.

"What is Madame drinking?" Madame is drinking the voices. Madame is drinking the waves.

Under the earth and far away. Beloved, stay quiet. I'll lay real roses over you.

Around my terrace now, the shimmering blue sea and sky are unbroken by images.

Glittering, unchanged, above the beige sand without even a bird's shadow, silent, distant, full of time and space. Beautiful world! You are me. Sinking down at night into a darkness from which I pull my selves--------like stars.